Aspen Allegations

A Sutton Mass. Mystery

Lisa Shea

Treasure every day!

Lisa

Cover design by Lisa Shea – the leaf is an aspen leaf I
photographed in Sutton.
Book design by Lisa Shea

"FLASHING IN THE DARK"
Written by Holly Hanson
Performed by Neptune's Car / Holly Hanson & Steve Hayes
Courtesy of Holly Hanson
© 2012 Wild Braid Music (BMI)

Visit my website at SuttonMass.org

In 2013, Aspen Allegations earned a Gold Medal from the
Independent Publisher Book Awards.

First Printing: March 2013

- 9 -

Print version ISBN-13 978-0-9855564-2-6
Kindle version ASIN B00BO0K7ZI

Treat each day as a blessing.
Tell the people you love how much they mean to you.
Live with your whole heart.

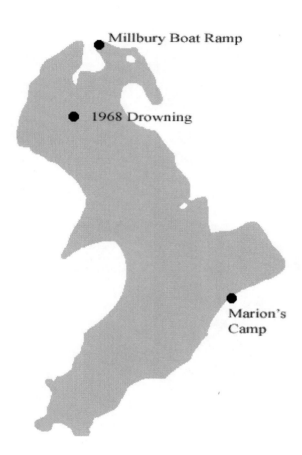

Millbury Boat Ramp

1968 Drowning

Marion's
Camp

Lake Singletary
Sutton, Massachusetts

Aspen Allegations

Chapter 1

What is life?
It is the flash of a firefly in the night.
It is the breath of a buffalo in the wintertime.
It is the little shadow which runs across the grass
and loses itself in the sunset.
~ Crowfoot, Blackfoot warrior

The woods were lovely, dark, and deep. My footfalls on the thick layer of tawny oak leaves made that distinctive crisp-crunch sound that seemed unique in all of nature. The clouds above were soft grey, cottony, a welcome relief from the torrents of Hurricane Sandy which had deluged the east coast two days earlier. Sutton had been lucky. Plum Island, Massachusetts, a mere ninety minutes northeast, had been nearly blown away by eighty-mile-an-hour winds. Here we had seen only a few downed trees, Whitins Pond once again rising over its banks, and the scattering of power outages which seemed to accompany every weather event.

I breathed in a lungful of the rich autumn air tanged with moss, turkey-tail mushroom, and the redolent muskiness of settling vegetation. Nearly all of the deciduous trees had released their weight for the year, helped along in no small part by the gale-force winds of Tuesday. That left only the pine with its greenery of five-needled bursts and the delicate golden sprawls of witch hazel blossoms scattered along the path.

It was nice to be outdoors. Two days of being cooped up in my house-slash-home-office had left me eager to stretch my legs. The Sutton Forest was far quieter than Purgatory Chasm this time of year, in no small part because hunting season had begun a few weeks earlier. The bow-and-arrow set were out stalking the white-tailed deer, and they had just been joined by those eager for coyote, weasel, and fox. I wore a bright orange sarong draped over my jacket in deference to my desire to make it through the day unperforated.

A golden shaft of sunlight streamed across the path, and I smiled at where it highlighted a scattering of what appeared to be small dusty-russet pumpkins. I stooped to pick one up, nudging its segments apart with a thumbnail. A smooth nut stood out within its center. A hickory, perhaps? I would have to look that up later when I returned home. I had finally indulged myself with a smartphone a few years ago when I turned forty, and while I liked to carry it for safety reasons, I preferred to leave it untouched when breathing in the delights of a beautiful day.

The woods were quiet, and I liked them this way. The Sutton Forest network stretched across the middle of the eight-mile-square town, but it seemed that few of the ten-thousand residents knew of this beautiful wilderness. In comparison, Purgatory Chasm, a short mile away, was usually bustling with a multi-faceted selection of humanity. Rowdy teenage boys, not yet convinced of their 'vincibility', dared each other to get closer to the edge of the eighty-foot drop into the crevasse. Cautious parents would climb along its boulder-strewn base, holding the hands of their younger children. Retiree birders would stroll Charley's loop around its perimeter, ever alert for a glimpse of scarlet tanagers.

Purgatory Chasm had an exhibit-filled ranger station, a covered gazebo for picnicking, and a playground carefully floored with shock-absorbing rubber.

Here, though, there was barely a wood sign-board to give one an idea of the lay of the land. The few reservoirs deep in the forest were marked, as well as where the forest proper overlapped with the Whitinsville Water Company property. That was it. Once you headed in here you were on your own. The maze of twisty little passages, all different, were as challenging to navigate as that classic Adventure game where you would be eaten by a grue once your lantern ran out of oil. A person new to the trails would be foolhardy to head in without a GPS or perhaps a pocket full of breadcrumbs.

In the full warmth of summer I would be alert to spot a few American toads, a scattering of dragonflies, and an attentive swarm of mosquitoes. This first day of November was both better and worse. The mosquitoes had long since departed, but along with them they had taken the amphibians and fluttering creatures that I usually delighted in on my walks. I had been rambling for a full hour now and the most I had heard was the plaintive *ank-ank* cry of a nuthatch. Maybe it, too, was wondering where the smaller tasty morsels had gone off to.

Still, with the trees now bare of their leafy cover, there was much to see. The woods were usually dense with foliage, making it hard to peer even a short distance into their depths. Now it was as if a bride had removed her veil and her beauty had been revealed. The edges of a ridge against the grey-blue sky showed a delicate tracery of granite amongst the darker stone. A stand of elderly oaks was stunning, the deep creases of the sand-brown bark rivaling the wise furrows in an aged grandfather's brow.

I came around a corner and stopped in surprise. A staggeringly tall oak had apparently succumbed to the storm's fury and had fallen diagonally across the path. A thick vine traced its way along the length of the tree, adding a beautiful spiraling pattern to the bark. The tree's crown stretched far into the brush on the left, but on the right the roots had been ripped up and a way was clear around them.

I moved off the trail to circumvent this interesting new obstacle in life, eyeing the tree. When I'd parked at the trail head there had been two trucks tucked along the roadside. One had been a crimson pick-up truck with no shotgun racks or other indications of hunting, at least that I could see. With luck the owner was just out for a walk like I was. The other vehicle had been a white F-150 clearly marked as belonging to the Department of Conservation. If the ranger was in here somewhere, hopefully he'd spotted the tree and was making plans to clear the trail. If I hadn't run into him by the time I emerged I'd leave him a note on his windshield.

My foot caught on a hidden root and I stumbled, catching myself against the rough bark of a mature oak. I shook my head, brushing my long, auburn hair back from my eyes. The forest floor was coated with perhaps two inches of oak leaves in tan, chocolate, fawn, and every other shade of brown I could imagine. My usual hunt for mushrooms had been stymied by the dense, natural carpet, and I knew better than to daydream while walking through this hazard.

My eyes moved up – and then stopped in surprise.

The elderly man lay on his back as if he had decided to take a mid-day nap during his stroll. His arms were spread, his head relaxing to one side. But his eyes were wide open, staring unfocused at the sky, long past seeing anything. The crimson blossom at his chest was a counterpoint to the dark green jacket he wore. The blood was congealed, the edges dry.

My hand went into my pocket before I gave it conscious thought, and then I was blowing sharply on the whistle I carried. It was only after a long minute that my mind began to clear from the shock, to give thought to the cell phone I carried in my other pocket. For so many years the whistle had been my first resort, the quickest way to communicate with fellow hikers.

I was just reaching into my other pocket when there was the whir and crunching of an approaching mountain bike. The ranger rode hard into view along the main trail, pulling to a skidding stop at the fallen tree. He was lean and well-built, perhaps a few years older than me, wearing a bright orange vest over a jacket peppered with foresting patches. His eyes swept me with concern.

"Are you hurt, miss?" he asked, his gaze sharp and serious as he caught his breath.

I found I could not speak, could only wave a hand in the direction of the fallen body. The dead man's hair was a pepper of grey amongst darker brown. He had been handsome, in a rough-hewn older cowboy sort of way, and in good shape for his age. Had he slipped on the leaves and fallen against a cut-off tree? Stiff and spindly stumps could almost seem like punji sticks, those sharp-edged spikes that the Viet-Cong laid as traps for unwary infantrymen.

The ranger gave a short shake of his head; I realized he could not see into the ravine from his vantage point. He climbed off his bike; his sure stride brought him to my side in seconds. He pulled up suddenly as his eyes caught sight of the body, then he slid down the slope, moving to kneel at the fallen man's side. He carefully laid a finger against the neck, pausing in silence, but I knew before he dropped his gaze what he would find.

He had his cell phone to his ear in moments, twisting loose the clasp on his bike helmet, running a hand through his thick, dark brown hair. "Jason here. We have a dead body in Sutton Woods, north of Melissa's Path. Just by where I reported that downed tree earlier. Get a team in here right away." He paused for a long moment, listening, his eyes sweeping the forest around him. "No," he responded shortly. "I think he's been –"

There was the shuffling of motion from above; both of us turned suddenly at the noise. A sinewy man stood there in day-glow orange, his wrinkled face speckled with age spots, a visored hunter's cap covering wisps of silvered hair. His eyes moved between the two of us with bright concern. "I heard the whistle. Is something wrong?"

In his hands he held a Ruger 10/22 rifle, the matte barrel pointed somewhere up-trail.

Jason settled into stillness. His eyes remained steady on the older man's, his lean frame solidifying somehow into a prepared crouch. The hand holding the phone gently eased down toward his hip. "Sir, I need to ask you to place your rifle on the ground and step back."

The hunter's worn brow creased in confusion. "I don't understand –"

"Sir," repeated Jason, a steely note sliding into his request. "Put down the rifle." His hand was nearly at his hip now.

The hunter nodded, taking in the patches on Jason's shoulders, and lowered the rifle into the layer of leaves. When he stepped back, Jason moved with a speed I had not thought possible, putting himself between me and the hunter, taking up the rifle as if it was made of bamboo.

The hunter looked between us in surprise, and then his eyes drifted further, drawing in the sight below us. His face went white with shock and he staggered down to one knee. "My God! Is he dead?"

"Have you been shooting today?" asked Jason in response, moving his nose for a moment to the barrel of the gun to sniff for signs of firing.

"Yes, sure, for coyote," agreed the hunter, his voice rough. "But I'm careful! I never would've shot a *person*."

Jason glanced for a moment back at the fallen man. "He might not have been easy to see," he pointed out. "Forest green jacket, blue jeans, he could have looked like a shadowy movement."

The hunter shook his head fiercely. "Ask anyone," he stated, his voice becoming firmer. "I call them my Popovich Principles. I look three times before I even put my finger into the trigger guard. I hear too many tales of accidents. I only took three shots today, and each time my target was solid."

My throat was dry. "Were you sure of your background each time?"

He glanced up at me, and his brow creased even further. "I thought ... but I'm not sure ..."

Jason looked over to me, nodding. "We will figure that all out soon enough," he agreed. "In the meantime, miss ..."

"Morgan," I responded. "Morgan Warren. I live a few miles from here."

"Miss Warren," he echoed, an easing of tension releasing his shoulders. He rested the rifle butt-down on the forest floor. "If you don't mind, we can all wait here for the police and make sure we get all our facts straight."

I settled down cross-legged with my back against an aspen tree, breathing in the scent of juniper, and closed my eyes. After a few minutes a sense of calm resurfaced. The woods drifted toward the peaceful, quiet, eternal sense that it had possessed when I first stepped onto the trail only a short while ago.

* * *

The police had come and gone, the medics had respectfully carried away the dead body, and the forest had eased into a dark blue twilight that resembled the depths of an ocean floor. Jason had remained at my side through it all. Now he stared with me down at the empty space at the base of the ravine. The scattering of witch hazel along the edges added a faint golden glisten to the scene.

"But I didn't hear a shot," I stated finally, as if that made all the difference.

He gave his head a short shake. "Mr. Popovich began his hunting back at dawn," he pointed out. "The victim was apparently shot a few hours later. The body was long dead by the time you reached it. He was undoubtedly dead before you left your house to come here. The M.E. will let us know for sure."

"He looked asleep," I continued. My thoughts were not quite coming in a coherent fashion.

He hesitated for a moment, then put an arm around my shoulder to comfort me. "Can I take you home?"

I shook my head. I was forty-three years old. Certainly old enough to be able to cope with this situation, as unusual as it was. And my home was a mere five-minute drive.

"I'll be fine," I assured him. But it was another long minute before I could pull my eyes from the spot and turn to navigate back around the fallen tree.

"We may need to ask you follow-up questions in the coming days, as we pursue our investigation," he murmured as we made our way up the trail.

"Of course," I agreed, my eyes taking in the forest around me as if it had recently sprung to life. Every twisted branch, every fluttering oak leaf clinging tenaciously to its tree sent a small surge of adrenaline through me. I wrapped my tangerine sarong even closer around my shoulders.

Worry creased Jason's eyes, and he ran a hand through his chestnut-brown hair. I wondered for a moment where his biking helmet had gone, and then remembered the police taking it and his bike back with them at his request.

A strange sense of loss nestled in my heart; I spoke to shake it loose. "I'm sorry to have kept you behind with me."

"Not at all," he demurred with understanding in his eyes. "I was happy to stay."

I lapsed into silence again, absorbed in the soft crunch of leaves beneath my feet, in the soft whistling of the dusk breeze as it scattered through birch and aspen. Jason was steady at my side. My shoulders slowly eased as we walked along the trail.

At last the trail widened before us. I'd never seen the vehicle gate at the mouth standing open, and it brought into focus again just what had happened here. I stared at it for a long moment before bringing my eyes up to the two cars standing side by side, his white F-150, my dark-green Forester.

He fished in a side pocket and brought out a card. "If you need anything – anything at all – you just call," he offered, and his eyes were warm as he handed the card to me.

I nodded, turned, and then I was back in the safety of my car, driving toward the security of home.

Chapter 2

I jolted straight up in bed, my heart pounding in my chest, the vision burned into my eyes. The dead man had been lying on his blanket of dark brown oak leaves, their crenelated forms lacing around the edges of his body. Then his glazed eyes had narrowed into focus, his head had turned, and he had stared right at me.

I could feel it, still, the power of his gaze, the pleading and desolation in his eyes. He had not wanted to die. He had so much still to share, to tell the world, and he had been cut short. I knew it with every cell in my body.

It took a few minutes before my breathing slowed, before I could blink into awareness of my surroundings. A gentle glow eased in around the double-shades that kept the room as dark as possible. I often worked late into the night, with the website maintenance tasks I handled from my home office, and the only way I could get ample sleep was to keep my bedroom as dark as a crypt. Glancing at my clock, I found it was nearly noon.

I pushed aside the heavy comforter and wearily pulled my yoga pants from the shelf, along with a robin's-egg blue top. I knew from years of experimentation that if I did not do my yoga session right when I got up that it would quickly become lost in the whirlwind which was my day. Email messages would flash urgently on my screen, software would crash, and a myriad of other problems would keep me engaged until I glanced out my window and realized the sun was, yet again, easing its way up over the horizon to signal a new day had begun.

I padded my way down the stairs, poured myself a tall glass of water, then unrolled my lavender mat before the sliding glass doors of my dining area. The view looked across my back deck and out over the tree-ringed yard. I gave thanks again to the life path which had brought me here. My neighbors' homes were barely visible on either side through the dense trees, and beyond the back yard the forest ran for a half-mile before it came up on Route 146. My quiet corner of the world was lush with wild turkeys, inquisitive chipmunks, and even the occasional deer.

I began my routine. First some gentle twists, loosening the ligaments, and then into tree-pose, the one-legged stance that Masai men used for hours when watching over their grazing animals. I stared out at the elderly oak tree, balanced, and let my mind go. The dark hole in the tree's center was where the local squirrel family raised its young. I recalled the early summer morning when I had been enjoying my routine on the back porch. I had watched their little heads peer eagerly from the dark recesses before streaming out, one after another, to explore their world.

A flash of color awakened me from my memories. A red-tailed hawk eased serenely across the center of the yard, pulling up with a careful wing adjustment to land in a nearby maple. I smiled, admiring his beauty, while also feeling the familiar twinge of worry for the many birds which came to my bird feeders. I sometimes felt as if I were putting a buffet out for the hawk as well as the smaller birds. And yet I could not bring myself to take down the suet, thistle, or sunflower seeds. Plenty for everyone, hawks included.

The sun salutations were next, and, as she always did, my striped cat Juliet came to take advantage of my helplessness while I held downward facing dog. She was nearly eleven now, and I could still remember the snowy morning I had found her on my back stoop, plaintively eating bits of suet I had dropped while filling the feeder. She had been rail-thin and shivering. I fed her outside for the day, thinking she was a neighbor's cat, but soon my concern increased and I had taken her in. I had put up signs, called the local vets, and talked with the neighbors. They told me this happened all the time. "City folk" from Worcester, tired of their pets, abandoned them in our woods thinking the domesticated animals would instantly turn into mouse-hunters and live a gloriously free life. Instead, most ended up being eaten by coyotes and raccoons.

So Juliet had become mine, and I had dealt with the allergies as a small price to pay for the steadfast love she had provided. Even now my skin tingled as she meandered between my arms, making sure to delicately trace her tail over every inch of my face and neck.

Into warrior pose II. This always reminded me of an archer, drawing back the string on her bow, focusing all of her attention on the shot ahead of her.

The shot.

My breathing caught. I wavered for a moment, then shook it off. This practice was about releasing thoughts – about losing oneself in the moment awhile. That training served me well through each day, helped me to focus and move through challenges as smoothly as I could.

I finished the warrior poses and sat down on the mat to do my seated twist. I loved this action; I could feel the vertebrae in my spine lifting and relaxing, settling more properly in their alignment. It felt good in a way few things did.

Then it was cat-cow, which to my amusement some yoga instructors were now calling relaxed cat and arched cat. Apparently women didn't like being called "cows". Were we that concerned about our appearance that even the names of simple animal shapes could hurt us? I did not mind at all the thought of being a serene, contented jersey in a highland meadow, breathing in the fresh breezes, nibbling on heather flowers and soaking in the joy of living.

And then, extended child pose. A relaxing of everything, forehead to the mat, arms stretched forward in an ultimate release to the universe.

The sobs came on slowly at first, a hiccup in my breathing, then they were shaking me loose, the tears streaming from my eyes in a river, my palms pressed flat against the mat in surrender. I could not tell where the emotion had come from; it simply was there, densely surrounding me. It was as if from a peaceful, blue day a roiling thunderstorm had materialized, the slate-grey clouds filling my senses, the rolling thunder going on for long minutes without rest.

At long last the storm began to break, glimpses of sky appeared through the rain, and my breathing was more than a desperate gulp amongst the cries. I lay slumped against the mat, pulling my shirt up to blot away the dampness of my face.

The phone rang.

I gave my head a shake to clear it, then pushed myself to my feet, taking the two steps to where the phone sat alongside the sliding glass door.

"Yes?" I asked shakily. Confusion laced through my thoughts. Nobody ever called me. My friends and family all understood I preferred email, especially with the odd hours I kept. For all they knew I was still sound asleep after doing a server upgrade until six a.m.

"Morgan Warren?" asked a deep voice which seemed strangely familiar. I could not place it and sagged with the guilt of my inability to recognize who it was.

"Yes," I said again, my mind not processing thoughts in a linear order. Was I supposed to say something else?

"This is Jason, the ranger you met yesterday," he supplied.

Suddenly the dominos began to settle into a line, the world adjusted itself into a clearer pattern. Yes. That had been the voice alongside me as the waves of police arrived, as the EMTs came to examine the body, as the hunter was taken off to answer questions at the station.

His voice came again in my ear. "Morgan, are you all right?"

I realized that I must have left a pause; my brain was not quite moving forward. "Yes," I lied automatically, for it was what people always said, wasn't it? Things were fine. Everything was going to be fine.

Now he paused for a moment, and when he spoke again a trace of worry had roughened his voice. "Morgan, do you have someone you can talk with?"

I ran a hand distractedly along my hair, smoothing it back into place. "I was going to go by Matthew's tomorrow."

His voice was short. "Oh." Another pause. "Well, if you need anything, you still have my card, right?"

"Yes," I agreed. I remembered now, the clean edges of the piece of paper, the whiteness of it against the twisting browns of the forest floor. The feel of his fingers against mine as he handed it to me – warm, sure, steady.

"I will let you go, then," he murmured, and his voice sounded far away. "Have a ... well, hang in there."

"You too," I answered, and then there was a soft click as the connection ended.

I put the phone back into its cradle. I had meant to see Matthew, it was true. He was in his late sixties and volunteered at the Sutton Senior Center, running computer training and repairing PCs for the community there. I was on a de-cluttering push and had found some spare power supplies and DVD drives that I knew he would put to good use. Besides, Matthew and his wife Joan were wonderful people to spend time with. Their home faced out over Ramshorn Pond. I'd spent many delightful afternoons sitting on their back porch, sipping tea, watching the resident heron glide slowly across the water.

But I did not know if I could bring myself to face the world quite yet, not after what had happened.

I finished my yoga routine, ending by sitting cross-legged and staring out into the yard. There was a gentle carpet of leaves, this one different from the forest, for I had a selection of maples in my mix which was mostly absent in the deeper woods. The edges of the lawn were a beautiful watercolor of yellows, crimsons, and fading greens created by the Virginia creeper which billowed there.

In the center of the lawn a square was marked off by black wire fencing; within it the remnants of the summer's tangerine-orange day lilies were held in place. A double shepherd's crook sprouted from their center. In warmer weather it held a pair of hummingbird feeders, and my yoga sessions were delightfully punctuated by visits of these buzzing helicopters of crimson and emerald. But the first frost had already come and gone, and now suet feeders hung there, luring in the nuthatches and chickadees.

Namaste.

I stood and made myself a protein shake for breakfast, as I always did, then walked the twenty steps into my home office, settling down before my computer, preparing to start my day.

I scanned my email, the normal litany of concerns and questions and suggestions jostling for my attention. But it was only moments before I had opened a browser window and hopped to the Worcester Telegram's website. Sutton was not large enough to have a paper of its own – we were but a small part of Worcester County, and only when something fairly exciting happened here would we get mentioned in the paper. I imagined that this might qualify.

Even so, it was not the lead story. A large section blared about "Election 2012", while the other feature was on how Hurricane Sandy's path through our region had not seemed to affect gas prices. The US unemployment rate rose to 7.9%. I had to look down further before I found a mention of it. "Tragic Hunting Accident in Sutton".

I paused for a moment before clicking. How would they reduce a life of a man – a life cut short in an instant – to simple black and white words?

They did their best. His name had been John Dixon, aged 71. He had grown up in Sutton and had worked as an ad executive for many years. He had enjoyed fishing and reading. He was survived by one son, also of Sutton.

I stared at John's photo, striving to replace the scene in my mind with this happy, smiling man. John had embraced life, had relished time with his son, had likely cast from the banks of Lake Singletary seeking the elusive rainbow trout.

At least his death had been quick, or so had murmured the EMTs as they bundled his body into the black bag. Straight through the heart, instant, perhaps even painless. Compared with other scenes they had visited, and given the myriad of choices life tended to offer, not a bad way to go after all.

I closed the browser window, pensive. I wanted to learn more about this man and how he had come to this sudden end.

Chapter 3

Ramshorn Pond stretched out before me in its autumnal splendor, gently fluffy clouds drifting across a sky the color of a Civil War silken ball-gown. Enough of the trees clung stubbornly to their foliage to give a dappled vermilion-gold effect to the edge of the water. Matthew's lawn eased down a slope to the banks of the pond. His wooden dock stood empty; the pontoon boat had been pulled out and winterized weeks ago. The water level had been lowered in preparation for the coming season of ice, and I could clearly see where the worn stone steps allowed one, in warmer months, to walk straight into the shallow depths.

I turned from the landscape and moved toward his door. The entrance was to the side of his two-story home, with the back offering a large porch overlooking the pond. I had sat there many happy summer afternoons, watching the hummingbirds flit at the feeders, relaxing after a day kayaking around the edges of the pond. Matthew and Joan offered warm conversation to go with access to their bucolic corner of the world.

The door was pulled open promptly to my knock, and Matthew stepped forward to wrap me in a warm embrace. He was in his late sixties, his blue eyes sharp and attentive within a face that showed the wear of age. A bit taller than me, he stayed in good shape with an active life.

"How are you doing, Morgan?" he asked as he stepped back to draw me in. The corners of his eyes creased in worry as he looked me over. "You look stretched thin."

I nodded, plunking down the hemp bag overflowing with computer gear. "I am not sleeping well," I admitted. "I suppose it is to be expected."

"You take care of yourself," he cautioned. "Come, have a seat."

Joan's voice called out from the kitchen. "Would you like some tea? The herbals I have are mint, chamomile, and raspberry."

"Raspberry would be lovely," I answered, settling down into their fluffy couch. I always enjoyed coming to Matthew and Joan's home. It was comfortable in a New England sort of way, with bulging couches one could sink into, a sturdy wooden table within easy reach, and a décor that spoke of nature and beloved family. And then, of course, there were the large windows which overlooked Ramshorn Pond. The beauty that surrounded them brought solace to my soul.

Joan moved into the room carrying a burgundy mug. "Here you go, my dear," she offered, placing it on a coaster before me. Joan was the perfect match for Matthew – warm, compassionate, with a quick mind and a lively heart. She sat down across from me. "Would you like anything to eat?"

I shook my head. "I just stopped by to drop off some spare parts for Matthew," I deferred. "A few power supplies, two DVD drives, an old graphics card, and a router. I thought he might find them useful for the systems he builds for the seniors."

Matthew nodded with a smile. "Indeed I shall. Your donations are always greatly appreciated."

He paused, giving me space, and I sipped my tea. Usually he swung by my house to pick up the odds and ends I had for him, to save me the drive. He settled down next to Joan, patient, waiting.

I looked down at the warm tea in my hands, watching the tendrils of stream as they drifted up from the dark surface. At last I spoke. "Did you two know him?"

Matthew looked at me with kindness. "Yes, we did," he stated. "He was quite popular at the senior center. Always coming and going with a new story to tell. The folks there have been talking of nothing else since we heard the news yesterday afternoon."

Joan's eyes sparkled. "He was something of a lothario," she added. "The ratio at the senior center is nearly ten to one in favor of the men. John certainly took advantage of those odds, and delighted in flirting with every female within sight." She blushed a soft pink. "Sometimes the main hall was called 'John's harem', with how warmly he was greeted there."

I thought back to the photo of him on the Telegram website, of the joy in his eyes, the smile on his lips. "So he had a good life?"

Matthew's voice was warm. "He did indeed," he agreed. "His son lived nearby, he fished weekly with his best friend Adam, and he had a large group of friends. He was even working on his dream project – writing his memoirs."

"Oh?" I asked, intrigued. "About his senior center dalliances?"

Joan laughed merrily. "Oh, no," she countered. "If he started in on that, there would be scandals! No, I imagine it was about his days in Vietnam and his travels after that. He spent years doing political work of some sort all over southeast Asia."

"He was drafted?" I asked.

Matthew shook his head. "He was one of the odd ones," he countered. "He actually enlisted. And it was even stranger, because he was merry."

My brow wrinkled in confusion. "I suppose it was normally the more serious ones who went off to war."

His eyes twinkled and he shook his head again. "No, no, I mean Merry, as in one of the hobbits," he corrected. "He and his three friends were a few years ahead of me in school, but they cut quite a figure in the late sixties. I suppose in earlier decades they might have styled themselves as the Four Musketeers, or even the Four Horsemen of the Apocalypse, depending on their nature. But these were the sixties, and we were rebelling against Sputnik and bomb shelters and a TV in every house."

He sat back against the couch, remembering. "They loved Tolkien's world, even carried around pipes, and had a stodgy old bulldog named Bilbo. They were inseparable. John was Merry, and it seemed every girl in school wanted to be at his side. He had this way about him, even then, a smile that had them melting."

"So, did they all enlist together?"

He shook his head. "No, I think Eileen's death shook them apart. John enlisted. Charles and Richard went off to college, and Sam Sares stayed behind to work on his father's dairy farm. They were all drawn back to Sutton in the end, but I never got the sense that their friendship ever rekindled."

I looked between the two of them. "Who was Eileen?"

Joan's voice was soft. "Eileen Hudson," she expanded. "A lovely girl, with long, straight blonde hair that seemed to come right out of a sixties fashion magazine. She drowned in Lake Singletary during a boating accident. It shook many of us hard, to think that life could end like that for someone our age. After that, several of the boys enlisted and a few couples married rather than wait."

I nodded in understanding. "I suppose seeing death tends to remind us of how ephemeral life is and to treasure each day," I mused.

My eyes fell on the bag of computer supplies at my side. "So John was going to start writing about all of these things, and then he's killed?"

Matthew's eyes sharpened with curiosity. "I thought his death was an accident?"

I pursed my lips in consideration. "The hunter had heard no other shots during the day, and he was absolutely sure that he had never taken a shot in John's direction. The only three shots he fired were to the north, after a coyote he was tracking."

Joan's voice was firm. "I would trust Popovich," she agreed. "He volunteers with our garden club and he is the most meticulous man I have ever seen. Every seedling is placed at the perfect depth, in soil the ideal pH. He leaves nothing to chance."

Matthew looked at me. "Have they found the bullet?"

I shook my head. "The M.E.s said it went right through him, and they had not found it when we left that night. I suppose I could check with Jason …"

"Jason, he was the ranger in the woods?"

I nodded. "Yes. I am very glad he was there. He was ... steady."

I gave myself a shake. Suddenly I wanted to be back home, wrapped by my own things. "I really should get going," I stated, taking a final drink on my tea. "Thank you for your hospitality."

Matthew stood and emptied the items out of my bag, handing it back to me. "You are always welcome, if you want to talk, or just look out at the pond," he offered.

"I appreciate that." I stepped forward to give him a hug, and then Joan. "I just want to be home."

My hand was reaching for my cellphone as the door closed behind me.

* * *

"Jason here," came his greeting as I headed toward Central Turnpike, and I found myself blushing for no reason at all. His voice sounded comforting and strong, like my thick, navy-blue robe I pulled around my shoulders when climbing out of bed on a wintry morning. It was a moment before I could answer.

"It ... it's Morgan."

He gave a sound of surprised welcome. "Oh! It's good to hear from you. How can I help you?"

"Did they find the bullet?" I blurted out.

There was a pause, and his voice was more careful when it came. "No, they did not," he stated. "We have had good weather these past two days, but there is no trace of it anywhere."

"And the M.E., is he sure it was the same kind of bullet that the hunter's gun shot?"

This time I definitely heard the concern in his voice. "I really should not be discussing the details –"

"I was there," I argued, my heart suddenly pounding, and I gave myself a shake, taking the left onto Central Turnpike, focusing on the road for a minute. My emotions were wild, untethered, like a five-year-old on a post-Halloween sugar high.

His voice was low and soothing. "I know you were."

"I just … I feel like I need to know the truth." I took in a deep breath, marshaling my thoughts. I could still see John's eyes, glassy, staring up into the firmament as if caught by surprise. Overlaid were the images from my nightmares, of his eyes gazing into mine with serious attention, as if he were relying on me for something.

Jason's voice came through my musings. "The M.E. has not issued his final report."

"What do you think it will say?" For some reason hearing his answer was suddenly all-important to me.

I came to the four-way intersection by the burnt-out husk of the Blue Jay Restaurant. I had gone there, back when it was whole, a comfortable family-style place with friendly staff and down-home food on the menu. Then it was gone in a burst of flame and falling timbers, and years had passed while its rotting shell fell in on itself. Now only the foundation remained. The owners had given up on finding a suitable buyer for it and had at last agreed to sell it to the town.

Given up. A tragedy, a violent loss, and then people simply gave up.

Jason's voice was cautious. "I don't know if I should –"

"But I found him!" I shouted into the phone, as if that made all the difference in the world. "I am the one who came to him, and now he comes to me, and I have to make it right. Something happened out there, and I don't know what, and it feels like –"

The road dipped down toward the soccer fields, there was a clicking in my ear, and the phone went dead.

I swore in fury, knowing my emotions were wildly out of kilter and not caring in the least. I flung the phone down onto the passenger seat, speeding up to get through the dead zone. In the past it had merely baffled me. How could Sutton set up kids' soccer fields - a full-contact sport if ever there was one - in a location where cell phones died like mayflies on a summer evening? Now the silent stretch of space edged me to a roiling boil.

I was back up the other side of the hill approaching 146 when my phone rang to life. I grabbed it.

Jason's voice crackled with worry. "Morgan! Are you all right?"

"Yes, yes," I half-growled. "Just the cell phone company trying to teach me lessons in patience."

Jason's voice eased into relief. "That's good," he breathed.

I drew my lips into a line, letting out a sigh. Jason had been kind to me; he did not deserve to be in the path of my lava flow. "Anyway, I'm sorry for –"

"No apologies needed," demurred Jason, his voice brooking no argument. "And you are right. You found him. You deserve to know what's going on. I will let you know as soon as I hear from the M.E."

A ripple moved through my heart, and I hadn't realized how tense my shoulders were until the knots loosened even slightly. "Thank you."

I let out a breath. "I should be going. I appreciate your ..." I paused, and my cheeks flushed. "Your being patient with me."

"Any time."

For some reason I had the sense that he meant it.

Chapter 4

I sat at my kitchen table, holding the mug of tea in my hands, looking out at the feeder in the side yard. A blue jay hung on the side of the sunflower seed feeder, hogging the seeds, swallowing them whole. A brave chickadee swooped to the opposite side, grabbed a hold of a single seed, then flitted away.

A movement caught my eye, and I smiled as a small flock of juncos descended on the cracked corn I had scattered on the larger rock at the edge of the property line. *Winter was coming.* The foraging of the small half-grey, half-white birds was one of the clearest indications we had that snow was just around the corner. Luckily I had already put away all the lawn items last week before Sandy descended on the region, so I was ready for the snow. Last year we had the infamous Halloween nor'easter which blanketed us with nearly a foot. Perhaps we were lucky that it was November fourth and we were still snow-free.

I sighed and sipped my tea, rolling my head along my shoulders. I hadn't slept well last night, and once again my yoga routine in the morning had failed to bring me peace. My hands still smelt of rosemary from where I had run them through my container plant before beginning yoga practice. I breathed in the pungent smell.

At last I grabbed one of my hemp bags and began filling it with the leftover cookie packs from Halloween. I had only had nineteen kids this year, in three large groups. This left me with quite a few goodie bags which needed to go to the food pantry before they ended up in my stomach. I knew that part of the lure was that the food pantry was located in the Sutton Senior Center, and I was curious to see what the talk was there about John's death.

* * *

The Sutton Senior Center is located on Hough Road. To its left was a playground, complete with softball field and slide. To its right lay a large cemetery. I often wondered how the seniors felt about that, sandwiched between the joyful activity of youth and a final resting place.

The building was low, long, and fairly pleasant. An administrative counter lay to the left as I came in, and I knew Matthew's computer lab and training area was through a door to the right. I moved to the counter, hefting my bag of goodies onto the wood.

I called out through the open doorway to the woman sitting in the office beyond. "A few things for the pantry," I let her know with a smile.

"Certainly," she responded brightly, coming over to meet me. "I am sure these will be appreciated as we head into the holiday season. Just leave them in that box there." She motioned to a cardboard box to the left of the counter.

I nodded, depositing the items where she asked, then moved down the hall to the main room. A scattering of round tables and wooden chairs were arranged on a blue-and-white diamond-tiled floor. There were perhaps fifteen people sitting and talking quietly. Most of the seniors were female, but there were a few men peppering the room. For today, at least, the predominant color of clothing was somber black.

One of the men looked up as I entered, and he stood to come greet me. He had dark hair with just a single streak of grey along his left temple. He was slender, but far from gaunt, and his dark eyes held a thriving strength to them.

"You'll be Morgan," he welcomed me with a gentle Texan drawl. "Matthew said you might be by. I'm Adam; John was a dear friend of mine."

"I am sorry for your loss," I offered, taking his hands in mine. They were thin, but far from feeble. "Matthew said that you and John spent a lot of time together."

He nodded in agreement. "Yes, we did. When I moved up from Texas, some fifteen years ago, John was the one who welcomed me and made me feel at home. He and I shared a love of fishin'."

He brought me over to one of the unoccupied tables, waiting for me to sit before he took his own seat alongside me.

I found it hard to begin. "What was he like?" I asked at last.

He smiled, his eyes misting for a moment. "He enjoyed life," he stated. He glanced around him. "He loved it here. He was the head honcho, and it seemed that everyone who met him adored him."

"But not his friends from his youth?"

The corner of his mouth turned up in a smile. "So Matthew told you about the four hobbits?" he asked, his eyes sparkling. "Yes, John would laugh about that. I think he felt he had outgrown that group; they had stayed within their little village while he had gone off and seen the world. He thought they could no longer relate to all the things he had done and experienced."

"And you?"

"I was in politics, like John. I grew up in Texas, became an Army Ranger out of high school, and then went here and there for quite a while. When I ended up in Sutton after I retired, John and I became fast friends." A shadow crossed his eyes. "He was taken far too soon. A horrible, tragic accident."

I leant forward. "So you feel it was the hunter?"

One eyebrow raised in curiosity. "Why, what else could it be?"

I lowered my voice. "Well, they have not found the bullet yet," I confided. "And the hunter swears he was not shooting in that direction."

His brows creased. "So you think someone did this to him deliberately?"

I shrugged. "I don't know what I think," I admitted. "It just seems very odd. He should have known better than to be in those woods in the middle of hunting season, dressed in forest green. Where was his car? And he just happens to be shot by the lone hunter who is aiming in the opposite direction?"

He nodded slowly. "I see your point. What do the police think?"

"The police are still investigating; perhaps they will come up with something soon. After all, it has only been a few days."

His lips pressed together. "From what I read, if a crime is not solved within the first forty-eight hours, the chances of doing so drop. Any traces of evidence are quickly washed away."

A woman's voice called out from the far end of the table. "Scrabble!"

He looked up. "I am afraid they need me to make a fourth," he admitted. "But if you are serious –"

I shook my head, not sure of anything at all. "I am still wound up from what I saw," I demurred. "I only have vague worries and unsettled feelings."

"Still," he pressed. "If you're fixin' to poke into this, I would be interested in hearing any news you come across. John was a good friend of mine. Perhaps this would be worth us looking into further."

I nodded my head. "Maybe when the M.E. report is finalized we'll know more."

"That's a good idea, to wait to see what it says," he agreed. "Can we touch base then?"

I nodded, and he took my hand for a moment before turning away.

* * *

The evening sky was filling with rich shades of blue, fading down to a delicate peach along the corrugated skyline of fir tops. I was driving south, toward Newport, Rhode Island, to have dinner with my mother and stepfather for her birthday. Route four was clear, and I drew in a deep breath, soaking in the beauty of the glistening sunset.

My cell rang, and I picked it up. "Hello?"

"Hey, Morgan, it's Jason."

My heart did a skipping step, and I pressed the phone closer to my ear for a moment. "It's good to hear from you."

"It's good to be heard," he replied, and there was a gentle smile in his voice. Then his tone became serious. "The M.E. report has been filed."

"And?"

"And the cause of death is a single gunshot wound to the heart. They are leaving the topic of accidental versus deliberate open. That cannot be determined."

I sighed. "They have no idea if it was the same caliber bullet as that hunter used?"

"It most likely was, but that doesn't get us very far. Many guns would take a bullet of that caliber. It could have been the hunter's gun – or it could have been a thousand others."

"What do the police think?"

He let out a breath. "Occam's razor is in play here, I think. We have a man dead in the woods with a gunshot wound. We have a hunter in those same woods, shooting a gun. Popovich heard no other shot, and saw no other person, since his arrival at dawn. Finally, we can find no real motive." He shrugged. "The police are leaning toward a tragic accident; some sort of a bizarre ricochet."

"Maybe he was shot elsewhere?"

"No, the M.E. says he was shot in that gulley and died instantly, right there."

I tapped my fingers on the steering wheel. "So Popovich should have heard if there was another gunshot. Unless John was killed before dawn?"

I could almost hear him shaking his head. "The M.E. puts time of death about eleven in the morning. We have several witnesses who drove past the entrance around that time frame, and the only car there was Popovich's."

"How did John get there, then?"

"Apparently his house is only two miles from the woods. His son says that he often liked to go there to think and relax. It wouldn't have been that unusual for him."

I shook my head. It just didn't feel right. "Without any bright colors on him?" I prodded. "In the middle of hunting season?"

"I know, it does seem odd," he agreed. "But still, odd enough to invent some sort of a ninja-assassin killer?"

When he put it that way, it did seem rather far-fetched.

My car started up over the Jamestown bridge and I looked down on the tiny island before me. "Now it's barely a speed bump," I murmured.

"What?"

"Crossing Jamestown," I explained. "I imagine in centuries past that it was a fairly long process, to get a ferry first onto Jamestown and then off on the other side. Now you barely notice you're on the island at all."

The car touched down on the island, and almost immediately came the signs about the fast lane for the upcoming bridge on the other side. "I bet I'm across in under four minutes."

"Heading to Newport?"

"Yes, to Zelda's Café. A birthday dinner with my mom and stepdad."

"I'll let you go, then," he offered. "Have a pleasant evening. Try to put this all aside, at least for a few hours."

The road turned a corner and the bridge stretched out before me, sparkling with tiny white lights as if it had been laced with Christmas tree decorations. "I'm on the other side already," I reported. "I wonder if the Jamestown residents would prefer the state tunnel over this road entirely, so we zoom through without disturbing their peace."

"Maybe they would," he agreed, a smile in his voice. "Have fun, Morgan."

"Good night," I chuckled, and with a click he was gone.

* * *

Zelda's was a small restaurant, the right half a rowdy bar with exuberant locals, the left half a nautically themed upscale dining area. Its walls were decorated with navy-blue stripes interlaced with white, and drawings of clipper ships added an interesting visual appeal. I noticed the Enterprise as I entered, and thought with a smile how that name had graced so many different vessels over the years. Just that morning I had heard from a friend who lived in New York City; he had still not regained power from Sandy and decided off-the-cuff to abandon home for a week's cruise. The Norwegian Gem had passed an aircraft carrier in the harbor, and my friend had enjoyed viewing the shuttle Enterprise which was housed on its deck. Apparently the Enterprise should have been covered for security reasons, but the hurricane had ruthlessly stripped away its protective grey shield.

My mom and stepfather were waiting for me. I exchanged warm hugs with them before we were led to our table. My mother was shorter than me, with neatly trimmed short, dark hair and a warm smile. My stepfather, Frank, was just slightly taller than her, and his Italian heritage shone through in his olive skin and aquiline nose.

"It's always good to see you," my mother welcomed as we settled down at the corner table. She turned to the waitress. "A bottle of Prosecco to start," she ordered. We glanced over the prix fixe menu, a staple of Restaurant Week in Newport.

Her mouth turned up in a smile. "I bet I can guess what you'll have," she teased gently. "Tuna appetizer, swordfish, and chocolate mousse."

I scanned the entries and nodded. "That's it exactly," I agreed. "Everything looks good, though."

"Did I tell you we saw a cougar in our yard a few weeks ago?" she asked, nodding as the waitress came over to pour out the bubbly. We gave our orders and the menus were swept up.

"Are you sure?" I asked. "I thought there was some controversy over whether cougars were really roaming around in Connecticut."

Frank leaned over. "It certainly looked like one," he confirmed. "We googled photos of cougars, and the sloped back and tufted ears were exactly what we saw. I saw a similar creature a few months before that, too, when driving back from Waterbury. A group of deer burst out on the road, ahead of me, and, behind them, a cougar was giving chase. The cougar pulled up to let my car go past, and then it set off after them again."

My mom gave a shake of her head. "There is a man on the commuter bus I take in to Hartford who is convinced that the state is responsible for the cougars," she informed us. "Some sort of a conspiracy. He feels the wildlife experts brought in cougars and mountain lions in order to curb the deer population, and now the state doesn't want to acknowledge it for liability reasons."

"If the cougars were endangered, maybe we should be pleased to have them back, to fill the web in properly again," I mused. "Sort of like the raccoons."

"Was there a problem with raccoons?" asked my mother. "We had a female raccoon which visited our yard quite regularly, and to our delight she then began coming in with her young kits. But then suddenly they all vanished. We wondered if one of our neighbors had had them trapped and relocated."

"It wasn't that long ago that raccoons were nearly wiped out by a disease similar to rabies," I explained. "We are lucky that they are rebounding."

Her brow creased. "Are raccoons really necessary to nature?"

I gave a soft shrug. "Everything has its place. If we lose a mid-level predator like a raccoon, it could cause the larger animals to starve. And, at the same time, it could cause the smaller rodents to blossom out of control."

The appetizers arrived, and I looked down at my tuna circles. They had a crispy tempura-style edging, and were served with a semi-sweet gyoza-style sauce. I would have preferred them straight up, with soy sauce, but this was an interesting enough variation. "Sort of like the bats," I added.

Frank was enjoying his clam chowder. "What about the bats?"

I took a bite of my tuna. Yummy. I turned to him, putting down my fork.

"Bats hibernate in caves in the winter. Recently, the bats have been infected by a white fungus. It interrupts their hibernation cycle and vast numbers of them have died." I gave a wave with my hand. "The scientists cannot figure out how to stop it and, if we lose the bats, we could end up with serious mosquito overpopulation."

His brows creased in worry. "I've always liked bats. I did not realize they hibernated in groups like that."

"At least some types of them do," I offered. "We get small groups of them passing through Sutton in the fall, on their way to wherever they hibernate. I always wish them well."

He nodded, then took another sip of his soup. "This is some of the best clam chowder I've ever tasted," he praised, smiling to us. "I think because it's Rhode Island clam chowder. It seems the Boston and New England varieties are creamier, while this is more brothy. It's just right."

My mom patted him on the arm fondly. "I'm so glad you are enjoying it, dear." She turned to me. "How are you doing, with the events of the past few days?"

It was if a shadow had been lurking in the corner of the room, and it suddenly billowed into a threatening pose. "I'm still coming to grips with it," I admitted. "But it seems that it may have just been a tragic accident."

My mother's eyes were warm and kind. "Everything happens for a reason," she commented. "What have you learned about him so far?"

"That he was engaging, and that he brought joy to many people," I related. "He was preparing to publish his memoirs."

Her eyes lit up. "You're a writer," she pointed out.

A warm kindle began within me, one which glowed with a golden light. "I am," I agreed, hope buoying me.

"You could write a biography for him," she encouraged.

It felt perfect. It was as if I had been staring at a jigsaw puzzle and suddenly a piece I had not seen on the table had been handed to me. "Yes, I could."

She raised her Prosecco, and we brought up our own. "To completing the story," she toasted, and the room echoed with the soft ring of glass on glass.

* * *

I had barely made it onto the Christmas tree bridge and the first straight-away of my ride home before I was finding him in my recent calls list and pushing the button.

"Hello?" Jason answered.

My voice echoed with joy. "I know what I'm going to do."

"And what is that?" he asked, a smile coming across the speaker.

"I'll write his biography for him," I revealed in triumph. "I will finish what he began; what meant so much to him."

There was a pause, and then his voice came, slow and steady. "That's kind of you to offer; I can see his death touched you deeply."

"He deserves to have his story told," I expanded. "I will ask his son for permission, of course. But I feel as if I'm involved, somehow, and this seems right to me. I hope it will bring me the closure I'm seeking."

"His funeral is tomorrow, with the burial at the Sutton Cemetery."

"I know; I intend to be there."

"So do I. I suppose we will meet there?"

My heart warmed at the idea, and I nodded, although of course he could not see the motion. "Yes," I added out loud. "I would like that."

"Then it's a date," he confirmed, and I smiled at the thought of a date at a cemetery. I supposed that all life was cyclical, with its beginnings and endings and rebirths.

My car rumbled onto the Jamestown bridge and I chuckled. "I blinked, and I missed Jamestown again," I teased him.

He gave a low laugh. "Those islanders may build their tunnel yet and be completely free of all you interlopers," he warned.

"I wouldn't blame them in the least."

The road stretched out before me, dark and deep, but I put aside the allure of keeping him on the phone the whole way. "Until tomorrow," I offered.

"I look forward to it," he agreed, and he was gone.

Chapter 5

Afternoon brought drifting clouds and blue skies as I drove past the Sutton Senior Center and pulled into an open spot amongst the long row of cars lining the cemetery. The senior center's lot had been full as well, and there were large flocks of dark-coated men and women streaming in. Apparently, John had many admirers who wanted to see him off.

I smiled in contentment, shutting the door of the Forester and snugging my black pea coat tighter around my neck. It was not yet the frozen tundra of December, but autumn was definitely leaving us behind. The air had a crispness to it, and the remaining brown leaves which skittered past me in the breeze had a hard-edged, sharp quality to them.

Jason was waiting for me at the entrance to the cemetery, taller than I had remembered, with a black wool coat and a navy-blue scarf. His eyes caught mine, a rich, dark brown, and they held for a long moment, first with a hint of pleased surprise in them, and then a growing contentment. He stepped forward to offer a hand as I approached.

"Morgan, it is good to see you again." His tanned cheek colored slightly. "Although I would prefer we eventually get together under happier circumstances."

"It looks to be a nice enough day for it, at least," I responded, taking his hand. It was sturdy and warm.

There was a call behind us, and Matthew and Joan approached, the pair bundled up in matching ski parkas. Joan's voice was rich and gentle. "There you are, Morgan. How are you doing?" Her eyes dropped to my neck. "That scarf is lovely."

I moved a hand to touch the soft fabric. "My one indulgence," I admitted. "It was hand knitted by a lovely woman out in the Berkshires who runs her own yoga shop as well as teaching knitting classes. Karen Allen."

Jason looked at me with surprise. "Not the actress?"

I nodded my head. "The very same. When I was young, that scene of her out-drinking and out-fighting the wild men of Tibet was quite inspiring to me. It made me believe that I could hold my own, if I enthusiastically gave it my all."

Matthew's eyes were bright. "And that you do," he agreed.

I turned and looked ahead to where the crowd had gathered. I recognized a group of grey-haired women from the senior center in a huddle. John's friend Adam was at their center, his tan coat glistening in the sun, offering a murmuring of words.

The priest made a motion with his hand, and I glanced up at Jason. "Shall we head in?"

* * *

The service was heart-felt, with the priest offering thoughts on life interspersed with his homily. The casket was lowered, dirt was thrown representationally on top, and friends and family slowly dispersed. Matthew and Joan made their farewells, and yet I found I could not leave. Jason stayed quietly by my side, not saying a word, and I stared down at the grave, lost in thought.

I had found a peace of sorts. My sleep had been even, my yoga practice rich with focus and purpose. John had apparently lived a good life, one full of family and friends, with smiles and good nature. It was a story worth telling. I would at least make my offer, and see what his son had to say.

There was a soft clearing of a throat behind us, and Jason and I turned together. A short, Asian man stood before us, perhaps in his early fifties, with clear, olive skin and gently sloping eyes. His dark hair was neatly cut and he wore an elegant, doe-brown wool coat.

"I do not mean to intrude," he began, his voice gentle. "Did you know him well?"

I shook my head. "I'm afraid not," I admitted. "I never had the privilege of speaking with him."

"Then how …" His voice trailed off as he looked between us. At last he spoke again. "You must be Morgan," he started afresh, his voice holding a hint of wonder.

"I am," I agreed, curious.

He put out his hand. "I am Jeff Dixon," he introduced. "I'm John's son."

I took his hand, trying to hide the surprise that swept over me, but his mouth creased into a smile and he gave a soft shake of his head. "Everyone has that reaction," he assured me. "My father met my mother in Cambodia. She was a civil engineer working on a water project. She was already pregnant with me, but my birth father had been killed in the conflict. John was the only father I have ever known, and he was the best I could have hoped for." His eyes glistened with emotion for a moment. "I will miss him dearly."

He drew in a breath and turned to Jason. "And you must be the ranger, then. Jason, was it?"

Jason nodded, shaking his hand. "I'm sorry for your loss," he offered. "If there is anything we can do for you, please just ask."

Jeff looked between us. "You have already done so much," he insisted with feeling. "If it were not for you, he could have lain out there for weeks while I went crazy with worry. By the time we found him, he could have been –" His voice caught. "There are coyotes and raccoons in those woods," he finished after a moment. "You were a blessing, to find him so quickly."

"Your father did not suffer," consoled Jason in a low voice. "The M.E. said death was immediate."

"Another blessing," agreed Jeff. "One I am quite grateful for. I told Popovich that he should not feel any guilt at all. Anyone could have made that kind of mistake. My father loved to hunt, and their positions could easily have been reversed." He looked down at the coffin for a moment. "A tragic accident. And he had his health problems. He was nearing the end."

He pursed his lips in a line. "Still, he was so set on putting down his memoirs before he went. It had become an obsession for him, this past month, after his last trip to the doctor's. When Matthew brought that old PC for him to work on, I almost thought to myself, 'well, this is it.' I had a sense that my father would work furiously to get out the words, and then I would find him one morning, lying in bed, a glowing smile on his lips, his writing complete and his soul departed." He dropped his eyes. "I guess fate didn't offer him those last few weeks."

A tremor ran through me at my impudence, but I put voice to my thoughts. "I would like to offer to write your father's biography for you, as a gift to his memory."

He looked up at that in surprise, his gaze searching my face. "You are a writer?"

I nodded. "I write content for websites, and have always been interested in doing biographies of local Sutton residents. It would be an honor to write about your father's life."

His eyes held bright hope, but after a moment he shook his head. "I'm sure you're quite busy with your other projects," he demurred. "I appreciate your offer immensely, but I would not want to take your time with this."

I tilted my head to one side, trying to read his mood. "If you do not want me intruding, of course I understand." I looked down at the coffin for a moment. "But this is something that I feel strongly. Your father's story should be told. It would bring me contentment to be able to work on it."

There was a lightening to his features with that, and he looked at me fully. "Are you sure? This is something you want to do?"

At my nod he stepped forward, offering me a warm embrace. "Then, absolutely, I would be thrilled," he agreed with a wide smile. "I'm sure I will be busy for a week or two, with all the issues and paperwork that have only begun. But once that's handled, I would be thrilled to sit with you and tell you what I know of him."

He put a finger to his lips in thought. "Maybe some of his friends would be willing to talk with you in the meantime," he considered. "They sometimes seemed hesitant to talk with me about his youth, as if a son should not hear such things. But with you being an outsider, they might be more open to frank discussion."

His eyes became serious. "I want his full story to be told, Morgan," he added. "He was not a man to polish horse dung. He loved to tell about life as it was, warts and all. He would want the entire saga told, whatever it held."

I nodded in understanding. "I will bring you whatever I find, and you can do with it as you wish," I promised.

Jeff turned to Jason. "And you will keep a close eye on her, as she does her research?" he asked with a smile.

Jeff looked to me, a brightness coming to his eyes. "It would be an honor."

* * *

There wasn't really a coffee shop in Sutton – the Honey Dew Donuts on Route 146 South had shut down once they sealed off the cross-over with jersey barriers. That left only the Bagels and Kebobs place in the small strip-mall by the post office. Jason and I sat across from each other, him with a black coffee, me with my orange juice and freshly baked blueberry muffin.

The place was an odd juxtaposition of aromas and sights. The décor was casual New England, with formica tables, a tile floor, and a long counter stretching across the back. One corner held a bookshelf with assorted titles, and the lone female employee stared at the TV in an otherwise empty room.

Jason looked at me across our small table. "So, where do we begin?"

My cheeks warmed at the "we" statement and I dropped my gaze to my muffin. "You do not need to be dragged into my project," I demurred. "I admit this has become important to me, but I'm sure you have better things to do with your time than to squire me around."

"I would be happy to do it," he insisted gently. "Despite what you might believe, rangers don't discover dead bodies every day. Mostly we move dead trees and occasionally help with a skinned knee or a lost hiker. It's rare that we have any trouble with hunters in this part of Massachusetts. In fact, I don't know the last time we had an acc … a situation like this."

I looked up at him. "So you are not so sure one of Popovich's shots had a wild ricochet?"

He hesitated for a long moment, then shook his head. "I've started wondering about it myself," he admitted. "That makes it even more important that I accompany you as you look into it. If there really is a person out there capable of shooting someone in cold blood, right now he or she thinks they've gotten away with it."

"It could still be an accident," I pointed out. "Maybe it was another hunter, he shot John by accident, then fled. Maybe some strange coincidence caused Popovich not to hear it."

His brows creased, but he nodded. "We should consider every angle. You never know when an unlikely situation could be the truth."

I took a bite of the muffin. "When I read a memoir or biography," I mused, "It always starts at the beginning. I think we should find those three friends of his from his youth and see what John was like then. That might help us understand why he volunteered to serve in Vietnam; how he endured the 'smell of napalm in the morning' and came out the other end."

Jason nodded in agreement. "Beginning with his childhood makes sense. Do you know how to find these people?"

"Matthew had said that one of his friends, Sam Sares, went to work for his father's dairy farm. I would have to guess that was Sares Dairy over on Nipmuc Road. They have a store area which is open daily even this time of year. I was thinking of taking a run over there tomorrow. Maybe we can lure him out for lunch or dinner and see what he has to say."

"What time would you like me to pick you up?"

I glanced up at that. He gave a soft shrug, spreading his hands. "It doesn't make sense for two of us to be driving all over Sutton," he pointed out easily, "and my work hours are flexible. I do most of my ranger work around dawn, in hunting season, to make sure the hunters are following state laws."

I nodded. "I tend to be a night owl, with the work I do on my websites," I admitted. "That way my changes are done when most people are asleep. Shall we say seven p.m.?"

"I will be there," he agreed. "We will see what Sam has to tell us about John, back before he had experienced Vietnam's thunder."

Chapter 6

I heard Jason's truck turning into the driveway as I sorted through my evening email, and a trip came into my heart. All around me were the familiar trappings of my world – the inlaid wood desk that brought me so much joy, the ivory-colored parakeet in her cage to my right, the striped grey cat curled up at my feet. And here was this strange man gently intruding on my world, easing his way into my routine.

He parked alongside my Forester, then gave a look around before heading up to my front door. I pulled it open as he knocked, welcoming him with a smile.

"Nice kayak," he offered by way of greeting. "Do you go out often?"

I nodded, glancing to where it sat in the yard on its rack. "As much as I can." My brows folded of their own accord. "Although Whitinsville closing access to their reservoir this past spring was a bit cruel. I used to love kayaking on the reservoir. The water was peaceful and quiet. No motorboats."

He smiled in understanding. "Still, you have a number of options in the area," he pointed out.

I nodded, gathering up my ski jacket. "Not any more this season," I countered. "The kayak needs to get into the basement before the snow comes down tomorrow."

"I would be happy to lend a hand," he offered.

"After we get through today," I suggested. "First we need to get out to Sares Farms to get a sense of what it is like. If Sam is there, we can see what he has to say."

"Ready when you are."

We piled into his truck and were on our way. We drove for a few minutes in silence before he spoke without turning his eyes from the road. "Do you have a plan?"

I shrugged. "Poke at the bushes and see what emerges," I admitted. "Right now we know little. The more we ask, the more we know, and we can see what shapes form."

He nodded, then glanced at the dashboard. "Do you mind a little music?"

I was intrigued to see what he had in there. "By all means," I offered. "Your car, your rules."

He hesitated for a moment, then reached forward to push a button.

A gentle acoustic guitar began, a folk-Celtic mix, and then a woman's voice rose above it. I blinked in surprise. The lyrics began.

I'm eighteen acres of wild country here
With wild summer roses in my hair -

"That's Neptune's Car," I said in surprise.

He glanced over at that, curiosity in his eyes. "You know them?"

"Certainly," I agreed. "Holly, the singer, she's from Sutton. She's amazing."

"My band played with them a few weeks back," he explained. "We were doing a benefit concert in Worcester, at the Boiler Room."

"You're in a band?" I asked, as Holly's beautiful melodies intertwined with her guitar player's deeper voice.

He nodded, slowing to a stop at the remains of the Blue Jay restaurant. The concrete foundations stared blankly from where the burnt-out husk had been removed. "I play bass guitar for a local band."

A comfortable feeling wrapped me. He was the foundation of the band, the reliable rhythm that eased through and beneath everything they did. It fit perfectly.

"What kind of music do you play?" I asked as we set into motion again.

He shrugged slightly, his eyes flicking to me for a moment in what might have been a nervous gesture. "A blend. Classic rock, modern music, blues. Zeppelin, Adele, Taylor Swift."

"Sounds lovely," I mused, intrigued.

He paused for a moment. "We have a concert coming up on Saturday, if you'd like to see us. It's a benefit at the Singletary Rod and Gun club, on the Oxford line."

"I would like that a lot," I agreed.

He smiled, then, and glanced over for a moment. Then he was back to watching the road, his gaze serious again.

"Did you want to do this quickly, so you can get to the fire station to vote?" he asked, and his tone was carefully neutral.

I shook my head. "I took care of that already," I let him know. "A close presidential election this year, and some interesting ballot questions. Medical marijuana and right-to-die."

"Hmmmm," he offered.

I smiled at that. I tended to hold my political leanings close to the vest, and with all the deluge of flyers and pamphlets in my mailbox for the past month, I appreciated that someone else was willing to keep low key on the topic.

When I did not respond, he smiled. "I voted as well," he stated, "and I see you are not belligerent about your politics. That's a welcome relief."

"There's a reason I thought about going out to talk with Sam today," I stated. "A good way to stay away from the TV and its non-stop coverage."

He turned left onto Nipmuc Road, and in short order we were driving amongst farm buildings and open fields. "Here we are," he stated after a moment. "This is their farm store."

My eyes lit up. To the right was a small pen, and behind it was a larger pasture with a pair of small horses. I went to the pen first. It was chilly out, and I pulled the neck of my parka closer. A small calf was in a plastic shed, curled up against himself. I felt his isolation. Cows are herd creatures; they feel safest when among a group of their own kind, bolstered by their members. He seemed alone and unsure.

"Hey there, little one," I called out to the white-and-black animal, and he blinked at me with large, brown eyes.

We strolled around to the back pasture, and one of the small horses ambled over to greet us. I stayed back, but Jason moved forward to the rail, waiting for the chestnut to approach him. The horse nibbled at his arm, the long pink tongue lapping along its length, searching for a carrot. Jason waited until the horse nuzzled him in the elbow before reaching out to gently rub along his nose.

"Friendly," I agreed, glancing back at the other horse which remained at the far end of the pasture. "I guess he thinks we might be bringing him a treat."

The front of the store held an assortment of decorative gourds as well as butternut squash. Inside the space was small but well maintained. Freezer space held home-made pies and cuts of meat. There was local honey, from tupelo to blueberry to orange blossom. There was fudge from Eaton Farms, another local shop. Several varieties of apples were on offer. And then there were items clearly brought in from elsewhere – pineapples, for example.

I was intrigued by the blueberry honey, and we brought a jar to the register. As the young woman rang it up, I asked if Sam was around. She nodded in answer, and after she handed me my change she headed into the back room.

Sam was much as I had imagined he would be. Stocky, creased, with greying hair and weathered skin. He was wearing blue jeans and a blue flannel top.

His voice was gruff but not unkind. "You wanted to see me?"

I put out my hand. "My name is Morgan Warren, and this is my friend Jason Rowland. We have come to talk with you about John Dixon."

A shadow drifted across his face, but he shook our hands. "A tragedy," he stated roughly.

I paused for a moment. "John had been working on his memoirs, and I have talked with his son, Jeff. I would like to do my best to finish that project, to honor John's memory."

A different look skated across the surface of Sam's skin at that; a confusing mixture of emotions that was difficult to decipher before it vanished again. "Oh?"

"If you have some time, it would be my treat at Tony's Pizza, to spend a few minutes learning more about what John was like when he was younger," I offered. "Nothing complicated. I would just like a sense of where the man began."

He paused for a long moment, gazing around him at the shelves of neatly stacked maple syrup and home-made fudge. "All right," he said at last. "That seems reasonable."

He turned to the young clerk. "I should be back in an hour or so." Then he was walking with us out of the building. He climbed into his crimson pick-up and in a few minutes he was following us back out toward Central Turnpike.

Jason glanced at me as we led the small train toward the pizza place. "So far so good?"

I nodded. "At least he seems willing to talk," I agreed. "Now to see what he says."

The intertwining harmonies of Neptune's Car kept us entertained, and soon we were turning into Tony's parking lot, perched high over 146. The sight of the parking lot surprised me. Usually the place was packed to the gills, especially at nine p.m. But tonight there were only two cars in the entire stretch. I glanced over at Jason.

He shrugged. "Election night, and the polls are extremely close," he pointed out. "Plus some interesting ballot questions. The staff is probably watching it on TV inside."

"And here I had hoped to avoid that all," I grumbled. We climbed out of the car into the cool late autumn night. Sam was close behind us as we headed into the building.

We stepped through the short entry hall and into the main building. The counter was to the right, with a long hand-lettered sign listing out the offerings of subs, pizzas, and pasta dinners. Italian marble tile spread along the floor, and the walls had wood paneling, decorated with assorted photos of baseball teams and other local events the restaurant had supported over the years.

Another couple was ahead of us in line, their voices holding disappointment. "But we called ahead of time so we could eat here," the man was saying. "Eggplant parm with ziti. That way we could have it here, with plenty of time before you closed at ten"

The man behind the counter shrugged. "Policy here is to put everything into bags," he stated.

The customer peered into the bag. "And we had asked for ziti, not spaghetti," he added.

The clerk set about dumping the food out onto plates for them, and soon the couple was settled in a corner. We moved up to place our own orders, with wine all around. The red was poured for us, and we took the glasses over to a green Formica-topped table, waiting for our number to be called.

Sam took a sip of his wine. "Well, what did you want to know?" In the small booth his face was tired. He seemed as old as the restaurant, the dull metal container of the napkins on the table reflecting his weary eyes.

I gave my own wine glass a gentle rotation. "What was it like growing up with him?"

He shrugged, glancing over at the counter, waiting to see if the green plastic trays with our food were out yet. "Well, he was Merry, of course," he growled, as if that explained everything.

"And you were Sam," I offered.

His shoulders tensed. "Of course I was," he snapped. "It was my name already; Samuel. And my father was a farmer. The others thought that was oh-so-cute. They had their plans to go off to college or the far east or wherever they were going to explore. And I was going to be stuck in *Sutton*." He took another gulp of his wine. "Sam the farmer. Sam the pack mule."

I looked at his hands, sturdy and firm. "You sound like you weren't too happy about this."

His breath came out in a snort. "Not happy?" He shook his head. "When I was a child, my friends were all boasting about being super-heroes or policemen. Any time I mentioned anything like that to my father, he scoffed at me." His voice took on a rough edge. "'You are a *farmer*,' he would snarl at me. 'Put that foolishness out of your head.'" He looked down into his wine.

There was a movement from the counter; Jason patted me on the leg before standing to fetch our food. I felt the warmth of his hand long after he had left our booth. He returned balancing two green cafeteria-style trays. He placed our food on the table and returned the trays to the counter.

I took a bite of my eggplant before continuing the conversation. "So, what was John like?"

Sam shrugged. "He was the popular one," he grumbled, poking at his spaghetti. "He could have shaved off his eyebrows and all the girls would still have flocked to him. He had that way about him." The corners of his lips turned down. "You know how they are. They barely saw me. I was stuck in the town they were striving to escape. They wanted adventure and excitement. Yeah, John had it all."

I asked softly. "Because he was going to Vietnam?"

He flinched as if I had shouted at him. "Nobody deserved that Agent Orange hell-hole," he growled, taking another long drink of his wine. The glass was nearly empty, and Jason stood without being asked, returning in short order with another full one. Sam barely seemed to notice. "Nobody wanted to head into that punji-stick deathtrap," he added, his eyes far away. "We had been raised on stories of the honors of World War II, of the bravery and heroism of a just cause. Korea singed the edges of that image." His voice dropped. "But this was something else entirely. Good did not always triumph."

Jason's voice was steady. "So why did he enlist?"

The flinch was there again, more pronounced, and he did not raise his eyes. "Eileen."

I held still. "The young woman who drowned?"

His voice was half laugh, half plaintive cry. "She drowned," he breathed, his face creased in pain. "She was stunning, like a Hollywood starlet somehow spirited into our quiet woods of aspen and maple. You should have seen her eyes. Liquid and full, rich with promises and dreams. Her whole life spread before her and she could have had anything she wanted. Then, in an instant she was gone. Her fingers were white, so white, like a porcelain doll. When she reached out ..."

There was a long silence then, and the mindless babble of the radio station's love-advice columnist pushed into my awareness. Some young girl was calling in, a high voice causing the announcer to take her for a child at first. But no, it was a pregnant woman, barely old enough to vote, asking for a song to dedicate to her unborn child. She did not yet know if it was a he or a she; the ultrasound had been inconclusive. From the kitchen I could hear the line cooks arguing over whether Obama would take Ohio or Florida.

Jason's voice eased into the pause. "Sam, were you there? Were you all there when she drowned?"

Sam gave a strangled cry, looking up at both of us. "Why are you dragging this all up after so many decades?" he challenged, his voice rough. "It's in the past. It's long dead. It should stay that way!"

He surged to his feet, and then he was turning, striding through the empty entryway, the door falling shut behind him.

I looked at Jason in surprise. He took in a deep breath, then let it out again. "We shook the bushes, all right," he agreed. "What did we learn?"

"That there is more to this story than I thought," I mused, looking down. After a moment I glanced around at the empty seats, the tables shined and cleaned. "Maybe we should head out ourselves. It seems tonight is not a night people want to spend away from home."

He nodded, moving to gather up take-out containers. In a moment we were back in his car. We had barely closed the doors when all the parking lot lights went out. Apparently Tony's was closing early, the staff eager to head home to monitor election results.

In short order, Jason was pulling onto my road. Guilt teased at me over the truncated dinner, and I gave him a nod. "I had not planned on watching election results, but if you want to come in –"

"Oh? What had you planned?" he asked, curiosity bright in his eyes. "The roads are practically deserted. It seems as if the entire state is glued to a TV right now."

"I am just glad to have the deluge of political fliers, phone calls, and pamphlets done with," I admitted. "I imagine they will be challenging and re-challenging results for weeks to come. Whatever they announce tonight, it will merely be the first of many stages. So I was going to watch the latest episode of Elementary on my DVR."

The corner of his mouth turned up. "Lucy Liu, the Charlie's Angel?"

He actually knew the show? For some reason the thought warmed me. "I enjoy the Sherlock Holmes stories, and while this version is a bit fluffier than usual, it does have its moments." I looked over at him. "Have you seen any episodes?"

He nodded. "All of them. I'd be happy to see tonight's with you," he offered. The words hung in the air with silvery luminescence.

It had been quite a while since another person had shared my space, since the world which had become narrowed to one was surgically stretched to admit another. I was a lake, silver and exact, unmarried by ripples. My heart flickered at the approach of a choice.

It was such a small thing, the joint viewing. And it was, after all, a night of issues. Matters of importance were being decided, as much as I tried to distance myself from the artificial trauma that was been stirred up by media of all shapes and sizes.

"All right," I agreed at last as he turned into my driveway. "I have popcorn," I added, "but not much else."

He smiled, and the warmth of it laced through my being. "That will be more than enough."

I closed my eyes for a moment, and the softest of hope perched in my soul.

Chapter 7

I was holding tree pose, thinking blissfully serene thoughts about how the deluge of robo-political calls would now be at an end, when the first delicate flakes of snow began to drift past the sliding glass door. There were only a few of them, just a gentle scattering of tiny white dots that skittered two and fro on the breeze, but I knew more would be close behind. The TV stations, barely content to let viewers rest their weary minds for a nanosecond, were now convinced that a nor'easter to end all snowstorms was barreling down on Massachusetts.

I refused to be drawn out of my routine and finished up the remainder of poses in my yoga set. I ended up sitting cross-legged, one hand resting palm-up on each knee, looking serenely out at the suet feeder hanging from the shepherd's crook. In the summertime a full flowering of day lilies surrounded it, but now the dark green foliage was low and flat. A fine layer of white coated each leaf. A chickadee was nibbling at one of the suet cakes, its black and white body fluffed up against the chill.

Namaste, I offered the little bird, hoping it would find a safe nook to tuck itself into against the coming winds.

I drew on boots and my ski parka, heading outside to my kayak. The tangerine-crimson-gold swirls of the molded plastic were decorated now with a silvery icing. I hefted it by one of its handles, giving it a gentle shake to free it of the snow. Then I walked it around to the basement slider and put it up on its rack. So much for my hopes of one more ride before winter settled in. Still, last year the first powerful snowstorm had struck before Halloween, so we had been given a week's grace this year.

Everything else had come indoors last week before Hurricane Sandy made its visit, so I was now set for winter. I checked the mailbox, smiling as I found only a few bills. The political deluge had stopped. I headed back in, shrugged off my coat and boots, and went to my computer to check on the status of the world.

Thank goodness. The stridency of the political battle had already faded into the background; the Telegram site barely had a mention of the winners of the various contests. Instead, their new focus was on the coming storm and how it would snarl traffic.

In my in-box was an intriguing note from Matthew. Apparently he'd gotten a call from Jeff, John's son. Jeff knew of Matthew's work providing computers to seniors, and he was also aware that his father's computer had been a recent donation from Matthew. He wanted to return the computer to Matthew so that another senior could benefit from it. Also, he thought there might be some notes on it about John's history. He was hoping that the three of us could get together and take a look.

I answered immediately, letting him know that I was interested, and asking when he wanted to get together.

I had barely begun to sort through my remaining email when the response came. Three p.m. I glanced at my clock. That gave me an hour to get ready.

Perfect, see you then.

* * *

The snow was falling more steadily now, and it gave a Currier-and-Ives feel to Ramshorn Pond. The trees ringing the water were laced with white, and the steady downward flow of sparkling confetti seemed to vanish like magic in the darkness of the water's surface. There was a strange car parked in Matthew's driveway. When he pulled open the door I could see that Jeff was already there, setting up the computer on Matthew's kitchen table.

Jeff turned with a smile. "It's good to see you again, Morgan," he greeted. "I am glad you're able to help us with this. And I hope you don't mind, but I invited —"

There was a movement from the kitchen, and Jason stepped into the room, holding a tan mug of steaming coffee. My cheeks flushed and my smile grew of its own accord.

His eyes were warm on me as he nodded his greeting.

Jeff went on, plugging the power cord into the back of the CPU. "Jason was telling me all about your meeting with Sam yesterday. Fascinating stuff. I suppose high school is never easy for anybody, no matter what era they grew up in."

"I imagine not," I agreed.

Joan's voice carried from the kitchen. "Some tea for you, Morgan? How about cinnamon?"

"Cinnamon would be lovely."

Jeff pressed the power button and the monitor flickered to life. He logged in and pushed the keyboard over toward me.

"I doubt my father had anything on this besides a browser and his story," he assured me. "The man had many talents, but computing was not one of them. He was barely able to use a mouse."

I sat down and in a moment Joan had placed a fragrant mug of tea at my side. The Windows desktop came into view, and I smiled. Jeff was right – few icons were installed beyond Word and Internet Explorer.

I launched Word and sipped the gently spiced tea as the software opened. I checked the list of recently opened files, then frowned.

It was empty.

I glanced up at Jeff. "Are you sure he'd started his work?"

He nodded. "Absolutely. I think he was three or four chapters in. He kept talking about how slow and steady won the race and how he would get there eventually. He was a hunt-and-peck typist, but he hung in there."

I opened up Windows Explorer. "And you're sure he was using Word?"

"I'm sure. That's why we installed it. He would occasionally email me questions about how to change fonts or adjust the margins."

I began poking around in Explorer, looking in all the typical places that documents could be stored. There was nothing. The system looked as new as the day Matthew had handed it over to John.

"Maybe he was doing it online instead?" I opened up Internet Explorer. I started looking through the browser history – and stopped. There were no history entries at all.

I thrummed my fingers on the table. "Did he know how to use the internet?"

He nodded. "Yes indeed. He was sending me Gmail messages from the house, and I know they were from this computer."

I shook my head. "Is there any reason he would have erased his history and files?"

Jeff frowned ridges into his forehead. "He was excited about his project and worked on it every night. It makes no sense that he would have wiped it out."

I checked the application list. No other browsers were installed.

Matthew leaned over my shoulder. "How about the recycle bin?"

Dutifully I went to the trash-can-shaped icon and opened it up. There was nothing there.

Jason's low voice rumbled into the mix. "Did he have another computer he might have used? A laptop perhaps? Or maybe something at the senior center?"

Jeff shook his head resolutely. "No. I am sure he was writing at home and working on this computer. He gave thanks to Matthew several times, in our messages, for giving him a way to finally share his story."

I pursed my lips. "Well, if it was this computer he was using, something has happened to what he was working on. Maybe he deleted it by accident …"

I went to the browser and did a quick web search for free hard drive recovery software. I pulled the USB thumb drive out of my purse and downloaded the software to the thumb drive. I then installed it to the same drive. If there really were remnants of files on the computer's main hard drive, I wanted to be as cautious as I could so as not to accidentally overwrite them with this new software.

In a few minutes the software was up and running. We all gathered around the monitor, staring at the software's progress report with anticipation.

Blip. A file name appeared on the screen.

JohnsAdventures.doc 2.3mb

Jeff's voice was high with excitement. "You found it!"

The software finished its run, finding no other files in a deleted state other than web cookies and sundry items. I clicked the icon to recover the Word document, and when it was ready, we opened it up.

There it was. The story was on Chapter 5 and ran about forty pages long. I glanced up at Jeff.

"Please send that around to all four of us," he stated. "I think we should all read what it says and see what we think. I can't imagine that he would have deleted this, with all the work he had put into it. And if he didn't, maybe someone else did."

I opened up a browser window and in a few minutes the document was on its way. I turned to Jeff. "Who would have had access to the computer?"

He shrugged, his eyes shadowing. "My father had an open door policy. Friends were coming in and out at all hours of the day and night. He loved having people over. There could have been any number of people near the computer since the last time he worked on it."

I looked down at the keyboard. "Maybe there are fingerprints on it?"

He shook his head again. "My father was always showing off his story to every person who came in. There are probably hundreds of fingerprints on that keyboard. I'm not sure that would help us."

My eyes went back to the monitor. "Well, at least now we know what he wrote; it's a start."

Jason's eyes were serious, staring at the black letters which traced along the whiteness of the page. "The issue could be with something that he had written, certainly – but it could also be something that was coming up in the story. Especially with John showing his latest work to every person who came by, perhaps someone needed to silence him before he reached the critical juncture."

Jeff paled, but nodded. "It could be that what was in the story currently is harmless enough, but that a later chapter would have revealed a secret."

Joan's voice was gentle. "Then this could be helpful to us," she pointed out. "If we see how far the story got, then it narrows down the time frame in which the secret existed."

I smiled. "Very true." I glanced out the window. The snow was coming down more enthusiastically now, and the sky was easing from river-rock grey to a darker charcoal. "Perhaps we should get home and share our thoughts via email once we each read through the document."

Jeff nodded, giving the top of the CPU a pat. "Matthew, feel free to remove that file again and find a new home for the system. I'm sure some senior will be thrilled to be able to email his grandchildren or play some solitaire."

We made our farewells, and Jason was at my side as we headed back up the path toward the driveway. "I came in with Jeff," he explained, nodding his head toward the crimson Sentra. "Are you sure you will be all right to get home?"

I glanced up at the downy flakes with fondness. "I've lived in New England for almost all my life," I responded. "If I was afraid of a few inches of snow, I would have left long ago."

He smiled at that. "Well then, drive safely," he offered. He stood, watchful, as I climbed into the Subaru and headed toward home.

* * *

I sat back on the futon, blinking at the screen, as the warmth of my laptop eased against my legs. I popped a cheese-and-Triscuit combination into my mouth, pondering what I had just read.

John's writing was rough, but showed an intense enthusiasm for the subject at hand. He had laid out what growing up in the late fifties and early sixties had been like in delightful detail, from the sound of Elvis on the radio in the living room to the flowered wallpaper which filled their kitchen with color. He had been a precocious child, riding his bike pell-mell all around the back roads of Sutton, splashing in Lake Singletary in the summers and sledding down the hill at the Baptist church in the winter.

The story had been cut off as John was entering his sophomore year of high school, fully entwined with his three "hobbit" friends. Sam had been right about his role in the group, and John had pulled no punches. He teased his friend endlessly for being the dullard of the bunch, trapped in a stagnant mire he would never escape. He was much more complimentary of the other two boys and their dreams of college and a future.

I tapped a finger to my lips, looking at the screen. Did that mean the trouble spot was during those high school years? Could they involve the girl who had drowned? Or could it be something that was coming later, either when he was traveling through Asia or when he had returned to Sutton?

There was no way to know. Joan was right, though. We had narrowed the field down somewhat, and now we would simply have to keep poking and prodding to see what we could learn.

Charles and Richard. Of the two, Charles seemed the easier to tackle next. He had retired from banking several years ago and apparently belonged to the local Lion's club. I found his name on the local website, with an email address. In a moment I had sent a request to meet.

My name is Morgan Warren. I am working on John Dixon's biography, with his son Jeff's permission. I would like to have dinner sometime when you're free.

It was only a few minutes later that a response appeared in my inbox.

Would love to share thoughts on John. He was a good man. On Friday I'm scheduled to play a round of golf at Blackstone National, if the snow melts in time. How about we have dinner there, at six?

That sounds perfect. See you then.

I stared at the document before me for several minutes before shutting it down. We would see what Charles had to say about his high school years, and if he had the same reaction Sam did to questions about the tragic death of their friend.

Chapter 8

The afternoon sun drifted with a pale blue light through the layers of clouds that coated the sky like a gentle blanket. The promised additional snowfall for today had never materialized, so we were left with the three inches which fell yesterday, now coated with a crusty top layer, like the glazing on a crème brûlée.

I gazed out my back slider with a smile at the frosting of white that now blanketed the landscape. Only two days ago my kayak was ready for another trip on the pond. And here we were, seemingly submerged in the heart of winter, with a flurry of birds making swooping visits to my various feeders.

I looked again at the snow. It had been said the Eskimos knew a hundred words for different types of snow. Of course that had been proven to be an exaggeration. The Inuit simply interlace words like we do in English, to have soft, wispy snow and hard, crunchy snow and everything in between. Still, it was an interesting thought. How many identifiably unique types of snow could there be?

Well, yesterday's three-inches had been a gentle snow – when you stepped in it there was no crunchy surface to push through. But it did form a solid impression of where your foot had landed, and there were no gentle cascades along the edges once you removed your foot. So maybe this could be called an easy-walking snow. Your feet went in, came out again, and if you wanted to you could retrace your steps.

Last night's rain-snow mix had turned that snow into quite another form. The hard-topped-crunch snow was something to be more cautious of. Going down a slope, one had to be sure to give one's foot an extra stomp to get through that hard layer, lest the foot slip and send the owner skidding down the hill on their backside. This would not be an ideal snowman-building snow, for example. Perhaps we would call this one-foot-stomp snow.

I rolled out my yoga mat, delighting in the wonderful scenery that nature had provided. Not only did the world glisten as if fairies had visited, but the evident wealth of bird life was staggering. Out the side window to my left I could see the main sunflower feeder. A steady stream of chickadee, titmouse, and goldfinch came fluttering in and out. These patient birds each took their turn, removing just one seed and flying off to work on it.

Suddenly a young male cardinal arrived, his muted brown feathers interlaced with the brighter crimson colors. He was less interested in sharing and took up residence on one side, glaring at any newcomers with a sharp, beady eye.

Below the feeder a flock of stealth doves – my name for the grey mourning doves – poked around in the snow for fallen seeds. Over toward the large rock was a group of juncos, their white bellies matching the snow over which they hopped with quick agility.

A movement on the two suet feeders on the maples caught my eye. Was that a fawn-brown nuthatch I saw, clinging to the tree? I'd never seen a brown nuthatch before! In a moment the bird hopped to a nearby branch, and I smiled. His stubby, cocked-high tail showed him to be a wren.

I moved through my routine, buoyed by the delightful movements of nature around me. A downy woodpecker came to sample the suet feeder, soon joined by a nuthatch. Blue jays watched from high in the trees, fluffing their bodies against the wintry chill. As much as I loved hawks, I was thankful that I saw none gliding in silent watch overhead. There was a virtual smorgasbord of feasting options for them, but I was grateful the gathering was able to enjoy their meal in peace.

When I was finished, I was loathe to leave the beauty that nature had brought to me. Instead, I fetched my laptop from the living room and set it up in the center of my natural-finish lauan dining room table. The walls were done with sage green paint, and the room featured a pine hutch. The stationary half of the sliding glass doors was fronted by a set of stainless steel shelves holding all of my porch plants. The large rosemary plant earned a top shelf location with its bushy leaves. Several jalapeño plants joined it there. I had once thought these were annuals, but an experiment proved that they thrived when brought in to winter. Even now they were creating green fruits for me. A rose plant on the corner delighted me with its delicate fragrance.

Lower shelves held a variety of basil plants, from the standard Italian basil to cinnamon and Thai. The bottom shelf held several petunia plants. These were another set that I had once thought annual and was pleased to see that they would flourish if only given a bit of warmth, love, and care.

I popped open the laptop and made a cup of Chanakara tea, laughing at a brief tussle between a red-bellied woodpecker and an enthusiastic chickadee. Sam's reaction had interested me, and I needed to know more about this drowning before I went in to talk with Charles. In years past, doing my genealogy research, I might have delved into microfiche stacks, spending hours in a dusty room with hard-backed chairs. Now I was sure that everything I needed lay at the other end of a search engine.

I googled, "Sutton MA Lake Singletary Drowning".

In less than a second my page was filled with results. I looked at the top one, and then blinked with surprise. The date on it was 1935. Intrigued, I clicked.

FIELD, J. The defendant was indicted for the murder on July 20, 1935, of Alice D. Sherman, by drowning her in Lake Singletary. The victim was the wife of the defendant.

I gave my head a shake. Wasn't this the plot of *A Place in the Sun* in 1951, where the man decides to drown a woman rather than deal with the difficulty of having her around?

The entry made fascinating reading. The page wasn't even about the court case itself. Apparently Newell Sherman had been found guilty of drowning his wife and had written a confession stating that. The page I read said, on July 22nd, he allowed a newspaper reporter to *photograph* his signed confession. Somehow he was hoping that this mistake on his part was enough to get the court to overturn his guilty verdict.

I shook my head. Even in 1935 it seemed people would grab at anything to avoid punishment.

Hmmm, was there more to this? Now I tried googling "July 20 1935 Alice D. Sherman."

It sounded more and more like a movie plot. An entry I found on the murder explained how Alice was born in 1912 and died in 1935, when she was only 23 years old. Her husband, Newell, took her out in a canoe, serenaded her, and then deliberately capsized the boat. Unable to swim, she sank. After that, he simply swam back to shore.

Apparently he had become enamored with a seventeen-year-old girl and wanted to run off with her instead.

I took a sip of my tea and sighed. Was life truly like this, to have a woman ruthlessly drowned simply because of a new infatuation? How about the young daughter and son who were left behind?

I offered a silent prayer for the innocent woman who had been slain and went back to my initial search. Eileen Hudson, who had been drowned in Lake Singletary in perhaps 1968.

There, the results began to pop up. I clicked on one of the links.

Eileen Hudson, aged seventeen - tragically drowned in a canoeing accident while out with friends. I began reading the names – and then stopped in surprise. John Dixon. Sam Sares. Charles Stone. Richard Watkins. The four hobbits. They had been out with her the night she had drowned.

The story did not seem to report any foul play, perhaps only an adolescent penchant for cheap wine before the fateful launch onto the lake in a trio of canoes. The night had been dark, with a new moon, and the boys had looked for her for nearly an hour before coming to shore to call for help. The body had been found two days later after authorities dragged the lake.

I pursed my lips. Here was something that others might not want to see the light of day. Sam had certainly seemed nervous enough when the topic arose.

I soon discovered that there was an online copy of the 1967 Sutton School Yearbook, for a small fee of course.

There she was, with sweet clear eyes which would never age. She wore her hair long and straight, as was the fashion of the times, and had a glow about her that would seem to lift her past any hurdle in life. She had not known, when she sat smiling for that photo in her paisley top, that fate would bring her to an untimely end.

She belonged to the drama club, and all four boys were there too, their faces eager and alive. What hopes and dreams had they held deep in their breasts? What futures did they see unrolling before them into the distant future?

The phone rang, and it was a moment before I moved to pick it up.

"Hello?"

"Morgan, it's Jason," came the voice, and I smiled. Funny how the mere modulation of air waves from a phone's speaker could do that to me. "I'm at the Market Basket in Oxford. Care for some sushi?"

I blinked. "How did you know I liked sushi?"

I could hear the smile in his voice. "You have yellow origami flowers in a vase in your living room," he pointed out. "As well as a Japanese kanji on the wall for tranquility. It seemed you might appreciate things Japanese."

I grinned. "All right, then, I adore sushi," I admitted. "I would love some."

"Be there in twenty minutes," he stated, and with a click he was gone.

I fished out the lychee liqueur from the bottom of the hutch, separated out some frozen peaches, and by the time he had arrived I'd created a pair of Champagne cocktails with a delightfully oriental theme to them. He settled in at the table as easily as if he'd been joining me for years, and we toasted the delightful day.

He took a bite of his tuna. "So, what have you been up to?"

I explained to him the research I had been doing and what I had found. His eyebrows went up as I gave him the details of the 1935 murder, but he did not interrupt and let me finish with everything I had found out about the drowning in 1968.

I turned the laptop toward him so he could see the images. "And here they are in the drama club."

He leaned toward the screen, wiping his fingers on a napkin. "A cozy bunch," he observed. "There were only ten members of the drama club. I imagine those five became quite close."

"And Sam apparently still feels strongly about what happened, even decades later," I added. "Maybe there's more to it than what the newspapers reported."

"Well, we can see what Charles has to say tomorrow," he mused. "He got out of town, at least for a while, going to school out in Kenyon, Ohio. He worked in Ohio for a decade after that before returning to Sutton to join OmniBank here."

My eyes lit up. "Apparently I wasn't the only one doing research," I gently teased him.

He grinned at that. "I thought it might be good to go into the meeting with a bit of background," he agreed. "I swung by the Sutton town hall. Everyone there knows everybody else in town, and their knowledge base stretches back decades. It's a bit scary."

I popped the last piece of salmon into my mouth and gave a grateful sigh. "Thank you so much for the sushi. That was quite tasty."

My phone buzzed, and I leant back to pick it up off the kitchen island. I glanced at the message and shook my head. "Charles has cancelled," I reported to Jason. "Says something came up."

He arched an eyebrow. "Think he has changed his mind about talking?"

I gave a soft shrug. "I guess we'll find out when I try to reschedule. Maybe I should try Richard instead?"

He nodded in agreement. "It's worth a try."

I typed in the message and sent the electrons flying off into the ether. "Well, nothing to do but wait and see what he says."

His eyes flickered toward the living room. "What else is on that DVR of yours?"

"Well, there is the Blue Bloods from last Friday I haven't gotten around to watching yet."

"Tom Selleck? You know, he is in a series playing Jesse Stone, a character created by Robert B. Parker –"

I grinned. "I own all the DVDs," I admitted. "I adore them. Jeff Beal's haunting piano music and the misty atmosphere of living on the Massachusetts coastline is soulfully presented."

He paused, and the look in his eyes struck me breathless. Then, at last, he spoke again.

"Shall we?"

He stood, offering his hand. My fingers fit with perfect precision into the cupped warmth, and I felt the rightness of it in the depth and breadth and height of my soul.

Chapter 9

I drew in a long, deep breath, basking in the golden sunshine which streamed down from a cloud-studded blue sky. Snow still melted at the edges of the Pleasant Valley Country Club's elegantly landscaped parking lot, but the white crystals had softened into a slushy, crunchy snow which would soon be gone. The nor'easter of two days ago was all but erased from memory.

We made our way up the long wooden stairs which led from the lower parking lot to the building proper, settled on the top of a hill like a manor house. A circular drive swept around before the main entrance, and I could almost imagine PGA legends being dropped off by their limousines, anxious attendants running to pull open the shining black doors, friendly faces ushering the talented sportsmen inside.

Jason's voice came from behind me. "Have you ever played golf?"

I gave a noncommittal shrug. "I have a set of clubs in the basement," I admitted, "and tried lessons a few times. But they never took."

"Were you personally interested in the game, or were you taking it up for some other reason?"

"Another reason," I evaded, moving to pull open the heavy door. Before us, like a split-level ranch home, lay two choices. To the right, head up a half-flight to the main reception area. To the left, down a half-flight to the restaurant. Down we went.

We had barely reached the maître d' stand when a hearty voice bellowed from further within the restaurant. "There you are! Come on over!"

The room was elegant in a comfortable way, with pool-table-green carpet and light tan walls with ivory wainscoting. The tables were set, but most waited empty. Only a few of the twenty or so tables were taken by middle-aged women talking animatedly. A wooden bar to the left was similarly sparse.

Along the right side wall a bank of floor-to-ceiling windows opened on a spectacular view of the putting green and golf course. The foliage was long gone, but the rolling hills of fir and pine were delightful, especially with the delicate lacing of snow just fading at the edges.

A large, well-built man stood before us, holding a glass of gin and tonic in one hand, his other outstretched to draw us in. He had a prime table along the windows, and we settled in across from him. Hands were shaken all around.

"Welcome, welcome," Richard offered heartily, settling back into his seat and waving a hand in the air. In a moment the waitress had come over, her jet-black hair framing a smiling face. Richard looked between us. "What'll you have? It's on me, of course. Have to do my part to keep this place flush." He grinned and took down a drink.

"Just water for me," I demurred. It was barely noon, and I was still blinking away the sleep from my eyes.

Jason nodded in agreement, and we picked up our menus to scan the offerings. Everything looked good. They had salads, sandwiches, as well as heartier dishes such as veal parmesan and filet mignon.

Richard barely waited for our menus to return to the table before leaning forward to jab a finger at Jason. "I could have told you not to bother with Sam," he teased. "That man barely knows which end of a chicken to lop off. And Charles is as skittish as a Catholic school girl fearing her first kiss. You should have come to me first. I could have set you straight on everything."

I glanced at Jason. Apparently Richard's network infiltrated every corner of Sutton. For a town of ten thousand people, it sometimes seemed as if I lived in Grover's Corners.

The waitress was back with our water and asked after our orders. Richard took the filet, medium rare. I asked for the salmon picatta, and Jason ordered a hamburger. Richard watched the waitress leave with an appreciative eye, then turned back to us.

"I imagine what you really want to know about was that night in 1968," he stated, sweeping us with his eyes as if beginning a presentation to an attentive jury. "It's all quite simple. We were drinking. I know we shouldn't have been, but there you have it. Some Boone's Farm cheap rosé on the beach, to celebrate Eileen's seventeenth birthday."

He paused for a moment, his eyes shining at the memory. "God, she was a beauty. Had this real Marilyn Monroe sweetness about her, and a figure to match." He shrugged. "And then we made the foolish but age-appropriate decision to go piling into our canoes and paddle around Lake Singletary while drunk."

Jason's eyes were steady on Richard's. "What happened then?"

Richard took another gulp of his gin and tonic. "There was some horseplay. Eileen was in John's canoe, of course, and I wanted her in mine. She laughed that bright laugh of hers and said there was plenty of her to share. And so she tried to cross."

I pursed my lips. "Where were Sam and Charles in all of this?"

He shrugged, a twinkle in his eyes. "Where they always were. In their own canoe, trying to keep up with us."

Jason kept his gaze. "So she tried to cross –"

The waitress returned with a tray, laying out salads for me and Richard. Richard tapped his glass and she nodded with a smile, heading off again. The salad looked delicious – glistening cherry tomatoes, fresh greens, and a good mix of other items as well. I smiled. Getting a decent salad was becoming a lost art.

Richard was stuffing a forkful of salad in his mouth. "She tried to cross, and she lost her footing. I grabbed for her, of course, and John dove for her as well. That capsized his canoe, I nearly overturned on top of them both, and by the time the splashing and yelling stopped she was gone. She was simply not there."

I took a sip of my water. "So you never saw what happened to her?"

He shook his head. "It wasn't that she was flailing for help and we couldn't get to her. She simply wasn't there at all. It took us all by surprise at first. We assumed she was teasing us – was hiding behind one of our canoes and would spring out with wild laughter. So we called for her. I remember Sam even sounded a bit angry, that she would upset us like that." His eyes shadowed for a moment. "But after a few minutes we realized she really was gone. And then we began to search in earnest."

The waitress was back with his drink, and he took a long swallow. "But that was it. There was no moon that night and a low fog had rolled in. We dove and swam, and called out, but there was never the slightest trace of her. Finally Sam insisted we go back to shore and get some help. So we did. But they didn't find her for two days."

Jason's voice was even. "What do you think happened?"

Richard leaned back, looking out the window. On a back green, a sprinkler head flared into life, incongruous against the decoration of melting snow on the edges of the grass.

"I think she was full of life and she thought she was invincible," he murmured at last, his eyes not leaving the bright landscape. "We all did. We never gave a thought to life slowing us down. Everything rolled out before us and we just had to grab for what we wanted. She was going to be a movie star and tackle powerful dramas, like *To Sir with Love*, only with female stars. I was going to be a lawyer and save the oppressed. Charles was going to go into stocks and bonds to finance all of our projects."

I kept my voice low. "And Sam?"

He gave a snort, turning toward us again, swirling his drink with a motion of his wrist. "Sam was going to wring the heads off of chickens."

Jason's voice was contemplative. "Do you think one of the others could have had something to do with her not coming up?"

Richard gave a guttural laugh. "Those miscreants? I doubt any of them had the brains to organize something that devious. Sam could barely look at her without blushing. Charles, for all his plans, could never keep his own bank account organized, never mind a more complicated task. And John ..."

I watched him. "And John?"

"John loved her," he finished, glancing up. The waitress was back and our plates were laid out. The food was richly aromatic; my salmon looked absolutely divine with wild rice and artichoke hearts across the top. Our waters were refilled and I took a bite. It tasted as good as it looked.

Jason enjoyed his burger for a minute before continuing. "Maybe John was jealous over something she had done?"

Richard shook his head. "John was completely convinced of his own powers of seduction," he countered. "He thought every girl within a hundred mile radius was helpless against his overpowering charms. Eileen could have been dating twenty other boys and he wouldn't have cared, because he would have been absolutely certain that they were only being used to tease him." He sliced through his steak, leaving a bloody streak behind the motion. "I think the poor guy was actually thinking of proposing to her."

I paused. "Do you think she would have accepted?"

He looked down at his steak for a moment. "You know? I think she would have. She was just that romantic, to want to head for the Hollywood Lights with her childhood sweetheart at her side."

I pondered this. "Would anyone have been upset by this?"

"Maybe Charles," he offered, putting another cube of steak into his mouth. "Charles was always jealous that John got all the girls even though he had no prospects. John's father was a mill worker in Whitinsville; their house was fairly run down. Charles had a notion that his wealthy family connections should gain him instant success in the romance department."

The Whitinsville mill reference sounded a chime deep in my memory, and it was a moment before I connected it to a thought. "Esther Magill worked at a mill in Whitinsville," I mused.

His eyes flashed with strong emotion. I realized it was the first time that something authentic had pushed through that pleasant mask on his face. And then the glimpse was gone; the placid retiree golfer was back with his forest-green collar shirt and cool ice-blue eyes.

"Ah, you mean that case from back in the thirties," he pondered, letting his eyes drift back out to the landscape. "Yes, we heard about that while growing up, of course.

I leant forward slightly. "Newell Sherman, the man who murdered his wife Alice, did so in order to win the love of Esther Magill," I clarified. "They both worked at the mills in Whitinsville."

"So they did," he agreed. "A tragedy, that. Left a pair of young children orphaned."

"What happened to them?"

He shrugged, taking a sip of his drink. "The son Dudley passed away in the nineties. The daughter still lives in Sutton." His voice dropped down a notch. "Must have been hard on her to grow up with that legacy," he added.

"Were any of you related to the family?"

He shook his head. "Although here in Sutton everyone knows everyone, of course. Dudley's sister-in-law worked right here at the Pleasant Valley Country Club for a while before taking over the Blue Jay. I'm sure I've run into her once or twice over the years."

The waitress swung by to clear away our plates and to refill the water yet again. I smiled at her. This had got to be some of the best service I'd seen at a restaurant in the area. I definitely put the restaurant on my list of places to return to.

Jason's voice was even. "So you're positive that there was no foul play involved with Eileen?"

Richard nodded his head. "We were young and foolish, but I don't think it occurred to any of us that we could die. The thought didn't enter our heads. When she didn't come up, there wasn't even a glimmer of an idea that she could be hurt. We simply thought she was joking with us."

He looked between us. "And now, if you have no more questions, I think I'll get in some putting practice while we have this sunshine. It may be the last I see until March or so."

We nodded, and he pushed himself up to standing, making his way toward the main door of the restaurant.

Jason watched until he had vanished from view before turning back to me. "What do you think?"

"I think he's a lawyer with decades of practice swaying an audience," I replied. "The only time we seemed to catch him off guard was when we asked about the 1935 murder."

"He did seem well prepared for everything else," agreed Jason. "So, what do we do now?"

"While we wait for Charles to come out of hiding, maybe we talk with John's good friend Adam again," I suggested. "Adam is the only one who doesn't have a vested interest in hiding the incidents of 1968. If Adam and John were as close as he says they were, maybe John has told him about that night. We could see if John's story matches what we've heard from Richard and Sam so far."

Jason raised an eyebrow. "I forgot to ask. Which hobbit was Richard supposed to be?"

I smiled at that. "He was Frodo, the man in charge," I responded. "The one that the others all turned to, the one they followed."

"Maybe there is more to the story than he's willing to share," he mused. He looked out the window at the streaming sunshine. "Shall I drive you home?"

I nodded. "I have a lot to get done today, and as much I would love to soak in a draught of sunshine, I am afraid I will have to stay indoors." I smiled at him. "Besides, I have to rest up tonight. I hear there is a happening gig in town tomorrow night and I wouldn't want to miss it."

He smiled at that, then stood, putting out a hand. I took it, my head rising, my heart lifting, and I was safe, settled, and incandescently content.

Chapter 10

I entered the main hall of the senior center and spotted Adam's single grey streak atop his lean frame. He still wore black, mourning the loss of his dear friend. He stood to give me a welcoming hug before settling down across the table from me. His voice was gravelly but strong.

"It's good to see you again. So, are you makin' any progress on finding out what happened to John?"

"I'm gathering up information, at least," I stated. "I can't tell yet if it's really progress. But I grow more convinced that his death wasn't just a tragic accident. It seems like there is something in his past which might be linked to it."

He took a sip of coffee. "I heard from his son, Jeff, that the computer was little help?"

"Well, it was certainly suspicious that someone had erased the file," I pointed out. "If there had been no harm in it, whomever it was would have just left the file there. If John had been killed for something that happened recently – let's say a jealous lover who didn't want last month's love triangle to be known about – they wouldn't care at all that John was writing about his childhood. There would be no reason for them to delete that file. So I think the fact that it *was* important to someone seems to indicate the flash point was in those teenage years."

Adam nodded thoughtfully. "That makes sense," he agreed. "So you think it has to do with Eileen's death? Something that was previously unknown, that John was only now going to bring to light?"

I gave a soft shrug. "Many people hold in secrets for decades, only to release them at last when they feel the end is near. From what Jeff says, his father seemed to be approaching that final barrier. It was why John was pushing to finish his memoir. Maybe he was going to finally unburden himself of something which had tormented him all this time."

"I know her death affected him greatly," mused Adam, looking down into his coffee. "It was the main reason behind his going off to Vietnam. He could not be around the familiar haunts any more. Apparently, everything he saw reminded him of her."

I leant forward. "What did he tell you about that night?"

He pressed his lips together in thought. "Not much," he admitted. "He said they had been drinking. That the other three boys began to get too rowdy for their own good, so he tucked Eileen into a canoe for her safety and took her out into the lake. He was fixin' to keep her out of harm's way until they settled down. Then the others all went after him, saying they wanted their turn with her."

"They were chasing him?"

He nodded. "Richard caught up with him first. Richard grabbed onto the side of John's canoe and insisted Eileen climb over into his. He got belligerent about it; Eileen was afraid and didn't want to go. Richard grabbed her by the arm to force her, John grabbed her other arm, and the next thing they knew both canoes had capsized."

I tilted my head to one side in thought. "That's not quite the way Richard told it."

He gave a low, dry laugh. "I am not surprised. The man could talk his way out of just about anything. If he had been the lawyer for Newell Sherman back in 1935, the man might have gotten away with murder."

"But it seems like John felt the drowning was an accident, then? Even if drunken horseplay was involved?"

Adam's face darkened. "Richard was responsible," he growled. "Richard made it seem as if John was the one at fault, when John cared for Eileen as if she was his little sister. John protected and watched over her."

"He wanted to marry her," I offered quietly.

His eyes flared at that, and he dropped them quickly to his coffee. "John? John adored his wife; Jeff's mother. He would have done anything for her. Who told you that John was besotted with Eileen?" He scoffed. "Was it Richard?"

"Was that not true either?"

He gave a quick shake of his head. "Eileen was under his protection, nothing more."

"Was she dating one of the other boys, then?"

"No," he answered shortly. "She wasn't dating anyone. She was dedicated to her dream of becoming a fine actress. She was pure like that; wholly enraptured in her craft."

"It's a shame she never had the chance," I mused.

He nodded somberly. "A great tragedy."

* * *

I pushed open the door to the Singletary Rod & Gun club's main hall, moving from the darkness of night to the bright light of the open room. Twelve long tables were on the edges of the space, and the band had set up on the stage before the dance floor. Jason spotted me and waved, coming down off the stage to greet me. "Morgan, I am so glad you could make it."

"Thank you for inviting me," I smiled.

His eyes moved down my outfit for a minute. I had worn a laced black top, black jeans, and low black leather boots. His eyes warmed with appreciation. "You look great," he murmured.

There was movement behind him, and in a moment I was being introduced to band-mates, girlfriends, and others who had come to hear them play. I knew I would barely be able to remember the collection of faces and names, but smiled and nodded before taking my place at the table.

The music started, and my toe tapped in appreciation. They were quite good, with the lead singer's voice rivaling Adele with its rich, powerful sound. They played a rich selection of songs, from I Saw Her Standing There to Barracuda to My Own

Worst Enemy. The audience filled the dance floor, and I joined the girlfriends as they danced, becoming lost in the music.

During one of the slower Pink Floyd tunes I turned to the dark-haired man alongside me. Bob seemed to be in his mid-thirties, with a closely cropped beard. "So, how do you know them again?"

"I'm a drummer, and I play sometimes with the lead singer and the rhythm guitarist," he explained, leaning forward. "I work with several other area bands as well. It keeps my skills expanding."

"I can imagine," I offered. "Did you grow up around here?"

"Right here in Sutton. Been here all my life."

"I'm looking into the drowning at Lake Singletary, back in the sixties," I explained. "As a favor for a friend."

"Oh, sure," he nodded. "My older sister went to school with Sam's younger sister. That affected him quite a lot, from what they say. Turned him nearly into a hermit. In fact –" He looked up, his eyes scanning the room. "There he is, over in the back corner. He fishes here sometimes." He lifted a hand in a wave.

Sam glanced up, his eyes sharpened for a moment as he met my gaze, and then his shoulders slumped and he nodded. He picked up his Bud and made his way across the darkened room, taking a seat next to the drummer.

His voice was low. "Bob," he greeted.

Bob turned to me. "Morgan, I would like you to meet –"

Sam's voice was gruff. "We've met already," he snapped. Bob looked up in surprise, and Sam modulated his tone. "She was asking about Eileen's drowning. I don't much like to talk about it."

Bob's brow creased in concern. "Sam, I'm sorry –"

Sam sighed and looked up, waving away Bob's concern. "No, no, I am the one who should apologize, for both tonight and for that dinner at Tony's. I'm not good at talking about that night. Haven't for many years." He took a pull on his beer. "But now John is dead, and the more I talk with my friends here at the club, the more I think poor old Popovich had nothing to do with it. John didn't deserve to die like that."

I leant forward. "What did happen that night on Lake Singletary?"

He ran a nail down the label of his bottle, scraping at it. "We were all fairly drunk," he mused. "Cheap pink wine, as I recall. Eileen was laughing and whirling in circles along the shore. She was a real, honest woman, like a Laura Ingalls Wilder novel come to life, with her dress drifting around her." His eyes became misty. "She had this joy in her heart, this way of speaking ... I could listen to her for hours."

"You cared for her," I murmured.

He half-smiled at that. "I'm sure we all did," he agreed. "She had a light about her, one you knew was rare in this world."

"How did the group end up in the canoes?"

He took another drink of his beer. "She wanted to feel the 'wind in her hair', she said. She ran down to where the canoes were tied up and jumped into one. It nearly went over right there on shore. John was by her side in an instant, taking the paddle from her and telling her to just sit in the bow. I think he figured he could keep her out of trouble that way. Richard was after them in a flash, calling out that he was the better paddler. There was only one canoe left, so Charles and I piled into that one."

His lips pressed together in a line. "I had to paddle, of course," he added with a trace of pique. "Charles just sprawled in the bow, staring up at the clouds and complaining that he couldn't see any stars."

"Then what happened?"

He looked down. "We had often tried to find the furthest spot one could get from shore, as a lark. I think we guessed it was about seven hundred feet, if you rowed toward the northern end and sat right in the center of the bulbous area there. And so we went, laughing and singing, calling out after each other, and the fog rolled in. It was a dark night and we could barely see the shoreline. It really was as if we were in our own world that night."

He sighed. "I caught up with them, and she was laughing in delight, standing up in the bow, teasing John and Richard without mercy. One moment she would claim she wanted to go over to Richard's canoe, and the next she insisted she'd rather stay with John. She was challenging them to prove who was the stronger man. The two of them were shouting out tales of climbing up Purgatory's rock face, of hitting home runs in baseball games, all the things young men do to prove their worth. I remember how her face shone with delight, how she was a goddess, standing there on the bow of the boat, having the men compete for her attentions."

His gaze became distant. "I'm not exactly sure what happened. One moment John and Richard were shouting out their triumphs, both of them staring up into her luminous eyes, and then Charles had grabbed a hold of John's canoe. I think he wanted his turn, or to get them to shut up, I never did know. He gave the canoe a shake, her hands went up in the air, and she was over the side before I could blink. John stood in a panic, and the whole canoe went over in a barnyard chaos of splashing and yelling."

I leant forward. "So Charles started the chain of events?"

"I don't think it was intentional," he stated quickly. "The guy was soused to the gills; he barely knew what he was doing. By the time we quieted down and realized Eileen hadn't come up again, we sobered up pretty quickly. We swam all around the area, diving as deeply as we could. But we couldn't find her."

His eyes shadowed. "I can't help but feel it was my fault. I was at the helm of my boat. I should have kept further away from Eileen's canoe. If I hadn't given Charles that opportunity, she would be alive today. She might have become a world-class actress."

There was a warm hand on my shoulder and I glanced up, surprised. Jason stood there, nodding to the men in front of me. I realized with a start that the band had taken a break; a laptop was playing filler music at a lower volume.

Jason's voice was rich with compassion. "You can't blame yourself for something another person does," he offered. "One never knows what life's twists and turns would be like. We tend to assume life would follow a perfect path if only X hadn't happened. But it seems likely that she would have fallen over, given the drunken state you were all in, with or without a shake of the canoe."

Sam let out a long breath. "She was dancing to music only she could hear," he agreed at last. "Weaving and spinning. I imagine you're right. She was teetering on that precipice."

Jason's eyes came to hold mine. "Any flap of a butterfly's wings would have sent her over, beyond the reach of a saving hand."

The throaty growl of Stevie Ray Vaughan's Pride and Joy intro filled the room, my boots clicked onto the dance floor, and Jason's fingers slid along my waist beneath my shirt. The touch of his fingertips against my bare skin turned me to liquid silver. I gasped, looking up into his eyes, and his smoky gaze told me he was intimately aware of exactly what he was doing to me. He spun me in a circle, pulling my hips in to meet his, and I was lost.

Chapter 11

Winter had released its icy grip for a day. It must have been nearly sixty degrees as I pulled into the parking lot at Purgatory Chasm – and winced. The place was absolutely crawling with people. There were family groups grilling up burgers by picnic tables, young lovers walking hand in hand, and two elderly women in teal sweats walking a pair of dachshunds.

Jason was waiting for me on a rocky outcropping, a navy-blue flannel shirt tucked neatly into his jeans. He smiled as he stood, coming over to join me.

A trio of youngsters nearly barreled into me as they scrambled toward the mouth of the ravine. I shook my head. "Isn't it Monday?"

"Veterans Day was yesterday," he pointed out with a twinkle in his eye. "They've all got the day off today."

I had completely forgotten. One of the down-sides of working from home is that I often lose track of when working-day folks have their days of freedom. I had gotten so used to weekdays being the quiet, restful days in the parks that it hadn't occurred to me it could be otherwise.

Purgatory is a granite chasm with walls reaching up to eighty feet high. The chasm was formed when, during the last Ice Age, glacial meltwater broke through a massive ice dam and rushed down through Sutton. Today it was densely peppered with people, as if a picnicker's sandwich had been left behind in a field and discovered by a ravenous army of ants.

I shrugged. "Well, we definitely won't be going down into the chasm proper today," I mused. "Shall we do Charley's Loop?"

He turned left, and we walked past the large, concrete-floored dining area with its scattering of wooden picnic tables beneath an open-sided, beamed ceiling. "Don't want to have children underfoot while making your way down the crevasse?" he asked.

A pair of young teenage girls strolled toward us, garbed in bright pink halter tops and shorts so tiny they could barely be called underwear. I waited until they passed before responding. "I find it incredibly stressful to go in when it's crowded," I admitted. "Not because of the challenge of the climb, but because of the carelessness of the others around me. The chasm is dangerous. There are jagged rocks and deep, narrow crevices littered all down its length."

My brow creased. "The last time I was through there, I saw a woman in her early twenties carrying a newborn in a chest wrap. A newborn! Just one slip of the mother's feet and the baby would have been crushed. It makes absolutely no sense how little care some adults have for the children they're responsible for. So every step I take becomes tense. I'm on constant alert to catch the arm of a tumbling college student in clogs, or to run for help if something more serious happens."

He nodded as we made our way down the path. The forest floor was carpeted with shades of brown, primarily red oak, white oak, and maple leaves. The deciduous trees had long since relinquished their robes, leaving behind only the fluffy pine and sturdy juniper to provide a rich green backdrop to the view.

His voice was rich in my ear. "The chasm does have a large warning sign at its entrance advising people of the dangers," he pointed out.

"Of course the sign is there; one would think that half the visitors aren't able to read," I sighed. "People head in there with flip-flops, or high heels, and then they wonder why the ambulance makes such frequent visits. It's as if they expect, if they're allowed to go in there, that it must therefore be absolutely safe. They figure if there was any danger that someone would have put up a fence to keep them away."

We came around a bend and heard high laughter off to the right. I looked over and drew to a stop. A group of teenaged boys and girls were jostling for position on a high outcrop jutting out over the chasm's depths.

Jason's brow creased. "Are you all right?"

"I was here last July fourth," I murmured. "I was just past this point when a man, standing on those very rocks, fell eighty feet to his death." I pursed my lips. "It was barely four months ago. Have they forgotten already? Are they so sure they're invincible?"

He rested a hand on my shoulder. Warmth eased through me, unwrapping the knot which had settled into my back. After a moment I nodded and we set into motion again.

Purgatory had a different kind of beauty as winter set in. Gone were the delightful scatterings of mushrooms in gold, crimson, and darkest violet. Gone were the flittering butterflies, the scarlet tanagers dipping low across the path as they chased in search of a dragonfly. Instead, with the rich canopy of maple and aspen gone, one could now see through the layers of trees to the rocks and clefts beyond. New landscapes were revealed in their stark, quiet glory.

I stopped by one rock, almost a curved sandwich shape with two distinct layers, a beautiful camouflage pattern of lichen speckled along its face. "I wonder if there are a variety of lichens to be found here, just as there are many types of wildflowers or mushrooms," I mused.

"We can certainly find out when we get you home," he agreed. "It would be a fun project for the winter."

We were arriving at the back end of Purgatory now, and we came across a dozen family members standing at the cross-roads, pondering which way to go. There were at least four children under the age of six. I gave a silent prayer that they would take one of the outer trails and not decide to go up through the chasm proper. At last they turned right, onto an easier path, and I breathed a sigh of relief.

I moved straight ahead. "Let's take the path that leads us toward Sutton Forest," I suggested. "It's the least traveled one here; we can see how the frog pond is doing."

He smiled at that. "I'm afraid all the frogs are long since tucked into the mud," he suggested, but he came to my side willingly, slowing as we approached the wooden bridge that crossed over a pool of water.

I breathed in deeply as we looked down into the reflections. Yes, there was the log to the left, often holding three or four frogs in a sunny streak of light. To the right were rocks they enjoyed warming themselves on. But Jason was right. There had been both last week's nor'easter and the cooler temperatures to contend with. Those poor frogs would have been sad indeed if they had not long since snuggled into a deep bed of mud. There was no doubt that the ground was fairly frozen by now, resistant to any efforts of small webbed feet to dig a shelter within.

He looked over at me. "Did you know that frogs have a type of anti-freeze in their blood that slows their respiration down to barely registering when they hibernate? That's how they make it through the long winter. Their bodies are barely alive. They simply hold still, patient, waiting for spring's warmth to reach down to them again."

Suddenly I could see the image in crystal clarity. A sense of waiting, the weight of mud and earth against one's eyes, not breathing, not feeling anything. Suspended in time, hoping against hope that someday there would be the softest of sensations, the minutest hint of warmth …

He turned to me with concern, his thumb rising to my cheek and brushing away a tear. "Morgan, what is it?"

His body was so warm, so close, and the last thin threads of my reserves melted away. I leaned in against his sturdy chest; his arms came up around me as if I had always belonged within them. The tender impression of his lips settled on my forehead, and a rich heat blossomed through me from that point, drifting down into the furthest reaches of my soul.

My voice was hoarse, and it took a second try before I was able to get words out. "I'm just so glad you found me," I whispered.

One of his hands gently stroked against my hair, and I looked up at him. His eyes were deep brown and smoky. His voice held a roughness. "I have been looking for you for a long time."

His lips moved down, I drew him in, and he was gentle and strong and heart-achingly tender all at once. I closed my eyes and became lost in the sensation. He smelled of musk and cedar and leather. It was a long while before he pulled back and looked down at me, his eyes full on mine.

I drew in another deep breath. "Cedar," I mused, a light tease in my voice. "I would think you would wear a pine scent so you could weave in and out of the trees like a deer, or a Nipmuc scout."

"I could wear juniper," he answered with a smile, his eyes not leaving mine. "Plenty of juniper here in Purgatory."

"None in the Sutton Forest, though," I pointed out. "At least I've never seen any on the main trails. It's all pine in there, on the evergreen side."

A memory flitted at the corners of my awareness and I stopped, clearing my mind of other thoughts. His brow creased and his eyes focused more closely on my face. "What is it?"

"That day we found John's body," I murmured, glancing left, down the trail that led across to the Sutton Forest. "I remember the rich scents of the forest just as I reached the ravine. I was marveling at how full they were – the pine and the juniper."

He gave a short shake of the head. "That part of the trail doesn't have any juniper on it," he corrected. "We were in there for days after the body was found. I am sure of it."

"But I know what I smelt," I insisted. "Juniper has that distinctive aroma to it. I would know it anywhere."

He glanced down the path for a moment, lost in thought. "So why would you have smelled it near the body?" He gave another shake of his head. "The toxicology reports came back clean. He had not been poisoned; not even been drinking."

I gave a shrug. "It had been a fine day; maybe he had been in Purgatory before he went over to the Sutton forest?"

"Or maybe the smell had not been from him, but rather from whoever killed him," Jason pointed out. "If it had been on the body, surely someone would have noted it and put it on the report. We were looking for every detail we could at the time. Maybe you happened to move next to a tree that the shooter had rested on."

I sighed. "I don't know," I admitted. "It could have been a wild flight of fancy, that I even thought I smelled it in the first place. Maybe it was just an unusual mushroom that I hadn't encountered before."

"Still, we should keep it in mind," counseled Jason. "You never know what might be important."

"As you say," I agreed. "We certainly have little enough to go on as it is."

A cloud drifted across the sun and I shivered. He pulled me close for a long minute. I was sliding my hands along his hips toward his back when a bright burst of laughter came from behind us. I stepped back quickly as yet another group of eight or nine children barreled down the path, pursued by a pair of weary adults.

I turned back toward Purgatory. At its base we veered left, starting the easy climb along the second half of Charley's Loop path. Rectangular yellow blazes cut into trees marked the way, and some intrepid explorer had added an orange letter "G" into the center of each one. Perhaps it was innate in the soul of each human to want to leave their indelible mark on the world.

A young couple came up behind us and I pulled aside to let them pass. The man was earnestly explaining to the woman that his house had burnt down once and that it had taught him how meaningless physical possessions were. I found the thought echoing in my head long after they had moved on. It was appealing, almost, the thought of all the flotsam and jetsam of life being swept away, of starting with a clean slate, filling it only with the things most important.

"My father said, once, that he wished his condo would burn down," I murmured to Jason, caught up in the thought.

"Oh, did he?" he asked, a hint of surprise in his voice. "Was he going through a rough divorce?"

I laughed out loud at that, surprised by the wildly different interpretation, and he turned to gaze at me for a long moment, a glow of warmth coming to his face as he watched me. Then he put out a hand, and I took it, twining my fingers into his.

"No, no," I explained after a moment. "I think he was relishing the idea of simplicity. Of shaking loose the myriad meaningless things we gather in life and settling himself back into what was important."

"That I do understand," he agreed. Together we moved up through the dappled sunlight, the golden afternoon sun creating leopard's spots against the twisting roots and slate-grey rocks.

We came up to my car, and he glanced at it before returning his gaze to me. "What did you have planned for the rest of the afternoon?"

"Just some chores and work," I stated. "Did you want to drive around for a while?"

He smiled. "I would indeed. I should take a glance at Whitinsville pond and also see what cars are at Sutton Forest."

I moved over to his truck; in a moment we were on the road heading north. I pointed as we passed a plaque embedded high in the rock face right along Purgatory Road.

"They really should put the plaque in a better place," I commented to him. "That sign commemorates how the Dudley family donated numerous acres of land to the Sutton Forest. Their son John H. Dudley was shot down in Sicily in 1943, during World War II."

"A worthy gift to commemorate, especially with this being Veterans Day," he commented.

I nodded. "But that plaque can barely be read from the ground, and with the road being so narrow here nobody ever walks along to be able to see it," I pointed out. "It's completely wasted where it is. There should be a sign among the actual hiking trails so that all those people enjoying the natural gifts around them know who to thank."

"I agree."

I looked ahead, and my eyes lit up. "Oh, can we stop at the duck pond?" He nodded. We pulled off to the right where a small pond edged the road, marking the far boundary of the Sutton Forest network. Beyond this began the residential homes and driveways.

"Oh look, two males and a female," I called out, spotting the mallards at the back of the pond. I clambered out of the truck, pulling my camera from my pocket. I took a few photos, then walked along the edge of the pond, marveling at how low the water was. In the spring it would be spilling over its banks, nearly crossing the road in its attempt to move downstream. For now, the water was several feet below the tufts of grass that edged the area.

Jason came up alongside me. "No frogs here either," he mused.

"Usually this is a prime frog-spotting location," I agreed. "Still, at least we have the three ducks. Do you know, all afternoon long, this is the first sign of any wildlife I've seen? Throughout our whole walk there was not one squirrel, not one insect, not one bird calling out."

The corner of his mouth twitched up. "There were certainly lots of voices raised high," he countered.

I nodded. "Exactly why I prefer weekdays," I stated. "*Real* weekdays," I clarified.

"You do have to share your forest, you know," he teased. "It is here for everyone."

"That it is," I nodded. "Holidays are a perfect time for families to come out, race around, and scream their joy out at the top of their lungs. I appreciate whole-heartedly that the kids are not glued to TV screens trying to blast holes in zombies." I smiled. "And it just means, if my personal aim is serenity, that I choose to visit at the quieter times. There's plenty of forest for everyone."

"I imagine that's why you're not in the Sutton Forest today, as well," he added, a sparkle in his eyes.

"Hopefully *none* of the families are in there," I agreed with warmth. "The hunters have their own time, and since their time is limited, I don't begrudge them."

We climbed back into the truck and once again we were in motion. We drove a loop around, turning left at the blinking light on Central Turnpike and pulling in at the entrance to Sutton Forest. There was a lone car parked there; Jason made a note of it before we moved on. Down we headed beneath 146, past a cloud of bright-pink fall foliage. Then we were curving around Whitinsville Pond. I smiled as we passed a pair of swans, watching as they dug their heads enthusiastically in the weeds, looking for some sort of tasty treat.

"You know, I bet to them a mucky fish is as mouth-wateringly delicious as a filet mignon with béarnaise sauce would be to us," I mused.

"You're probably right," he agreed with a low laugh. "And to a robin, that early morning earthworm is the sweetest ambrosia in a neatly wrapped package."

He turned to look at me. "Does that mean you're interested in dinner?"

I shook my head reluctantly. "I do have things to get done tonight," I demurred. "And the next two days I'm busy as well, with friends. But if you're free on Thursday –"

"Thursday it is," he agreed promptly, nodding. "It's a date."

"Is it?" I asked, my cheeks warming.

He put out a hand, and I took it in mine, twining my fingers between his. He was silent for a long minute, running his thumb gently along the top of my hand.

"It is," he said at last, and the sound of his voice warmed me to my very core.

Chapter 12

I took a sip of my raspberry tea, staring at the glowing monitor on my inlaid-wood desk. It had been a long day, but I had begun to catch up on the work that had stacked up these past two weeks. A comforting sense of accomplishment blossomed within me.

I glanced up at the pair of windows which lay before me and my brow creased in curiosity. I'd lived in Sutton for sixteen years and had seen about every face it could show. The coy, gentle mists of spring, the sultry, humid evenings in the summer, the nose-searing, frigid tundras of deep winter. But this was something new.

The sky was glowing salmon.

I stared at it for a long moment, then picked my camera up off the desk and headed to the front door. As I came down the front steps, I looked up – and stopped.

There before me was a fully formed rainbow. I could see every detail of it, the shimmering colors from ruby red through tangerine orange to the duskiest violet. The trees in my front yard played peek-a-boo with its shape, but it was clearly there.

I smiled with delight as I walked across the lawn to my driveway, then out to the street, strolling a few houses down to the left to get a better view over my neighbor's house. Most homes in my neighborhood had left their trees intact around them – Sutton was a "Tree City" after all – but this particular neighbor had cleared out slightly more than the rest and this afforded me a better view of the full rainbow. The traffic on our street, always light to begin with, was non-existent at the moment. It was only 4:30 p.m. and the commuters had not begun their homeward trek. The street and the rainbow were mine alone.

I wondered how many people were slogging away indoors on tasks for a demanding boss. How many were glued to their computer screens, as I had been, missing out on nature's beauty? Was a large portion of the population playing Farmville or watching reruns of Survivor and missing out on this glowing kaleidoscope of beauty?

Suddenly there was an odd ache in my heart; I wished Jason was there by my side. For so long I had been self-reliant, had forced myself to appreciate the glory of nature on my own. I would sit by the waterfall at the Blackstone River, thrilling at the rush of power and strength of the spring's deluge, and thinking that perhaps it was meant for me alone. I had strived to take pleasure in the solitude, for lingering in sadness over it seemed to do no good. And yet ...

I breathed in deeply, the colors before me seeming to flutter and pulse. It was spectacular. Perhaps my photos would hold some small measure of the beauty, and I could share them.

A thought came to me, warming me to my core. Maybe Jason *was* watching this very rainbow. He spent a lot of time outdoors; from our walks I knew he was just as much in tune with the world around him as I was. Surely he would have noticed the rich pink tinge of the sky, the beautiful half-circle of reflected light high above.

We were sharing it together.

At last a faint chill seeped through me. I had run out of the house without putting on a jacket and we were half-way into November, after all. Giving one last thought to those who had missed this stunning display of light and refraction, I turned.

And stopped.

I was now facing west. Before me was one of the most stunning sunsets I had ever witnessed. The entire sky was ablaze in golden color. There was brilliant yellow, soft tangerine, rich orange, softer amber, and a plethora of colors I could not even find names for. It was richer than any painting I had seen. The clouds streaked and stretched through the colors, adding a flame-like texture to the display.

I smiled, and then began laughing as the beauty of it thrilled through me. Here I had been staring at the rainbow, feeling sorry for those who were missing the kaleidoscope that was right outside their window. And I, myself, had been holding my back to one of the most stunning displays of nature in my life. It had been right there. It had literally required only the slight turn of my head to see. And I had almost missed it. I had been completely unaware of its presence.

Had I kept my head pointed toward my computer screen for a mere ten minutes longer, I would have missed every second of both the rainbow and the sunset, completely oblivious to the beauty today offered.

I shook my head, drinking in the rich colors as they throbbed and eased, as they shifted and shimmered. Nature had created this magnificence. It had laid this banquet before me with no questions asked, no demands, a simple offering of heart-stopping glory. All I had to do was to look up. I merely had to have an open mind, an aware set of senses, and a compassionate heart. I had to be ready to receive. And here it was, the pine trees along the margins of the sunset providing a dark, crisp-edged counterpoint to the flow of colors.

I wrapped my arms around myself, the chill fading from my senses as I soaked in the beauty.

At long last the colors faded into ochre and rust and I headed back indoors. As I opened the front door I heard my cell ringing and went to pick it up.

The voice burst from it the moment I answered. "Morgan! There you are. You missed it!"

I smiled widely, my heart swelling within me at the compassion in Jason's words. "I was outside," I soothed him, moving to walk toward the dining area to look at the lingering remnants of the sunset. "I saw it all. I even took a few photos."

He sighed in relief. "It was spectacular," he murmured. "I was worried you would be so caught up in your coding that you wouldn't realize it was happening."

"I very nearly was," I admitted. "But the salmon sky caught my attention, and then I was hooked. The rainbow ... the tangerine sunset ... it was stunning."

"It was indeed," he agreed. There was a pause, and then he added, "I wish you had been with me."

My chest expanded at his words, at the echo of my own thoughts. "We shared its beauty," I pointed out. "We were together through that."

A longer pause, and his voice was rough when he spoke again. "So you are heading out to have dinner with friends tonight? In Marlboro?"

"Yes, it's a monthly meeting. A support group, of sorts, for women who run their own web-based businesses. We share social networking ideas, marketing techniques, that sort of thing. It helps me immensely to have that brainstorming and cheerleading support."

"Well, you have fun," he offered. "And drive safely."

"Of course," I agreed, and we hung up.

I stood by the sliding glass door, staring across at the clouds as they drifted into dusk.

* * *

Sorento's was on Main Street in Marlboro, having taken the place of other Italian restaurants that had tried and failed in the past. Common wisdom was that ninety percent of all restaurants went under in the first year, and certainly, whatever the statistic was, keeping a restaurant in business in this modern age was no easy matter. In this world of Yelp and TripAdvisor a few poor reviews could turn away legions of potential patrons. In addition, with the recession, many were choosing to cook at home rather than eat out.

I walked into the small lobby, glanced right at the bar, then moved left into the restaurant proper. It appeared I was the first of our group to arrive. A waitress came over to the Maître d' stand, took my name, checked off the reservation, and led me to a table in the center. The restaurant was a nice mixture of elegance and comfort. The polished wood floors, fresh flowers on the tables, and well-dressed wait staff indicated this was not a pizzeria aimed at young kids. The presence of the casual bar right next door as well as the long stretch of decorative mirrors relaxed any thought of a stuffy formal experience.

My two friends arrived only minutes after I did, and we settled down to review the menu. Geraldine was one of the most brilliant women I knew. She ran a top-notch hosting firm and was always deciphering the innards of a complex system problem. Whenever I ran into issues with SQL, PHP, or internet traffic, Geraldine could free my tangled technical skein with one quick yank.

Tanya was talented in a different way – her area of expertise was web design. She had created several sites for me which were stunning in their beauty. She hailed from Sweden, and there was something about her clean design and use of natural colors that called to me.

We ordered glasses of Prosecco and, when they arrived, gave a toast to friendship. "You know," said Geraldine, after taking a sip, "it seems like all day long I was hearing people criticize each other or point out problems. I made it a point to thank my Dell rep for being so prompt in helping me out. I think we too rarely offer praise to people for being there for us."

"That's true," agreed Tanya. "With Thanksgiving coming up, many people on Facebook are taking out time each day to offer thanks to someone for being a warm force in their life. I think we should do that more often. We are quick to judge – but slow to appreciate."

I looked between the two women. "I appreciate you, Geraldine. And I appreciate you, Tanya," I toasted. They smiled, returning the words.

Tanya turned to look at me. "So, you have had quite the excitement since last month," she prodded. "Tell us all about it."

I explained everything that had happened since I found John in the woods that first day of November. They listened attentively, and the waiter brought in our appetizers of eggplant in marinara sauce. The food was delicious, and I paused occasionally to take bits of the rich dish. By the time I finished he was clearing away those plates to lay down our main course.

Geraldine selected a piece of cheese off her antipasto plate, nibbling it in thought. "So you still have to question Charles, the man who works at Omnibank?"

I nodded, taking a bite of my veal marsala. I sighed in satisfaction. So often veal came out tough or rubbery at a restaurant, but it was smooth and tender. Just right with the Portobello mushrooms. "Yes, hopefully we'll be able to meet on Friday. He keeps putting me off."

Geraldine glanced at Tanya. "If I recall correctly, Charles was the one embroiled in that minor snafu a few years ago."

I looked between them. "What was that? I don't think I heard about it."

Geraldine smiled. "I tend to be the political junkie, while you avoid all talk of politics," she gently pointed out. "It involved some loans given to a certain senator. Apparently Charles and the senator were old friends and there were numerous irregularities in the loan structures."

Tanya nodded. "I remember that. I never got the sense that Charles did it for political gain or to get any favors. From the press conferences, he seemed baffled as to why anybody cared about what he did. He thought he was simply helping out a friend who deserved the money and that it was all right to bend the rules a little."

Geraldine chuckled, taking a sip of her drink. "I don't think the poor man even realized at the time that he *had* bent any rules," she added. "It seemed like he got the position he had through family connections and didn't quite grasp how things were supposed to work. It's more likely that he had a secretary or underling who normally handled that type of issue for him, to make sure it was done properly. Maybe that person was out on vacation for a week or two and he was allowed to run amok."

My eyes brightened at the image. "Sort of like the sorcerer's apprentice, with Mickey wanting to take his turn at running things?"

Geraldine nodded in delight. "That's it exactly," she agreed. "Charles gave me that very vibe. He had both a desire to be liked and a confused bafflement why his efforts didn't quite work out the way he wanted them to."

Tanya took another bite of her salmon. "Maybe you should bring him here for dinner," she mused. "This is delicious. Would you like a bite?"

I offered my appetizer plate to get a portion of her salmon. In a moment I was concurring with her appreciation of the dish.

Geraldine leant back in her chair. "Well, be sure to let us know how it goes," she stated with a warm smile. "I imagine your time with Charles should be fascinating."

Chapter 13

I pulled into the dark parking lot at The Oregon Club, sighing in resignation at the cars jammed side-by-side. It seemed like everyone had come up with the idea to head into rural Ashland on this late-autumn Wednesday night. There was not one free spot in the entire dirt rectangle. Finally I wedged myself in against the main road, hoping that for the next few hours the drivers kept their wits about them and did not stray into the gutter while texting an important message to a long-lost girlfriend.

A sign by the door said to ring the bell, so I did, then headed in. My friend Kathy was already waiting for me in the narrow hallway. A few years older than me, she offered a warm, gracious hug. We had known each other since our days at Worcester Polytech, over twenty-five years ago. At the time, having women attend an engineering school had been something of a novelty. Nowadays the college had cancelled their women-in-engineering support program as being unnecessary. How times were changing.

A waiter dressed in black arrived and showed us over to a corner table in the main dining area. The Oregon Club had once been a speak-easy, in decades long past, and the establishment clearly thrilled in that connection. The quiet building had begun life as a residential home and the original room layout was still plainly visible. The walls were gently moss colored, while the dark-wood tables sported white cloths with runners of earth-toned, textured fabric. On one wall hung a huge stag's head sporting sunglasses and a dark hat.

We ordered splits of Mionetto's Prosecco, then got to perusing the menu. So much of it looked delicious. We finally settled on carpaccio and a goat cheese dish to start. Kathy ordered "The Steak" while I decided on duck breast. The waiter headed off to fetch our items. In short order we were clinking our flutes together in celebration of friendship.

She took a sip, admiring the bubbles, and then leant forward. "How are things going with your ranger?"

"Today is exactly two weeks since we met," I mused, looking down into the thin stream of bubbles which ascended through the pale amber liquid. Two weeks. Two weeks since my eyes had risen, calmly, quietly, and then beheld a sight which would change everything. There was a line now in my life, dividing the period before I had seen John Dixon's body and what had followed.

I could feel the rough texture of the oak tree's bark beneath my fingers, breathe in the crisp juniper and pine, see the gentle golden glistening of witch hazel along the edge of the ravine.

Were there details I was missing? An odd sound I heard as I strolled along the quiet path, dismissing it as unimportant at the time? A glimmer of something that didn't quite belong?

Kathy chuckled in amusement. "That smitten with him already, are you?"

I flushed, looking up and smiling. "I apologize, my mind had wandered ... but, yes, there is definitely something about Jason that calls to my soul."

The corner of her mouth tweaked into a smile. "So, serious?"

I tapped a finger on the edge of my glass in thought. "I know people talk about falling in love at first sight, but I think I need more than that. I know I, myself, have layers and complexities. I would hesitate to think that someone could draw in everything I am in one quick glance. I would hope that the man I am drawn to has just as many facets to him; that it would take proper time to absorb them all."

Kathy nodded. Her deep plum sweater shifted as she moved. "I imagine at first glance you could get a fair sense of character," she agreed. "You could see if he snaps at a waitress, makes a racist comment, or his car is peppered with bumper stickers promoting causes you are strongly against. But you're right, you wouldn't know at a glance if all of the delicate inner workings align properly with yours."

I smiled. "Certainly after two weeks I can tell we're generally compatible. We both adore nature. He is compassionate toward others, understanding, intelligent, and patient." I took a sip of my Prosecco. "I'm sure that for some people that is enough to call it a good match. We all have different expectations in life. Not too long ago, many women would be happy to find a man who held a steady job and didn't beat her at night."

The waiter came by with our appetizers. My carpaccio looked delicious, with rich, pink meat and shaves of cheese. Kathy's goat cheese dish was served in a fist-sized ceramic pot of candy-apple-red, complete with matching lid.

Kathy took a bite and smiled in delight. "This is really good," she enthused. Then her eyes came back to mine. "I imagine, when women first won the vote, they were thrilled beyond belief to finally have achieved that victory. I also imagine that by the time the fifties came around, women of that era were blasé about that hard-won privilege. I'm sure some didn't even bother to vote because they were too busy driving their kids around to sports and arranging dinner parties for their husbands. They lost sight of how far they had come in life."

"I wonder what the women of the sixties would think of us now," I sighed, taking a forkful of my carpaccio. "There they were, burning their bras, fighting to attain equal rights with men. Eileen wanted to change the world, making movies about racial equality and inspirational women."

I shook my head. "Now, forty years later, our young women are anorexic, caking their faces with make-up, cramming their feet into stiletto heels, and posting naked photos of themselves on Twitter. Rather than caring about equal representation and glass ceilings, they are obsessed with acquiring breast implants and hiding any sign of wrinkles or aging."

"It does seem that women often strive to reach an imaginary ideal that few can achieve," agreed Kathy.

I thought of the many beautiful, brilliant women in my life who were larger-than-average and who were penalized as a result. "I can only hope that these issues in society are cyclical," I mused. "It was not that long ago, culturally speaking, where the generous curves of Rubens paintings were thought to be an ideal in health. An ample body size represented fertility and womanhood. Maybe we reached a 'low point' in the late sixties with the emaciated stick-figures of Twiggy and, later, Kate Moss. Maybe we are now on an up-trend from that and over time we will become more and more appreciative of a naturally full woman's form."

"We can only hope," offered Kathy. "It's hard watching young women grow up today, striving vainly to squash their body into society's mold – the perfect chest size, the perfect leg length, with smooth, unmarred skin of the exact right tone. No woman can ever achieve all of those things."

The appetizer plates were removed and our main dishes arrived. Again they were cooked to perfection, with a rich garlic flavor to the green beans. Duck is one of those dishes that can be hit-or-miss at restaurants, and I was pleased to see it was done just right. I was two-for-two with my experiments for the week. Apparently the gods of food creation were on my side.

Kathy's eyes twinkled. "So, what do you think of Jason?" she asked, deftly steering the conversation back on track.

"He certainly seems like a man I could grow fond of," I agreed, nodding my head. "Two weeks is enough to have moved past all the normal weeding-out processes. I can see that, as we are now, we're nicely compatible."

"So what comes next?" Kathy spread some olive tapenade on a slice of bread and took a bite of it.

I gave a soft shrug. "Now things grow more intricate. Most pairs can find common bonds to last in a short term. They like the same music. They enjoy the same sports. They laugh at the same TV shows. They feel comfortable in each other's presence. Meet enough people, and that level of closeness can be found pretty much anywhere."

"You are a poet at heart," she teased me gently. "You're seeking something far deeper."

"That I am," I agreed softly. "There are two truisms about a person. The first is that they do not change. The second is that they do not remain the same."

She laughed at that, a low, rich sound that sparkled like sunlight on an autumn lake. "So true."

I sliced as I spoke. "People change for all sorts of reasons. I used to adore driving around and exploring all corners of New England. Now I am content to take hikes in my neighborhood instead. I used to love flying out to Seattle or California or Costa Rica to explore different landscapes. Now, when I travel, I count the days until I'm home again among my beloved hills and mossy valleys."

My mouth quirked into a smile. "Even small things. I used to adore scallops; now I find them rubbery. I used to crave macadamia nuts, but somewhere along the way I ate too many of them and I'm no longer interested."

"So you want a man who tolerates your changes?"

"I want more than that," I stated, finishing off the last green bean. "I think many women are content with tolerance. They're thankful that at least they have someone to come home to. They're glad that at least he likes dogs, or at least he enjoys science fiction. But to me, I don't want someone who just puts up with me. Life is so short. We're here for a mere blink of an eye, the alighting of a dragonfly on a wavering reed. Our time here flares with the brilliance of a dying star and then it snuffs out into ebony stillness. I want someone with me who feels that heat of the cosmos and at the same time who breathes in the peace of the eternal life around us. I want him to treasure who I am now, certainly – but who also will admire and respect me in thirty years."

Kathy smiled. "So he can't adore you simply because you kayak."

"Exactly." I clinked my glass to hers. "Let's say he was thrilled that I was a woman kayaker and at last he could kayak with someone. And, even more than that, let's say he was additionally impressed that I enjoy the music of Neptune's Car, and that I was fond of the Serenity TV show. To some men I might be an ideal woman and a perfect catch."

"But all of that is ephemeral," mused Kathy.

"It is indeed," I agreed. "In three years I might have a hip issue and be unable to kayak any more. My tastes in music might slide so that I'm listening to Celtic guitar music all day long. I might get hooked on a military drama set in Afghanistan that looks into the interaction of the strong male US culture against the women who live their lives in burquas. If what he was drawn to was my outer shell, he might need to 'tolerate' me in my new form. For me, that would not be enough."

"You would be the same within, the same compassionate, warm, intelligent spirit," she pointed out.

"The world is full of millions of women with those same basic traits," I countered. "Someone who found those basic traits unusual would have been someone who did not meet many new people. And someone like that would always have the risk of actually getting out and around, someday, and realizing just how rich the world actually was. I would not want someone who settled for me because they mistakenly believed that what I offered, at that level, was unique in the universe."

"So what you do want is …"

I smiled wryly. "There's a reason I have been single for so long after my divorce," I pointed out. "I have dated countless men, and many are convinced I am just right for them. Sometimes, after the first date, they know with all their heart that we are a perfect match. And yet I know we are not."

I thought about Eileen, about her dreams of inspiring others to a better life. I considered the four men who surrounded her, passionate moths inexorably drawn to her glowing flame. Could one of those men have felt, deep within his soul, that he was Eileen's soul-mate? What might he have done when she gently turned him away?

There was still Charles left to query. When Eileen had vanished from sight that foggy evening, had his life become a barren field? Had his subsequent mis-steps reflected a shattered interior?

The waiter approached, shaking me out of my musings. He laid down my chocolate mousse, Kathy's crème brûlée, and we were in heaven.

* * *

I took the left from Route 122 onto Depot Street, thankful that the interminable project to fix the bridge had finally been completed. Previously, I'd had to make a long detour to find another way across the river. On the down side, the arched bridge used to have a fun, sharp bump in it that, when hit at the right speed, could almost send a car airborne. I had enjoyed that, some dark nights when nobody else was around. Now the bridge's curve had a far gentler arc to it. And perhaps in my growing maturity I found I did not much mind the change.

I moved up the long, sloping hill, gazing at the large homes around me, occupying land which had once been farmland. So much of the rural nature of the area was changing. Large colonials with three-car garages were creeping into orchards and wheat fields as if a wave of kudzu were sending curling tendrils over native plants. I knew that progress was inevitable, but still, some part of me resisted. I was pleased to see several black-and-white cows still occupied their comfortable, marshy pasture as I approached Central Turnpike.

I pulled to a stop at the five-way intersection, and grinned widely. They were at it again. Several years ago the house on the corner of the street had become infected with an abundance of holiday zeal. The owners had filled their yard with lights, statuary, and Christmas decorations of all shapes and sizes. Then, a year or two back, they had abruptly stopped. I had wondered if the neighbors had complained, or if the local police had declared such an ostentatious display at a major intersection to be a road hazard. Maybe it had been simple economics. It must cost a fortune to run all of the gadgetry they had.

Whatever the reason, it seemed to have been resolved, for here it all was, laid out in a glorious profusion. The entire house was coated with lights which streamed from base to roof. The lawn was nearly covered with trees, reindeer, trains, houses, and any other holiday-themed item I could dream up. There was even a sign announcing which radio station to tune to in order to hear their custom-designed broadcast.

None of it was lit yet, even though it was well past dark. I could clearly see Orion high above. Perhaps the family was waiting until December first to begin their visual offering? I gave a small nod in their direction. I would look forward to sharing in their celebration of the season. Until then, I would be content with a sky filled with silver glitterings.

Chapter 14

I was just pulling on my black pea-coat to head out to dinner with Charles when the phone rang. Charles's voice sounded tight and rushed. "So sorry, something came up," he stated. "I can't make it tonight. How about tomorrow afternoon?"

"Sure," I agreed, my curiosity piqued. It seemed that Charles had an unusual number of emergencies in his life. What was going on?

I dialed Jason's number and in a moment he had picked up. I informed him, "Charles has bailed again."

"Good," he replied. "I would rather be there when you two meet, just in case. I'm not sure I trust any of these men."

I smiled at that. "I'm sure I'm perfectly safe in the middle of a restaurant," I pointed out. "Little chance of him slipping arsenic into my veal marsala while I'm looking out the window."

I could hear the hesitation in his voice. "Still, I would feel better if I was there. Is he going to try for tomorrow?"

"Yes, in the afternoon. Are you free?"

"Absolutely. I will see you then," he agreed.

There was a noise in the background, and his voice was apologetic. "I'm sorry, the meeting is starting up again. I need to go."

"Of course, you have fun," I assured him. "This will give me time to do some research reading."

"Enjoy your evening," he offered, and then there was a click.

I breathed in the relaxation of having a surprise block of free time. Maybe it was a chance to treat myself. With the first snow come and gone, the first fire was long past due. I headed down into the basement, grabbed a log from the stack, and brought it upstairs. I checked the flue, then cleared a few items which had somehow gotten stacked in front of the fireplace area. Once the log was lit, I pulled the iron-chain curtain in front of the fireplace, then moved into the kitchen. I shook half a bag of salad mix into a large bowl, added some raspberry-walnut dressing, and a few olives. I poured a large glass of water and brought my meal back into the living room.

After settling the tray on my lap, I reached over and picked up *An American Tragedy*, a 1925 novel by Theodore Dreiser. The story followed a man who clawed his way up from nothing, accidentally impregnated a poor woman, then decided to kill her in order to be free to pursue a rich heiress.

The novel had earned considerable acclaim, and I could see why. I was about a third of my way through the book and so far it had been gripping. I had expected the book to be fairly short, a summary of how the main characters met and tragically ended. Instead, Dreiser had taken us back to the very beginning. We met the anti-hero Clyde Griffiths when he was young and formative. He and his three siblings were moved around from place to place by their strictly religious missionary parents. They were dirt-poor, scrounging for pennies, and Clyde was acutely aware of just how many social and material goods he was missing out on.

In modern times we often think of it as normal to view characters through the lens of psychology and sociology. What was their childhood like? What was the culture around them like? However, back in 1925, this was not necessarily the norm. Freud was just developing his theories. Dr. Spock was barely out of diapers himself. Dreiser's other writings had been panned or even banned for being too realistic and revealing.

However, here he had finally found a way to create a ground-breaking, genre-bending story which would help readers realize how important a character's full history was. Dreiser based his story on the actual 1906 drowning-murder of Grace Brown by Chester Gillette. This sensational story was followed as closely by the public as the OJ Simpson trial was in 1985. By using this lurid source material, Dreiser hooked the readers' attention and showed them why background did matter. The unveiling of Clyde's youth, and the great hurdles and traumas he encountered along the way, helped readers understand Clyde's mentality in later years. Clyde was not simply an "evil man". Rather, he was a human being, with all the jealousies and fears and desires that many of us have. In his case, a combination of his difficult childhood, his encounters with a less-than-warm society, and of course his own choices amidst that chaos guided him to an unfortunate path.

As I ate, I read about Clyde's tenuous crossing into adulthood, as he was able to find his own way. It became clearer by the page that he was losing the ability to hold out against the lures of money, beautiful women, and risk. As so many reality shows tragically demonstrate, people often make reckless decisions when life-changing wealth is dangling before them. They lose their moral bearings when an ideal partner could be theirs forever.

Clyde's story was not new, or even unique. What made the story powerful was that we saw how he slid into this crevasse, and how the high walls made it challenging – if not impossible – for him to change his way.

The fire crackled and popped, its gentle warmth easing out into the room. My salad finished, I brought the bowl and glass into the kitchen, then decided on a special treat. I had bought pinwheels a while back – an intoxicating combination of marshmallow, chocolate, and crunchy cookie base that harkened to my youth. I took one, poured a gently curved glass of tawny port, balanced my blue-glass plate with its single pinwheel treasure, and I settled back down before the fire.

I read until Clyde had reached the crux of the story. He had seduced Roberta, the young, innocent factory worker who he supervised. She welcomed him into her life nightly, hoping against hope that he would marry her. At the same time, Clyde had begun attending parties with the social elite, fox-trotting with the elegantly decorated butterflies, making his plans to wed one and solidify his position in society.

It seemed so simple to Clyde. What he had always dreamed about was right there in front of him. He didn't even have to stretch out to grab it. It was simply sitting there, a luscious peach hanging on a tree, its fuzzy surface warm in the summer sun. And all he needed to do was turn his back on his inconvenient obligations.

I put the book down, taking a long sip of my port. No wonder so many journalists had called the Alice Sherman drowning in 1935 "An American Tragedy". One story neatly mirrored the other. Had Newell Sherman read this book? Had it inspired him to finally take action, and reach out for the seventeen year old girl who drew him so strongly?

I thought again of the four men who surrounded Eileen, transfixed by her musical voice, coral lips, and rose-blushed cheeks. She had become a woman beyond reality to them. Would they be driven to twist from their moral compass as a result?

It was beginning to seem possible. Undoubtedly at some level each of us eventually faces a similar cross-roads. Two roads diverge. We have an opportunity to do something which calls strongly to our soul – and often all it requires is a subtle turning. Not even a "bad act" necessarily, but rather the slipping off of an obligation, a hesitation before returning a phone call, an excuse made to something one had agreed to.

And then there was the other side of things. How many times did we obligate ourselves to do a task when we really didn't want to? How many times did we say 'yes' out of a sense of guilt or duty or pressure to put forth a certain appearance to others? So many steps in our lives can be laid out for us by others. Our parents point us toward a certain profession as we're growing up. Our friends label us with a character trait or flaw. The world around us attempts to lay out steps for us, and often it is easier to follow that path than to strike out in our own direction.

How many times, then, do we end up on a rocky, unkempt path which doesn't lead us to where we really want to go? And then, when that perfect cobblestone walkway appears, leading to what we desperately dream of, are we too stuck in the ruts to be able to shake ourselves loose?

In Dreiser's story, Clyde had a dream - what many would call the "American Dream". He had grown up scrounging for bread, shivering at night, and wishing he could have a pair of shoes he could be proud of. His parents wouldn't send him to school. He had little assistance beyond the brain in his head and the drive in his heart.

His progress in life came from his own initiative. He lobbied hard to get a job and pursued improvements at every corner. He didn't complain. He put his head down and focused on doing the best he could.

So where did he go wrong? Yes, he broke the rules about dating an employee – rules that often seemed they were made to be broken, considering how often this happens in real life. He was fond of her and she of him. Certainly he pressured her to go further than she wanted, and shouldn't have.

So, in a way, she was also caught up in her own pursuing of the American Dream. In the 1920s, much as in 1906 in upstate New York, a woman planned for marriage and family. If a young woman took a job, it was thought that this task was just a temporary situation, a way for her to build some independence and pay her own way until she found a man to support her.

So Roberta was on her own path to her dreams. She came to this factory job with the expectations of her family riding on her shoulders. She would move up in the world, find a suitable husband, and have him support the extended family.

She honestly fell for Clyde. He was handsome, smart, stable, and had a good job. His connections with the wealthy owners gave her great hope for rising high above her family's run-down farm. Yes, he had said he didn't want to marry her – but they were still in the beginning stages of courtship. She had faith that over time he would grow to love her and want her forever. That was what she saw as her American Dream.

My thoughts flicked back to the 1906 drowning in New York, and I took another sip of port. A woman with dreams, a man with dreams, and they were like a set of Ukrainian stacking dolls, laid out in a row. The smaller doll looked longingly at the next doll size up – while that doll had his own eyes turned even further up the chain. And the woman he sought barely noticed him, because her own eyes were seeking out something better.

My mind slid forward to the tragic drowning in Sutton in 1935. Again, Newell Sherman was a man with a strict religious upbringing, a choirmaster, and a scout-master. When the perfect dream had come along, how desperate had the longing been within him?

And then, in 1968, there was young Eileen, her eyes shining with hope for the quintessential American goal, that of becoming an actress and using her presence to inspire millions. The four men who surrounded her had their own dreams as well. To speak before the Supreme Court, to stride the streets of Wall Street, to navigate the Saigon River, and poor Sam who simply wanted any say over his life. Had their dreams become tangled like a loose skein of yarn? When one person pulled hard to get free, had the rest knotted up, never to be pried loose again without a sharp cut?

I knew somehow all of this connected together. There was some thread I was missing, some answer which connected, through dark shadows, to John Dixon lying beneath a grey November sky.

I shook my head. It is said that there is nothing new under the sun. Babylonian courts struggled with issues of betrayal, greed, jealousy, and revenge. Philosophers in ancient Rome complained about the inattentiveness of their youth. Unmarried couples in the middle ages were scolded by the church for being too wild and free. Had we really not learned anything in three thousand long years about finding peace, serenity, and joy in what we had in life?

I took the last bite of the pinwheel and looked down at the empty plate. It seemed that we still faced the same challenges our ancestors had. We struggled with moderation, with investing our precious energy into what was truly important in life. We were forever struggling to set aside instant gratification for values that survived the eternal subtle etchings of a desert wind into a rippled sandstone bluff.

Chapter 15

I carefully cradled the Tupperware container of two dozen devilled eggs on my lap as Jason pulled to a stop before the low, white ranch house. The clock on the dashboard of his truck was just clicking to six p.m. – we were exactly on time. The evening was crisp and bright, with a quarter-moon crescent shining boldly through the night sky. Orion's belt was studded with its glistening trio of stars.

We walked the short path to the front steps, and the half-hearted bark of a dog sounded as we knocked at the door. There was a call of "come in!" but I found the knob wouldn't turn under my hand. There was bright, merry laughter from inside, and then the door pulled open. Meredith, Jason's talented lead singer, stood waiting, a green-print apron over her flowing skirt.

"There you are, welcome," she greeted. "I forgot to unlock the door!" Jason hefted the half-case of wine in his arms, moving to tuck it against one wall. The home was a study in comfortable formality. We had come into the elegant dining room, filled with a sturdy, dark-oak table set for ten. Gold-chased plateware, glass salad bowls, and jewel colored napkins adorned each setting. Behind the table stood a large curio cabinet, also of heavy, carved oak, featuring curved glass sides and a collection of sapphire-blue dishes.

Meredith's husband came out to greet us. He was nearly six feet tall, bordering on thin, his ebony-dark skin pointing to his Masai birth. He offered a wide smile as Jason introduced us.

Jason's eyes moved over the collection of pots simmering on the stove. "I hear your famous ribs will make an appearance tonight?"

Simel's smile widened. "Indeed," he agreed. We could hear a soccer game playing from the TV in the next room. Simel's fondness for the sport was almost legendary with the band, and I had half expected to find a TV set up in the dining room. He turned to the fridge, covered with photos of family members. "Would you like something to drink? A beer? Water?"

I shook my head. "Nothing yet, thanks."

There was a knock on the door, and others began to arrive. The rhythm guitarist was tall and slender, in his late forties, with a dark-haired wife he'd been with for nearly twenty years. The lead guitarist was shorter, more muscular, with a girlfriend whose cooking skills were top-notch. Last came the drummer, easy-going, smiling, with his girlfriend who had joined him only in the last month or two.

There was laughter and cheery conversation; I felt welcomed and drawn in by the merry group. Clearly they had been playing together for a while and were comfortable with each other. The two guitarists talked animatedly about how they had been taken advantage of by dentists who maintained a "drill, fill, and bill" focus in life. Apparently both had been pressured to have unnecessary dental work done in order to fund the dentists' children's passages through Harvard and Yale.

I could commiserate. Back ten years ago I had been required to switch dentists, and began using a new one out on Route 9 in Westboro. On my very first visit there he insisted that I had two cavities and needed a crown. This despite me having a cavity-free record for the previous decade. I was concerned at the time – perhaps my last dentist had been lax? Maybe he had been ignoring serious issues in my mouth? I let this new dentist do the work he recommended. However, I felt so uncomfortable with his atmosphere during the crownwork that I did not want to return. So I switched dentists again, to yet another one in Westboro that a friend of mine recommended. For the ten years I had been with him since that, I had never again had any cavities nor other dental work needed. It made me wonder if that one dentist on Route 9 had been of the "drill, fill, and bill" variety – and that my teeth had been quite fine as is.

Meredith announced that the food was ready and we moseyed around to the kitchen, waiting our turns to take portions from the fragrant-smelling containers. There was warm garlic bread with gently browned tops, freshly made meatballs simmering in a tomato sauce, the rose-colored ribs, and the rhythm guitarist had brought a large, white bowl of Caesar salad. Soon we were settled at the heavy table, three bottles of wine among a pair of silver candelabras.

Meredith leant forward, a smile on her face. "So, Morgan, any news on the murder in the woods? You were talking to friends of the victim as last I recall."

I shook my head, taking in a forkful of the salad. It was just the right combination of crisp lettuce and creamy dressing. "I seem to be stalled," I admitted. "It was easy enough to meet up with Sam, the farmer, over at Tony's Pizza. And you might have thought that it would be Richard, the lawyer, who would be the hardest to pin down. But no, we had lunch with him over a week ago at the Pleasant Valley Country Club. He was quite willing to talk and answer any questions we had."

Meredith's brow creased. "So who are you having a challenge with then?"

"It's Charles, the banker," I stated. "He wants to meet us at the Blackstone National Golf Course. They have a mid-priced restaurant there, the National Grill. But it's been over a week now and there seems to be one excuse after another. We were supposed to meet several times and it never quite works out. Even this afternoon he backed out at the last minute. It makes me wonder if he's got something to hide."

The rhythm guitarist looked up, his pale grey eyes matching the light grey of his t-shirt. "Charles? Charles Stone, of OmniBank?" he asked. I sought for the guitarist's name in my memory, and finally dredged it out. Paul. I remembered his Facebook posts now, rich with images of sunsets taken from his back porch.

"Yes, that's the one," I agreed.

"Well, that should be easy, then," he pointed out, taking a bite of the crisp garlic bread. "Charles will be at Blackstone National tomorrow, participating in the turkey shoot."

I blinked at that. "They'll be shooting turkeys? At a golf course?" I knew they had wild flocks of turkeys that roamed the greens – I'd seen them many times while driving past the course. It had never occurred to me that they might allow hunting on their lands.

Paul's smile stretched wide, and at my side Jason gave a low chuckle. Jason's voice was warm. "No, no, a turkey shoot isn't like that. It's a style of golf tournament. In some cases participants all pay their entry fee with an actual frozen turkey, and the meat gets donated to a local food bank. In this case it's the opposite. Everyone who participates pays a fee to play, and the winner gets to take home a turkey for Thanksgiving."

"Oh," I murmured, my cheeks flushing. "I suppose I have read too many stories set in Revolutionary War times, when they had actual turkey shoots. Sometimes they would tie the poor animal to a post, at a far distance off, and shooters would pay to take a shot at it. Whoever killed it was allowed to keep it."

Paul took a drink of his malbec. "In any case, I know Charles will be playing at Blackstone tomorrow. If you show up there, hopefully you should be able to corner him after his game is done. He probably wouldn't want to make a fuss with all his friends around. You could find out what you wanted to know."

I nodded in agreement. "That's a great idea; thank you so much."

Paul waved a hand expansively. "I believe in karma," he stated. "Not necessarily that if you're evil in this life that you come back as an ant. But more that what you do each day in this current life affects how people around you treat you and how smoothly your own life goes."

He looked across at the lead guitarist. "Take for example last Monday. We had cancelled our normal weekly practice, but Todd here misunderstood and showed up at my house right on time. I could have been annoyed, of course. I could have told him to head back home, so I could lounge and watch some TV. But instead, I was happy to see him. I told him, sure, we could practice for a while and enjoy each other's company. We worked on some songs, mixed up some drinks, and had a great time."

He took another sip of his wine. "It's those moment-by-moment decisions that shape our lives. Maybe the next time we play one of those songs we'll be that much better because we invested the extra practice time. Maybe our friendship is that much stronger because we relaxed and talked together, just the two of us."

He gave a small frown. "Sometimes it's a little depressing to see what gains people's attention. I will post an image of a spectacular sunset – a gift of nature – and I'll get a few likes on it. Then someone else will post a nasty rant full of swears and hostility and that post will get a flood of them. Why are people so eager to notice the negative?"

I spoke up. "I liked your sunset," I pointed out. "There are people out there who do appreciate beauty." I thought about it for a moment. "Perhaps some people feel so trapped by life that all they can do is vent and complain about it and attract others who feel the same way. And maybe people who enjoy nature and beauty, and are serene in their lives, find little need to post about it on Facebook or to spend time there watching for other posts to like."

I pursed my lips for a moment. "So maybe the unhappy people spend hours on Facebook sharing their unhappiness and finding satisfaction in reading about the unhappiness of others. It makes them feel less alone. Conversely, maybe those who are content and joyful, who love nature, spend their time out enjoying life. They aren't as drawn to immerse themselves in the Facebook world."

Jason smiled over at me. "I imagine you're right," he agreed. "I would much rather be out hiking in the woods with you any day, instead of sitting in front of a computer screen writing or reading other people's posts."

"Certainly I do check in on my friends," I admitted. "They live all over the world now. Facebook is an easy way to see who needs help with something, who has reached a goal, and who I can simply offer a warm thank-you to. But in terms of my entertainment for an evening, I would much rather put a log on the fire, pour a glass of tawny port, and curl up with a fascinating book."

Meredith smiled at me, her cheerful face dimpling. "So what are you reading?"

I gave a low chuckle. "Well, this book definitely counts as fascinating," I explained, "although not necessarily cheerful. It's called *An American Tragedy* and was written back in 1925. It's about a young man who gets an impoverished farmer's daughter pregnant, but then falls in love with a rich debutante. He decides the only way out is to drown the pregnant woman so he and the heiress can live happily ever after."

Meredith's eyes lit up. "Wasn't that the plot for *A Place in the Sun*?"

I nodded. "Exactly; the movie was based on this book. It's fairly dense – over eight hundred pages – and I'm currently up to the wrap-up of the trial. The book explores the interlocking layers of people and situations. The man was chasing his American dream, of having a beautiful wife and wealth beyond reckoning. The pregnant woman sought her own American dream – a husband, a home, a white picket fence and her kids running around merrily in the yard. Little is cut-and-dried in the book. The man doesn't set out to cause harm, but events snowball around him until he feels trapped. He just can't see any other way out."

Paul shook his head. "There is always a solution," he countered. "One just has to keep brainstorming new options until the right one appears."

"I suppose it also depends on a person's creativity levels," I pointed out. "If a person simply cannot see beyond the box they are currently in, they can feel as if they have no options. All they can do is scream their anger at the gods."

Paul's eyes lit up. "Like those posters on Facebook."

A grin creased my cheeks. "Exactly like them," I agreed. "It's easy to sit back and spew anger about what life has done to you. But look at us! We have ample clothing, we have delicious food, and we have warm homes to live in. Millions of people on our Earth dream of having even a small portion of what we take for granted. To complain about the few issues we have in life seems churlish. If anything, we should relish the opportunities for joy we have, and if there is a hurdle in our lives, we should approach it with fortitude and find a way to rise above it. Few problems were ever made better by kvetching and griping about them. The people who roll up their sleeves, take a deep breath, and do something constructive are the ones who find success in their lives."

Jason chuckled. "And they probably aren't spending their time posting about it on Facebook," he pointed out.

I turned and gave him a toast. "Probably not."

His eyes were warm, chocolate brown, and shimmering with hidden depths. My pulse quickened in response, and I was suddenly quite grateful that it was the weekend. Judging by the heat in his gaze, we might not be getting to sleep until very, very late.

Chapter 16

A flurry of trepidation skittered through my chest as Jason drove us down the long, rutted drive which led to the Blackstone National Golf Course. The flag at one of the tees fluttered hard in the wind, and I knew it was barely above 40°F out there. I hugged my black coat tighter around my shoulders. I was glad Jason was here with me. The entire situation with Charles had been building for so many days that it felt as if a blizzard were bearing down on us.

The building stretched out before us, low, white, with the pro shop entrance on the lower level and the more formal main entrance on the upper. We parked the car and then headed around toward the front doors. Once through the short lobby we reached a pair of staircases which descended into the main hall area.

The empty room was set up for the turkey shoot dinner, with long rows of tables covered with white cloth. A fire blazed merrily in the fieldstone fireplace, a wreath of ivy centered high above it. One table to the side held several sets of golf clubs being auctioned off.

We moved to the left, into the bar area. A lone young woman sat at one of the six high, round tables, watching football on the TV and eating a small lunch. After a minute or so she looked around and smiled.

I was half-afraid she would not serve us. "Lunch for two?" I asked.

"Yes, certainly; sit anywhere," she motioned with a wave of her hand. We took a small round table by the large glass windows overlooking the course. The grass was a vibrant emerald against the soft blue of the sky. I settled into my high cherry-wood chair, keeping my coat on. The room was chill;

undoubtedly the course building wasn't made to withstand the brutal cold of winter. The expectation would be that, by then, they would have shut down for the season.

The menu was a single page print-out with a collection of casual fare on it. I decided on a Cobb Salad, while Jason got a bowl of chili. I glanced at my watch, and then we settled in to wait.

It was only a few minutes later when a heavy-set man in a forest green collared shirt ambled into the room. His face was lined; his short hair was brown peppered with grey. He walked up to the bar and waved a hand. "Captain and ginger," he called out to the waitress.

Her black pony-tail shook in apology. "We're all out."

His face tinted red. "What? But -"

She shrugged her shoulders. "We have Blackheart," she offered.

The sharp downturn at the corners of his mouth showed his lack of enthusiasm for this, but he nodded. She placed the drink before him, then headed over into the kitchen.

I glanced at Jason before raising my voice to be heard over the TV. "Charles, why don't you come join us? The next round is on me."

His face lit up in delight and he took the few steps to our table in a slow, rolling gait. "I would be happy to," he agreed, settling himself down on the seat. "Here for the turkey shoot, then? I'm up in about a half hour. Do we know each other from the Chamber of Commerce?"

I put out my hand. "I'm Morgan Warren and this here is my friend Jason. We were just having dinner with Richard last week over at Pleasant Valley."

He perked up a bit. "Pleasant Valley, now there's a course," he mused. "That ninth hole is a lot of fun. Great restaurant there, too." He glanced back toward the bar with a snap in his eyes. "They always have Captain, when Richard invites me out there."

"I'm sure they do," I soothed him. "My lunch there was a lovely afternoon. Richard and I had a great time talking about what his childhood was like."

The waitress came bustling over with the chili and salad. The chef had ringed the edge of the salad plate with jalapeno circles, interspersed with cucumber wheels topped with cherry tomatoes. He had even sliced the bottom off of each cherry tomato so it sat sturdily in place.

The waitress looked over at Charles. "Something for you?"

I waved a hand toward Charles. "Put it on our tab. After all, you're a friend of a friend."

He brightened and looked at Jason's chili. "I'll have some chili as well," he agreed. When the waitress had gone, he confided, "Not as spicy as one might hope, but still, it's tasty and warm." He glanced out the window at the course laid out before us, shivering slightly. "It's going to be a cold one out there today."

The waitress was back in a moment with Charles's chili, and for a few minutes we were all eating, Charles taking regular, long drinks of his cocktail. The furrows in his brow began to relax. I eased us into the topic.

"So Richard tells me that you hung out with his crowd – with John and Sam – in high school," I noted.

He nodded, taking a nacho to scoop a dollop of chili from the bowl. "Yeah, he was always lording over us," he agreed. "All that silly hobbit stuff. As if we were going to have a grand adventure or something."

"And there was Eileen too," I added.

He glanced up at that; his brows came together as if he were sorting out a problem in his head. At last awareness came into his eyes and his hand froze part-way to the bowl. "Wait, are you the woman who has been calling me?"

"I just want to hear about what high school was like," I soothed him, keeping my voice even. "Sam and Richard have already told me all about it."

He blew his breath out at that, shaking his head. "I'm sure they did," he grumbled, taking a long pull on his drink. The ice cubes rattled emptily within the glass, and the waitress promptly came over with a refill.

He looked morosely at his chili before taking another bite. "I bet each told you how Eileen was passionately in love with him, ready to run off with him at a moment's notice, and it was someone else's fault that she died," he groused.

My eyes lit up with interest. I leaned forward, careful not to pressure him. "You seem to be the only one who cares about Eileen," I commiserated. "The others barely seemed concerned at all."

"Of course they weren't," he scoffed, finishing off half his glass in one long swallow. "They had their plans and dreams. She was just arm-candy to them - a trophy to show off and discard. But she wasn't like that."

"Of course she wasn't," I encouraged.

His eyes unfocused slightly. "She was a rational woman," he remembered, his fingers running along the edge of his glass. "She was so unlike the other flittering butterflies at our school. When she said she'd be somewhere, she was there. When she made plans, she followed them through." The corners of his lips turned up in a smile. "You should have seen how she kept her bank accounts. They were as neat as any accountant I'd ever met."

"So she banked with your family?"

He nodded, stirring his chili absently. "About a week before the accident she came in to withdraw all her funds. I remember how upset I was. Had we done something to make her lose faith in us? But she was the gentlest of souls. She explained that she was preparing to go away and she needed to have the funds in cash to be able to make the trip smoothly."

I raised a brow. "Where was she going?"

A soft smile traced his lips. "Hollywood of course. We were coming up on graduation and she was making her plans. She knew exactly what story she wanted to work on, too – the story of Helen Keller. How a woman who was blind and deaf could reconnect with the world and inspire others." His cheeks tinged with pink. "I told her she would be fantastic."

I glanced at Jason before looking back at Charles. "Did the others know?"

He gave a quick shake of his head.

"It was our secret. She understood what it was to rely on someone and to be relied on. I was the only one who knew, the only one she could trust."

"So then the party on the beach was a farewell celebration of sorts?"

He nodded, his gaze again looking off into the distance. "Yes, and only she and I knew about it. It was a special connection between us. She promised me she'd write often, once she got herself settled into Hollywood. I could see it all, as if she were taking the first step onto a golden cobblestone path. She would become a star, of course. I would go out to visit her. As her talents expanded, I would manage her finances. Take care of the business side."

"She must have trusted you immensely," I murmured.

He nodded his head eagerly.

"So then she wanted to head out in the canoe?"

He took a sip of his drink. "Yes. She wanted one last trip on the lake, to soak it in before she left. She wanted to spend one last evening surrounded by the scenery she loved so much."

His eyes darkened for a moment. "And of course John, that grab-every-girl dandy, jumped up immediately and told her she would ride in his canoe. Richard was in the water a second after them, insisting he would take her instead. That left me to wait for Sam to get his rear end up off the sand and over to our canoe. The man had no stamina at all! He was huffing and puffing just to try to catch up. By the time we were out in the center, John and Richard were already at it. They practically had her by each arm trying to pull her in half. I shouted at them to stop it, to stop it! She just wanted some peace and quiet!"

He fell back in his seat, his shoulders slumping. I took a drink of my water, waiting, letting him share his story in his own time.

At last he began speaking again, his voice rough. "When she went in, she gave a heart-wrenching cry. I still hear it at night when I lay awake, staring at the ceiling. And then she was gone. There was the hollering of the others as they went in, the splashing of the canoes overturning, but there was not another sound from her lips."

A thought came to mind, but I waited a long moment, allowing Charles to work through his memories before giving it voice.

"Did they ever find her money?"

"What?" he asked, baffled, looking up, seeing me as if coming back from a long way off. His gaze became more focused. "You know, I never thought about that. No, I never heard of that, and her parents were in the bank back and forth after that time for the insurance settlement and such. I would have noticed it with the paperwork we were doing."

"How much was it?"

"About two thousand dollars," he stated. "She worked hard, holding down an after-school job during the school year and then moving to full time in the summer. She was a waitress at the Blue Jay, and with her dependability and good service she made great tips."

I imagined the tips were probably due to other assets she possessed, but thought it wise to keep silent.

His brow wrinkled in consideration. "That's over eleven thousand dollars, in today's money," he added. "Quite enough for someone to get their start in life."

I nodded, my mind tucking away the information. This could add an entirely new motive to the mix. If I could keep Charles talking, he might have yet more details for us.

"A tragic night," I sighed. "If only Eileen had decided to stay on shore, how differently things might have turned out."

He gave his head a sharp shake. "Eileen had every right to take a last trip around that lake," he insisted. "She loved it there. She spent every free moment she could in the summer down at Marion's Camp, enjoying the beach." His eyes darkened. "No, it was John and Richard who caused her death. Their jealousy and need to possess her killed her. You should have seen them dragging at her arms. Each wanted to own her. They never understood her at all."

The waitress came by to gather up our empty plates and he glanced up at the clock. "Tee time for me," he stated, climbing to his feet. He looked between the two of us. "Well, I hope I have been some help for your project. She deserves to be remembered."

"I will make sure to include all your insights in the story." I pursed my lips for a moment. "Is it all right if I share the news about her desire to go to Hollywood?"

He nodded sharply. "Absolutely. It would serve those two right, for them to realize she was about to leave them behind. She was going to stream across the sky like Halley's Comet, and the world would have marveled at her talents."

I met his gaze. "I'm sure she would have been celebrated as a leading actress."

His shoulders slumped slightly, and then he turned, heading out to the main hall.

The bar area settled back down into a silence, with only the running patter of the TV providing background noise. For some reason my eyes settled on a whitewashed wood sign hanging on one of the walls – "cold beer". It could have been there twenty years ago, or sixty. So much in life stayed the same, while humans hurried through it, so sure that their presence made a difference or held enormous importance.

Jason looked over to me, his dark eyes steady. "What do you think? Was he evading us because the missing money is the key?"

I tapped my finger to my lips for a moment. "It could be. On the other hand, it could be that the other boys really did not know that she was about to leave them forever. Did they somehow find out that evening, and the news stirred them into a frenzy?"

Jason put out a hand to me, drawing me to my feet. "So what's our next step?"

I smiled at him as we made our way out to the main hall and then over toward the pro shop. "I think we should have another visit with John's good friend Adam and powwow with him. He knew John best. He had heard John's stories many times over the years. Maybe once we catch him up on what we've heard, something will stand out."

Jason nodded, drawing to a stop. I glanced over, then smiled. A thirty percent off sign had caught his eye. "Need a new shirt?" I asked.

He shrugged with a wink, moving over to riffle through the options. "A good deal is always to be appreciated," he pointed out. He looked over at me. "Maybe we should include John's son, Jeff, in tomorrow's meeting as well. I know his father didn't share much with him about this event, but you never know what might jog loose a memory."

"That makes sense," I agreed, coming up alongside him. "So you'll be there?"

"Where you are, there I will be," he murmured, his voice dropping. The sense of it wrapped snugly around me, the most comforting of quilts on an evening glistening with snow.

Chapter 17

I pushed open the glass doors leading into the Sutton Senior Center, smiling at the holiday wreaths that hung along the walls. The woman at the long, tall white counter to our left waved a greeting as we passed. A small room on the right held Matthew's computer class, and he nodded to us, his calm instruction flowing unabated to a small group of attentive students.

The larger room ahead was perhaps half full, and we spotted Adam immediately at a table by the far wall. Jeff was already there, and both waved us over with welcoming smiles.

Adam stood as I approached, holding out a hand. "So good to see y'all again. I hear you have some progress to report!"

He shook my hand firmly, then Jason's, and we all settled ourselves around the table. I took in a deep breath, then began.

I laid out everything we had learned, from start to finish. Adam and Jeff followed my words eagerly, and both clearly were brimming with questions, but they didn't interrupt. When at last I had finished, Jeff sat back, his eyes round.

"I had no idea at all," he sighed at last, looking between us. "My father had never spoken of that night. I had heard *of* it, of course. It was a legend at my summer camp – a ghost story the boys would scare each other with. But my father refused to talk about it. After a while I stopped pressing him, and honored his wishes."

Adam nodded in understanding. "Your father didn't want you to think of him in that situation," he explained gently. "He didn't want you to be rowin' along the edges of Singletary, staring at the water, thinking of him reaching for Eileen's hand. He hoped you would be free of the shadows that haunted him."

Jeff shook his head. "Still, it was a burden he carried, and maybe, somehow, I could have helped."

Adam gave a wry smile. "Nothing you could have done would have helped to lighten his load," he gently advised. "Your father was a writer. He felt things with a passion. He was going to carry that grief with him every day."

I leant forward slightly. "Jeff, so you mean all of this was completely new to you? There was nothing even remotely familiar about any of it? Your father never talked about missing money, or why he fell out with his friends, or why they never reconnected when he returned to Sutton?"

Jeff gave a slight shrug. "I'm afraid my father sought to shelter me in many ways. When I asked about his old friends, he simply said they drifted apart and had nothing in common any more." He glanced over at Adam. "He said that Adam was all he needed. The two of them were as thick as thieves."

Adam smiled, and nodded at the compliment. "Your father was an amazing man and I treasured his friendship," he returned. "It is still hard for me to believe he's gone."

I turned to him. "Did he share more of his story with you, perhaps? Was some of this familiar?"

He nodded. "Yes, there were times, after a long night of whiskey and fishin', that he would reminisce some about his youth. He would talk with sadness about the night Eileen drowned, or the demons that drove him to head off into the army." He glanced over at Jeff. "But he always tempered it with the thought that he met your mother because of it, and together they had raised you. He was quite proud of you and all you've achieved."

Jeff looked down for a moment, his eyes misty.

Adam ran a hand through his hair, his brow furrowing. "Something you said, though, triggered a memory. What was it ..."

Tension drew across my chest. It took an effort for me to stay silent, to let him follow those tenuous wisps of thought backwards in his mind, to reach their source.

"Ah, yes," he stated, brightening. "You were talking with Charles about the missing money. The money he said Eileen had taken out of the bank before she met her tragic end. It brought something to mind that John had been complaining about one night."

"Oh, and what was that?" I asked with interest, leaning forward.

"We were driving by Sares Farms one afternoon, and I needed to stop in to get some fresh tupelo honey for one of the ladies in the bridge group. She'd been fixin' to bake her delicious cookies again, but she was out. I let her know I'd be happy to pick some up. In any case, as we pulled into the main parking lot, one of the workers drove by in one of those large tractors. The kind that you can attach twenty different things to. John stared at it, shaking his head."

His gaze grew thoughtful. "When I asked him what was wrong, he said that Sam had bought a new tractor just like that right after Eileen had died. John thought it was right disrespectful for Sam to have done that – to celebrate the death by buying himself new toys, as it were. It was part of what led to their falling out, and to John decidin' to quit town altogether once he graduated."

I glanced at Jason in surprise. "I got the impression that Sam's family was quite poor at the time," I murmured.

Jason nodded in agreement. "That's how it seemed to me as well."

Adam's voice was somber. "John always said he fed his desserts to Sam in the lunchroom because the lad barely had anything to eat. It did seem, from what I heard, that times were tougher than a week-dead snake for that family."

I pursed my lips. "And yet, somehow, Sam was able to buy an expensive new tractor for himself as a graduation present? Did he ever say where he got the money?"

Adam shrugged. "John never mentioned; he was just upset at the meanness of it all. To him it was the final straw."

I looked over at Jason. "Maybe we should take another trip out to Sares farms then, and have a little chat with Sam."

Jason smiled. "I wouldn't mind some fresh tupelo honey, myself," he teased. "We could make ourselves some cookies tonight and eat them by the fire."

"That we could," I agreed, warming at the thought.

* * *

The sky was soft grey with dense, rolling clouds; the air had a definite snap to it. Winter was on its way, although so far we'd been lucky to have only had the one snowfall. In another month Sutton would be blanketed, and if we were lucky the white carpet would remain through mid-February at least. I adored the snow. I loved the crispness of its crunch, the way it frosted the trees with white sparkles, and the way it turned our town into a Currier and Ives painting.

As if to highlight my romantic daydreams, one of the houses we drove past on Central Turnpike had two ponies out in the front yard grazing the winter grass. I laughed in delight to Jason, pointing them out. "Other towns have a surly boy pushing a lawnmower around to keep their grass short," I commented with a grin. "Here in Sutton we take a more ecologically sound route to lawn maintenance."

"And the grass gets free fertilizer as well, fully organic," added Jason with a chuckle. "The best of all possible worlds."

We pulled into the parking lot of the store. I headed over to the calf pen first, gazing at the doleful eyes of the young animal. Jason waved a hand to the two horses in their ring, and one came over at a slow amble, content to nuzzle Jason's hand for a few minutes.

At last I sighed. "All right, then, down to business," I noted, and we turned to enter the building proper. Jason moved to the shelves at the back to sort through the various local honey options, and a young, lithe woman came out to greet us, her blonde pony-tail swinging with her step.

"Is Sam in today?" I asked with a smile.

"Sure thing, he's out back," she offered. She headed briskly through the rear door, and it was only a minute or so before she returned with Sam in tow. He half-checked his step when he saw who was waiting, and the look on his face held resignation and acceptance in it. "So, back again," he began without preamble. "I imagine you have some more digging to do in a past which would be better left buried."

I pitched my voice to remain gentle. "Jeff just wants to know what happened to his father," I pointed out.

Sam's shoulders eased slightly. "Of course the boy does," he agreed, his tone softening. "He's a good kid. I see him around, and he's respectful - a rare trait in our smartphone-obsessed modern times."

He nodded his head toward the front door and we walked together over to the side of the horse ring. The darker horse came over to nuzzle him. He put a hand in one pocket of his long coat, drawing out a carrot. The horse's ears perked up with delight; in a moment his large, rubbery lips had closed around it.

Sam gave the horse a fond rub on the forehead. He spoke without rancor. "So, what have Charles and Richard been telling you? It has to be one of them that has set you back on me again."

I had the impression that Sam was a no-nonsense, tell-it-like-it-was man, and I decided that a straightforward approach might work best. "Before Eileen had her accident, she had been planning to go to Hollywood. She withdrew all her savings - $2,000 – from her bank account."

Sam glanced up in surprise. "She did? Who told you that?" He gave his head a shake. "Never mind, I remember she banked at OmniBank. Undoubtedly it was Charles who knew about it. He had his fingers in every pie that bank possessed, and many others as well. I'm surprised he didn't have himself as co-signer on her account, to help her *manage her funds*." He gave a snort.

"So you didn't know about that?"

"That she was going to Hollywood? Well, sure, we all knew she was going someday, but it seemed a distant dream. I sort of figured she'd hang around town for a while, do that waitressing that she was so good at, and plan for it at a slow clip. I had no idea that she was going to leave right after graduation."

I strove to keep my voice neutral. "And the money?"

He ran his hand down the horse's mane. "Well, two thousand dollars. That is quite a lot. I had no idea she could make that much money being a waitress. Heck, that could have bought a new car back then, and not just a cheap one, either. It would have paid for a good quality vehicle."

I kept my eyes on him. "Maybe even a new tractor."

He gave a low laugh, and then stilled, turning to look at us both. His gaze hardened and he slowly shook his head. Finally he ground out, "That weasel. Is that what he's been telling you?"

"You did get a new tractor, right after the tragedy?"

He turned his head and spit into the horse ring. "My family got that for me as my graduation present," he snapped, a shadow falling over his face. "It was their bribe to keep me here. They knew how jealous I was of Charles's going off to Kenyon University, and Richard heading down to Georgetown. Everyone was going somewhere and I was stuck at this farm, stuck just as surely as if my boots had sunk deep in a mire and I couldn't pull them out."

His hand twined into the horse's mane. "I remember how empty I felt that night I came home and found it waiting for me, a red bow sitting on top. My family was so proud, so thrilled at what they had done. To them it was a dream present, something none of them could imagine having. But to me it was an enormous ball and chain. That was what that tractor was to me. It was trapping me, holding me down, and I could never get free."

I focused on keeping my voice gentle. "I thought your family was quite poor ...?"

He grumbled deep in his throat. "Oh yes, I'm sure the others were delightedly enthusiastic about making that clear. My clothes never fit right. My socks always had holes in them. I barely had half a lunch to eat. But we did all right. We raised chickens and pigs and we kept the farm running. It wasn't always easy. The world was changing to large farms and heavy machinery, modernizing. We were struggling to get by on a small scale, with hand-cared-for animals."

He looked across the horse ring, to the fields stretching out beyond. "Yes, we were poor, but we had equity here in this land. Acres and acres of it. So my father went to the Bank of Massachusetts and took out a mortgage so I could have my tractor. He trusted in me to improve things enough to offset the loan amount." His shoulders tightened. "Yet another burden laid on me without my permission or desire."

"That would be why Charles didn't know about it," I mused.

"You bet that's right," he agreed heatedly. "Charles didn't understand the meaning of privacy. He would dig through any records he wanted and make snide comments to people after he had discovered their most personal secrets. Half the time I don't even think he did it to be cruel. He had just been that way for so long that it had become second nature. He had become used to knowing everything and assumed it was there to be talked about."

He was quiet for a moment, then looked up at me in surprise. "Wait, so you're saying that her family didn't find this $2,000 in her room after she died? Surely she would have kept it there." He leaned against the railing, thinking for a moment. "Even if she did have it on her when we got into those canoes, which seems quite unlikely, there was never a time that anyone could have gotten it from her. We were all right there." His eyes drew somber. "And then, of course, she went into the water only a short time afterwards. I know they didn't find anything odd on her when they pulled her up. Just the clothes on her body and that gold cross she always wore."

"If the money was missing, and you didn't take it, how about the other three? Did any of them suddenly seem to come into wealth?"

Sam gave that some thought. "Well, Richard got a shiny new Lincoln Continental when he graduated, but his family breathed money. I imagine they could peel off the bills for that without even noticing they were gone. And Charles, despite that trouble he got into at the bank, never seemed to be in want of cash. I think his missteps were more due to absent-mindedness and a lack of concern, not a desire to have more money in his own account."

"Still, one would think that the money would have to go somewhere," I pointed out.

He looked up. "And you're sure the family didn't find it?"

I shook my head. "Charles's family was close with Eileen's parents, and they went over all the finances together after the tragedy. There was never any mention of a sum like that."

He ran a hand along the rough wood fence, pondering. "Her parents are both dead now, of course, so we can't ask them," he mused. "But I suppose her younger sister is still around somewhere."

"She had a sister?" I asked, surprised. "Nobody has mentioned her until now."

He gave a wry smile. "Nobody ever gave her much thought," he agreed. "Eileen was blonde, gentle, with large eyes like a resting doe. You could imagine her standing in a forest, Snow White like, with bluebirds fluttering down to keep her company." He glanced down. "But Cheryl was something else altogether. Short, dumpy, with mousy brown hair that was barely brushed. Eileen had to keep her bedroom door locked to keep Cheryl from rifling through her things, and half the time that didn't work. The girl had an ingrained nasty streak – every other word out of her mouth was a swear, and her favorite pastime was to gossip about others."

"So not someone you encouraged to hang around with your group, then," I commented neutrally.

He gave a low chuckle at that. "No, definitely not," he agreed. "There was no love lost between those two. I'd have to say, I would imagine Cheryl was almost happy when her sister met her untimely end. She was no longer being compared with the glowing Golden Child of her family. No longer dreading the day that Eileen went off to Hollywood and became a famous celebrity."

I glanced over at Jason. "Maybe we should go have a talk with Cheryl, then," I suggested. I looked back to Sam. "Does she work somewhere nearby?"

He shook his head. "Last I heard, she worked in Sturbridge, at the Publick House. It's a restaurant, dating back to the mid-1700s. A lot of history there. I know because one of my staff went to a wedding there a few months ago, and Cheryl served them."

"Well, then, luck is with me," I offered. "My father adores the Publick House, and I arranged for him and his girlfriend to meet me and Jason there for Thanksgiving dinner. They do the full turkey with all the fixings, and it's his favorite dish when we go the rest of the year. So it seemed only appropriate to let him enjoy it on that special day."

"You'll probably see her then," he agreed. "That's definitely a day they rake in the highest tips. Everyone is feeling generous and thankful that they didn't have to do three days of cooking to pull off the meal. She'll be there."

"Well then," I mused, turning to smile up at Jason. "I guess we'll see if we can't talk with her, and learn some more about what might have happened, all those years ago."

Chapter 18

I gazed at the sky as Jason and I drove north on 495, heading for Haverhill. It was the day of my monthly writing group meeting, and Jason had chivalrously offered to drive me the hour each way so we could spend some time together. He had a park he wanted to visit in the area, so it was a good excuse for him to get out of his typical neck of the woods.

"Look at those blues," I stated, my eyes tracing the various shades. "What would you call that?"

The corner of his mouth twitched in a smile. "Sky blue," he grinned.

I gave him a swat. "You can't describe a sky as being sky blue, that's cheating," I teased him. "How about robin's egg blue?"

He gave it thought. "I think robin's egg blue is creamier, perhaps warmer," he stated. "That is decidedly a cool, pale blue."

I looked to the right. "And then, over there, we have a darker, richer blue. I've given up on knowing what to call that. Kathy, my poet friend, calls that *Maxfield Parrish blue*. But even that seems like a cheat, to simply reference an artist who tends to use the color a lot. Surely, though, the color has a real name. Something in nature should be that color other than the sky of course."

He nudged his head at another portion of the sky. "That over there might seem like a Caribbean sea blue," he mused.

"I suppose that's true," I agreed. "So now we're calling sky the color of water. What's next, calling a light-colored water 'sky blue'?"

He chuckled. "Being a writer is complicated stuff; my life is much easier. I head out into the woods and look for deer tracks.

You see the tracks, you know they were made by a deer, and that's that."

I grinned. "I think you're simplifying things a bit," I teased. "You're able to tell which are turkey tail mushrooms, you know which tracks go with which animals, and if we ever got lost, I know you'd be able to find us a way out."

His eyes came to meet mine for a moment. "I'm honored you have so much faith in me."

"I do," I agreed, and meant it with all my heart.

Minutes eased by in a comfortable silence as the sky drifted from sky blue to ice blue to Caribbean sea blue in a veil of light grey clouds. Soon we were pulling off the River Street exit, and he was dropping me off at the entrance to the 99 Restaurant.

He gave me a nod. "I'll be back at six, then?"

"That sounds great." I gave him a wave. "Just call my cell if you end up running into traffic or something. I've got books to read, so I'll be fine."

"Have fun," he called, and then I was heading inside.

I shook my head as I moved through their lobby area. Now they'd installed a TV even in this small waiting area. It seemed as if bars and restaurants were installing TVs in every corner of their building, as if patrons couldn't possibly survive without a television signal for more than five seconds. Whatever happened to allowing imagination a fertile place to grow, or, God forbid, an actual conversation?

The next door opened into the restaurant proper, and I glanced to the left. Our habitual booth was already opened up into a double-wide layout, and Anne sat at the table, munching on a bowl of popcorn. I smiled and headed down to sit down across from her.

"Good day," I greeted, laying down a copy of my literary magazine. "Here's the latest issue for you to look through, if you'd like."

She picked it up eagerly, and paged through the poems, photos, and stories. I gave the popcorn a gentle push so it was a bit further from me. It was bad enough that I ate it sometimes, but it wasn't even that good. It was fairly stale with a hint of chemical sharpness.

The waitress swung by, a middle-aged woman with bobbed blonde hair. "Merlot for you, dear?"

"A cabernet today, thanks," I responded.

She nodded and was off. I leant back, relaxing after the long drive. The booths were comfortable enough, with ridged wooden backs. The music was set on "popular" today, and I smiled as Carley's "Call Me Maybe" came on. The wealth of parodies on YouTube were staggering, with my favorite being the Cookie Monster singing "Cookie Maybe". I found myself tempted to find it on my cell's YouTube to show to Anne, but I resisted.

In a moment the waitress had returned with my wine. Right behind her came Simone, another one of our group members. Simone plunked into the booth beside me, smiling her welcome. "You would not believe the week I had," she greeted. "My whole family has suffered through the flu for the past month; I've had no energy. Today is the first day I was able to get in motion."

The waitress came by again, and we put in our orders. Our salads with ranch dressing showed up almost immediately, and Simone smiled in amusement as I pushed the croutons off to the side.

I shrugged. "I'm not that hungry right now, so I might as well eat the parts I really enjoy," I pointed out, taking a bite of the lettuce. I turned to Anne, who had put the magazine aside. "How are your students treating you?"

She shook her head, running a hand through her grey hair. "When I retired from teaching college in person, I thought the online courses would be a fun way to keep my fingers in the process," she sighed. "But the kids online are just as bad as the in-person students. In the spring there was that girl who was grumpy with my quizzes, so she took to the forums to openly discuss cheating on the tests. She tried to incite all of the other students to join in. I thought that was outrageous, but now I have a student who is even worse."

"Oh?" I asked, taking a sip of my wine. "What is this one doing?"

"She's an older woman, and she's having trouble understanding the material. I've been teaching this course for over ten years, and people have never had problems with the areas she's stuck on. I think she's just not carefully reading the material. She's gone to the dean twice now, both wanting him to force me to give her an A and also to get a full refund at the same time."

I shook my head. "Can't you drop her from the class?"

The corners of her mouth turned down. "No, I'm not allowed to drop someone simply for being obnoxious. I'm stuck with her. I fully expect, when the course finishes up in mid-December, that she will come back and agitate to get a better grade than whatever she earns."

"Maybe this will be a learning experience for her, that she can't bully her way through every course," I pointed out.

Anne sighed dejectedly. "She told the dean I was the meanest teacher she's ever had."

I looked over to Simone. "This sounds like a winning formula for her," I teased. "Each new teacher she runs into can be the new meanest teacher and she can always make that complaint. If teachers cave into her, not wanting to deal with the grief, she gets a string of As and maybe even some free classes as well."

Anne took another handful of popcorn. "Well, I don't care," she stated firmly. "This will be my last class, and then I won't have to deal with it any more. I can focus on my painting and my poetry."

We finished our salads, and the waitress brought over our main dishes. I had the salmon with asparagus, the same thing I'd gotten every month for the last two years of meetings. It was, as usual, fairly tasty.

Anne looked over at me. "So how are things going with your investigations? What was his name again?"

"John Dixon," I replied. "I'm still not sure about the drowning of his friend Eileen, back in 1968. Sometimes it seems as if it was suspicious. But then at other times it seems simply like a tragic accident, one that ripped apart a group of four close friends. Who knows, though. Maybe they would have separated as they left high school anyway and gone off on their own paths."

Anne cocked her head to one side. "John Dixon? And Eileen drowned at the end of high school?"

Curiosity perked within me. "Do you know of them?"

"Wait, let me see if I can find it," she murmured, digging through the bag at her side and pulling out an iPad. "I think my publisher was talking with me about that book recently to get some feedback on a cover concept."

I sat back in surprise. "I had no idea John had gone that far in his project. I thought he was barely getting started."

Anne was focused on her tablet. "It was all hush hush," she murmured. "They were friends from way back, I think Vietnam. When John mentioned his project, my publisher leapt in with ideas."

She slid a few screens and then stopped, nodding in acceptance. "Ah, here it is." She passed the tablet across the grey table toward me.

I looked at the image in interest. If I'd given thought to what the cover might be like, I'd have imagined a canoe sitting alone in the middle of a lake, or maybe smooth ripples. But the book was taking a different tack entirely.

It was an image of John and Eileen when they were both around sixteen. They were standing in a garden lush with orange day lilies and bright crimson peonies. John was tall, dressed in a sapphire linen shirt, his dark hair shining in the golden summer sun. He had his arm wrapped possessively around Eileen's waist. She was laughing out loud, leaning into him, wearing a white peasant blouse and a long, olive-green skirt. Her hip-length blonde hair was caught by the wind, blowing like a curling banner.

The title on the page was "Sixty-Eight Love Affair".

"Wow," I said, gazing over the image. "This isn't quite how I imagined his work. I thought he was writing about the tragedy."

"That is what my publisher initially thought too," agreed Anne. "Apparently John was pushing hard to focus on the romance, about how he and Eileen were soul-mates. He wanted to lay out how they were partners since they were quite young and how he was her one true love. She and he would have settled down in a house on the lake, raised kids, and lived the perfect American Dream. Then tragedy struck and he lost it all."

I pursed my lips together. "Did anybody else know about this angle?"

"I don't think so," she stated. "He was sharing the intro excerpts of his book with many people, to get feedback on his writing style, but he wanted to keep the main storyline, cover, and title a secret. He said that way it would make the largest splash when it was finally released." Her eyes dropped to the tablet for a moment, to the image of the laughing couple. "I got the sense that he thought the other men would be jealous of him and he was looking forward to that."

"I agree they probably would have been a bit put out by this take on their childhood," I pondered. "Each of them seemed to think that she was fond of them and had a special connection with only them. For John to claim her as his one and only might not have sat very well."

I took another sip of my wine. "I wonder, too, how Jeff would have felt. He probably wanted to think that it was his mother John loved. The idea that John spent his entire life pining after a dead woman probably wouldn't be settling."

Anne took back her tablet, tucking it into her bag. "John also kept saying that he had a secret to reveal in the story, one which would be shocking to all of his friends." Her mouth tweaked into a wry smile. "I guess we won't know what that was now," she mused. "He didn't leave behind any notes?"

I shook my head. "Just the story he had finished up until now, which cut off several years before the tragedy," I agreed.

"There was nothing in there that was surprising at all. So his secret must have been planned for a subsequent chapter."

Simone looked between us. "You mean he had no notes at all?" she asked. "When I write stories, I always have reams of notes to work with. I keep a list of important dates, descriptions of locations, and that sort of thing. That way I can glance at it and know my writing is consistent. Sure, he was writing about a history that he lived, but even so I can't imagine he had memorized every date or every name. You're saying he had no notes at all while he worked on this? Just one Word document that he filled out page by page, like a modern day Kerouac?"

Her words made me pause, and I sat back for a moment. "Well, there didn't seem to be anything on the hard drive," I pointed out. "Just the one file containing his story."

Simone pursed her lips. "He was sharing that story with people, right? As he wrote it?"

I nodded. "Yes, he was doing that quite enthusiastically. Whenever people came over to visit he would read his latest chapter to them to get their feedback."

"All right, then, he probably wouldn't have made much of an effort to hide that file, then," she noted. "There weren't any secrets or surprises in that file. But his notes file, the one that held his upcoming revelation, he probably kept hidden somewhere. That way, if someone used his computer for something, to check Facebook or send off an email message, they wouldn't accidentally come across it. I bet he tucked it in an odd corner, with a name that wouldn't be recognized."

"You might be right," I agreed. "I'll have to check with Matthew and see if he's already reformatted the hard drive. This is certainly worth looking into, at least."

The waitress came over. "Any desserts tonight?"

Anne looked at me and smiled. "I will if you will," she offered.

"All right," I conceded with a smile. "Two hot fudge sundaes, please."

The waitress chuckled. "Coming right up, girlies."

* * *

It was nearly eight p.m. by the time Jason and I pulled into Matthew's driveway. To my delight he had answered my call and said not only was the drive not yet reformatted but that he was home for the evening and would be happy to have us stop by. Joan was off playing mahjongg and he would enjoy the company.

Ramshorn Pond was dark and silent under the sprinkling of stars, and I wondered if the heron was out in the reeds somewhere, tucked in for the evening. We had seen a hawk in a dead tree on the way home; it had been fluffed up like a football, keeping warm against the encroaching winter's chill. All signs pointed to a frigid season ahead.

Matthew pulled the door open with a smile, ushering us in. "I have it set up on the kitchen table for you," he greeted. "Some tea?"

"Sure, I would love some peppermint," I agreed.

Jason chimed in. "That would fine for me as well."

Matthew headed toward the kitchen. "Coming right up."

I settled into the chair before the keyboard and turned on the computer monitor. The Windows screen burbled to life. I brought up Windows Explorer and began with a system-wide search for anything touched since October 1st. I figured that would give me a month's worth of files to start with.

The screen filled with results as Matthew brought over our tea and settled into a chair beside me. "Anything interesting?"

I shook my head as I scanned down the list. There were updates made to Internet Explorer, updates to the operating system, and various tweaks to Flash and the anti-virus software.

Matthew pointed with a finger. "What's that one?"

The file name was autoexec.bat, and I shrugged. "It's an operating system file," I explained. "Older systems had them to set up drivers and initialize settings."

"Yes," he agreed, "but look at the size of it. It's four meg."

I paused in surprise. I hadn't even looked at the size. The file name had seemed so natural that I had skimmed right past it in the long listing.

I right clicked on it and told it to open with Word.

Enter password to open file.

I pursed my lips. "All right, that's not a batch file," I agreed. "It's a Word document, and someone thought it special enough to password protect. Even his main Word document didn't have a password on it."

Jason leant forward in interest. "All right, then, what do you think the password is?"

I typed in Eileen and hit enter.

The password is incorrect. Word cannot open the document.

I tried Eileen1968, EileenJohn, JohnEileen, and a variety of other phrases. No such luck.

"Hmmm," I pondered. "I wonder how many guesses I get until this thing locks me out."

Jason gave a dry chuckle. "Might want to find that out before you start hacking your way into the file."

I did a quick google search. A few minutes later I shook my head. "It appears I can just keep guessing to my heart's content," I commented. "They even have tools that will sit there guessing away at passwords for you all day and night. Eventually they get in, as long as the password isn't too long. For example, no matter what combination of case, numbers, or symbols you use, if your password is only six characters long, it can be hacked within a day."

Matthew glanced at us. "Might be worth a try."

In a few minutes we had downloaded a tool, installed it, and set it loose. The numbers started spinning as it listed how many combinations it had tried, how much time had elapsed, and how much time remained for passwords of varying lengths.

Jason looked at the output, shaking his head. "Even if you mix case and symbols, it looks like you have to get to eight characters to have it be safe for twenty years. If you reach nine characters, since the hacking utilities go through the shorter combinations first, you'll be safe for your lifetime, even if it's just two or three words put together. So it sounds like it's best to have a password that's easy to remember, a phrase, and nine or more letters long. You don't need anything special about it at that point. The hackers simply will never get that far in their processing."

I smiled. "I imagine in thirty years we'll have all our data embedded in our brains, and won't be using hard drives at all."

I looked up at Matthew. "All right then. Send me an email if it does anything interesting in the next day or two? Once we get past that point, we might as well give up. If it's something longer, we're not going to take up your kitchen table for years to figure out what it might be."

"Sounds good to me," agreed Matthew. "We're going away to our son's for Thanksgiving, and will be in and out tomorrow. So it's fine to keep it going for a while at least."

"I'll be interested to see what's in there, if we're able to get in," I mused. "Just what was it that John was so excited about revealing?"

Matthew shrugged. "We may find out, or it may be lost forever. If he chose a twelve character phrase, the aliens may have taken over the planet by the time anybody knows the answer."

I chuckled. "Thank you for your help, in any case. Let's hope his password was of the short-complex variety, and he felt that was enough."

Chapter 19

It was the night before Thanksgiving, and the Milltown Tavern in Millbury was an absolute madhouse. It was also the cleanest I had ever seen the neighborhood pub. The wood floors were shining with polish, every table gleamed, and even the air smelled fresh and crisp. The team at the restaurant had done their utmost to prepare for the waves of home-comers.

For surely it seemed as if half of the people stuffed into every corner of the pub had come home for the holiday. There were greetings from old school friends, cheers of welcome from across the bar, and the bartenders worked at a frenzied pace trying to keep up with the constant stream of requests for refills.

I sat at the table nearest the dance floor, watching while Jason lugged in speaker cabinets and amplifier units. Only the rhythm guitarist was here; it was barely six p.m. The others wouldn't be coming for a while yet, as the band didn't go on until nine.

I looked over the one-sheet menu, considering my options. They had lobster on the menu, as well as scallops and haddock, but I finally decided to go with a New York Sirloin with steamed vegetables. There was little chance of a bartender coming to check on me in this throng; I pushed my way through the crowd to get to the bar. It was a center island in the middle of the building's floor. To its right was the dance floor and tables, while the left area held a large TV and smaller stools for the non-dance crowd.

"A New York Sirloin, and what comes with it?" I called out over the noise.

"Oh, we don't have that today," she shouted back.

I glanced down at the menu. "OK, a Delmonico," I amended. "What are my options?"

"Fried, mashed, rice –"

I shook my head. "I'm sorry, I meant what vegetable."

"Oh, tonight's vegetable is carrots."

I winced. I used to hate carrots with a passion. Recently, with a great amount of effort, I had pushed myself so that I could at least tolerate them. Barely. Apparently the efforts had been worth it, if they were going to be half my meal. "All right," I agreed, and got a Diet Coke before heading back to my table.

I pulled out a stack of origami paper and began folding paper cranes. It was a way I passed the time, and I hoped that the crowds would appreciate having a free gift as part of the evening's entertainment.

The lead guitarist arrived, with his girlfriend Morgan right by his side. I found it fascinating that we shared such an uncommon name. She came over to sit opposite me, dressed for fun, with an elegant, draping top in crimson over a pair of jeans. She and her boyfriend were training for triathlons and it showed in her lean form.

I put aside my paper folding. "What are you two up for Thanksgiving?"

"Going to see relatives," she said. "And you?"

"I usually have Thanksgiving dinner with my father," I said. "I figured we'd go out to the Publick House in Sturbridge. It's an inn dating from 1771, and George Washington stayed there. My dad loves their turkey dinners even at other times of the year, so I thought that he would appreciate their full spread."

"That sounds lovely." She looked around. The drummer had arrived, but his girlfriend, Abigail, wasn't in sight. "Is Abigail coming?"

I glanced around. "I didn't hear either way."

She went up and talked with her boyfriend Todd for a moment. "Apparently she's sick," she reported as she came back to the table. "It's just you and me tonight."

"I hope she's feeling better soon."

The bartender came by. "I'm sorry, we don't have carrots today after all," she stated. "We only have corn."

The options were moving as far down the starch chain as possible, apparently. "Can I have a garden salad instead?" I asked.

She nodded, and in a moment she was off again.

The steak arrived, and the salad was just right. I was only able to eat half the steak, but Jason was thrilled when I waved him over and offered the rest.

In short order the band was doing its sound checks, and soon the gig started. The floor filled up almost instantly with fans eager to have some fun. Jason had said that Meredith had been feeling sick, but you couldn't tell by hearing her voice. She was fantastic, hitting the notes with ease, ripping through classics like Rock and Roll and Barracuda.

There was a movement to my right, and suddenly a handsome Asian man was coming toward us.

"Jeff!" I cried out with a smile. "I'm so glad you could make it. Morgan, this is Jeff; he's involved in that matter I'm researching."

"Of course," agreed Morgan, moving to the side of the dance floor with me. Her voice became somber for a moment. "I'm so sorry for your loss."

"Morgan is a great help in my research," he stated, nodding to me. "I think we might have some more information to go on soon."

"Oh?" asked Morgan. "What happened?"

"A new file we found that might have interesting information in it," he explained. "We're in the process of accessing it."

"Good luck," offered Morgan.

I heard the opening notes to "My Own Worst Enemy" and my ears perked up. "Time to dance!"

Morgan nodded and Jeff moved to sit at our table while she and I danced. Soon Meredith took a break to help her voice, and the band drew two guest singers out of the crowd – a man and woman who fronted local bands. Both were phenomenal.

Finally the band took a break and Jason came over to the table. "Jeff, great to see you," he greeted, offering his hand.

Jeff smiled in welcome. "Jason; your band is fantastic. I love your music mix."

Jason sat down at my side, giving me a warm hug. "How are you doing?"

"I'm having a blast," I told him. "You guys are alive tonight, and the crowd is loving it."

He looked out over the stuffed room. "This is probably our largest crowd ever," he agreed, "although I think it's the pre-Thanksgiving timing rather than our mad skills."

"Ah, but if you guys were awful they all would have left," I pointed out. "They're all staying, even though they could go elsewhere or even head home to prepare for tomorrow's festivities."

He gave a warm smile. "True enough. I suppose they must like us."

Meredith, the lead singer, came by. "Hey there, Morgan," she greeted. "What does your t-shirt say?"

I looked down at the black Japanese kanji on the face of my ivory shirt, and held out the cloth so she could see it more clearly. Below it, in black letters, was the word "Peace".

"Very nice," she praised. She looked out over the origami cranes which stretched down the center of the table. "And these are yours?"

I nodded. "Yes indeed." I had made a small sign to lie next to them, stating *free – please take one*. "I figured people might like them for their loved ones, with the holidays being tomorrow."

"A nice idea." There was a call from further down the bar and she headed off.

Jason looked over at Jeff. "No word from Matthew yet?"

Jeff shook his head. "I wouldn't expect any," he pointed out. "I don't think that program will make any progress for another few days. Although I suppose you never know. The password might be something beginning with the letter B, and we could hit it fairly quickly."

I chuckled. "That seems a good incentive to begin your password phrase with the letter Z, and to have it be fairly long but easy to remember," I stated. "Something like *ZebrasLoveGrass*. A hacker program would be working for thousands of years before it got to the Zs, never mind going through all the letter combinations leading up to that."

Jeff raised an eyebrow. "That's assuming modern processor speed, though," he grinned. "It could easily be that ten years from now the manufacturers would have made some sort of a quantum leap in processing speed, and programs could try every combination known in the universe in under an hour."

Jason nodded. "After all, isn't the saying that all the processing power used to put man on the moon in the Apollo mission is now held in a typical calculator?"

I smiled. "How things change," I agreed.

The drummer gave a wave, and Jason gave me a quick hug. "Back to work." He stood and moved over to the stage area.

Jeff came around next to me, patting me on the arm. "I'm going to see if I can make my way to the bar without being squashed like a bug," he chuckled. "Want anything?"

"Bacardi and diet coke, please." He nodded, turned, and began wending his way through the crowd.

The band played a slow song, drawing couples onto the floor, then the male guest singer was up again. I got to my feet. It was Ramble On by Zeppelin, a song I adored, although admittedly hard to dance to. I was the only one who made the attempt. I figured I should do my best to help the guest singer feel at home – it must be a bit disappointing to take the microphone and watch the dance floor clear! Luckily the following songs, also Zeppelin, were more dance-able and the floor was soon crowded again.

Finally there was a slow song break and I made my way back to the table. Jeff was in the seat next to me, and he leant over. "Was a lime in that okay?"

"Just perfect," I agreed. I took a long sip of the drink, thirsty from dancing. There was an interesting scent to it, one I struggled to put a name to. It was like a forest, crisp …

"This smells like juniper," I said at last, puzzled.

He chuckled, leaning forward again. "I think that might be me."

I gave a sniff near his chest and smiled. "Yes, it is," I agreed. "It smells nice."

"They were giving out after-shave samples at the senior center," he commented. "My father hated the aroma, so he gave me his. I finally decided to give it a try tonight. I think it's not half bad."

I drew in an exaggerated breath and expressively sighed, giving him a wink. "Maybe I'll have to get some for Jason."

The beginning notes of "The Middle" sounded, and I was back on my feet, dancing as if no one was watching. The second set ended with enthusiastic applause and cheers.

Jason came back to sit at our side. "Enjoying the music?" he asked Jeff.

"Absolutely," he agreed. "Unfortunately, I've got a busy day tomorrow. Adam has offered to have me over for a full Thanksgiving dinner, since it will be my first without my dad. So we're going to start early on it." He stood, smiling down at us. "Thank you so much for a delightful evening. I'm sure we'll be in touch."

I gave him a hug. "Drive safely!" He nodded, and made his way through the crowds to the door.

Jason watched him go. "Jeff is a good guy," he murmured. "It's a shame his father was taken from him like that, and so near the holidays too."

"Adam is taking good care of him, it seems," I pointed out. "And with that new aftershave he was wearing, maybe he'll lure in some women as well."

Jason's eyes twinkled in amusement. "Oh? Anything I should look into getting?"

I shook my head. "While I did tease him about that, I love the way you smell naturally. You smell of woods and moss and safety. He just smells like juniper."

His eyes drew down to focus on me. "Juniper?"

I blinked. "Yes, why?"

He glanced around, then lowered his voice slightly. I had to lean forward to hear his words. "You said you had smelled juniper near the body," he pointed out.

I froze in surprise. I had completely forgotten about that. "But surely I just smelled an actual juniper tree; they are scattered all over Purgatory Chasm."

He shook his head. "I have been back over the stretch of trail where we found John's body several times now," he stated. "There are no juniper trees near there at all. The only evergreen there is pine."

He drummed his fingers on the table. "Maybe, if Jeff likes the scent, his father did too. Maybe it was something on his father's body that you smelled."

I shook my head. "No, Jeff said that his father hated the aroma. I can't imagine John would have put it on."

His brow creased in concern. "Jeff seems like such a nice guy. It's hard to imagine that he would have been involved in his own father's death. Maybe he had just talked with his father earlier in the day and didn't mention it to anyone for some reason? Maybe they had argued? What had he said about his activities for that day?"

"He said he was in Boston attending a series of seminars. He was there when he got the call from the police about his father," I explained.

Jason's gaze shadowed. "He could have always skipped out on one of them." He looked toward the door for a moment. "It's about an hour drive each way, but certainly it's doable. He could claim that nobody happened to see him because of crowded sessions or something like that."

"I suppose," I agreed doubtfully. "But what would be his motive? Getting his inheritance more quickly?"

He nodded. "There's that, of course. The recession has hit everyone fairly strongly. I've heard Jeff saying that money was tight."

"I suppose it could be about this book, too," I mused. "He adored his mother and he treasured their memories together. Now John was going to come out with a book all about how much Eileen meant to him, how he worshipped her, and how she was the one true love of his life. Would Jeff really want to hear about this day-in and day-out, to have his father talking about it non-stop? What if the book actually became popular?"

"So why would he have given us the PC, then, if he was so worried about its content? Why not keep it himself, as a spare computer of some sort? Nobody would have questioned that in the least."

I pondered that, taking another drink of my cocktail. "Maybe he didn't want it in the house, reminding him of the novel and all it represented. And maybe he felt he'd done such a great job of deleting his father's files that the story never would come to light again. The system would be given to a 90-year-old grandfather, used occasionally for email, and soon it would fail or become obsolete, ending up in a landfill somewhere."

"And then we began digging up the files, but luckily they didn't tell us anything, so he felt safe," Jason added. "He has been watching us this entire time to see if anything else materialized. Maybe his visit tonight was a sign that he's getting worried." The corners of his mouth turned down in a doubtful frown. "I'm still not sure I think the theory could be true."

"Well, if this program actually works, we might know then," I pointed out. "We can make sure Jeff is there when we open the file, and watch his reaction."

"That's a good idea."

I pulled out my smartphone. "I'll email Matthew right now," I told him. "Let him know not to open the file until all four of us are present. That way we can see what any reactions are."

"That sounds best," he agreed. "Better to keep an open mind, and look at this from every angle. It's definitely a strange situation all around. To think that an event from 1968 is still having repercussions in this modern year."

A wave from Meredith, and he looked up. "Time for the last set." In a moment he was up on stage again.

I looked around the pub. It was heading toward eleven p.m. now, and the room was definitely quieting down. Most weekends I imagined the pub was buzzing until well past midnight, but this was a Wednesday, after all, and tomorrow was Thanksgiving. Jason and I had made 1:30 p.m. reservations at the Publick House, and we were barely going to get any rest in between getting home from the gig and heading out. I was sure that many other people were going to have full days tomorrow and needed to get at least some sleep.

Morgan and I had fun dancing through the last set, and soon the band was packing up. At last I was offering hugs good-bye to the rest of the band and Jason wrapped an arm around my waist.

"Ready to go home?" he murmured.

His fingers did a circling slide against the edge of my hip, a sigh escaped my lips, and it was all I could do to nod.

Chapter 20

We pulled down the narrow driveway of the Publick House Inn and Restaurant in Sturbridge, Massachusetts at one-thirty on the dot. Jason dropped me off by the back entrance, then headed off to park the car while I pressed my way through the crowds to the door. It was only worse inside. Elderly women in thick fur coats, young girls in fluffy fuchsia dresses, and everything in between blocked the way in.

The Publick House could be an absolute maze, but I had been here enough times to have learned its floor-plan. First I wended my way up the stairs, then down the long corridor toward the front of the building. A jog right to move along the time-warped floorboards, passing the large, open reception area often used by weddings. Then a left-hand turn into a narrow alley which seemed to be a covered-over passageway connecting the old building to the slightly-less-old annex. Finally, a right into the inn proper with its reception desk and main dining area.

I spotted my father and his girlfriend, Zelda, sitting on a dense, stuffed couch in the crowded waiting area. I wriggled my way through and gave them each a hug.

My father smiled at me. "It's good to see you." He was in his mid-sixties, his tall, lean frame still retaining much of the tone it'd had during his volleyball years. His once dense curls had become sparser over the years, and had shaded from dark brown into a soft grey. "They wouldn't check us in until everyone had arrived."

I looked around at the mob. "No wonder," I agreed. I turned to his girlfriend. "How are you doing?"

"We're retired, so every day is much like the last," she teased. Her grey hair was cut close in a short style and her frame held a comfortable weight on it.

"I'll go get us set," I offered, and after a few minutes of working my way through the crowd I got into line for the maître d' stand.

The woman took my ticket and glanced at her register book. "Table 804," she noted, and waved at a young man standing nearby. "Go check on 804," she called out. He headed into a room behind him and was back in a few minutes.

"They're still eating dessert," he reported.

I stepped away from the area. Apparently it was going to be a little while before we were able to get seated. There was a pat on my shoulder and Jason was there.

He smiled at me. "I heard. That gives us time to talk a bit, then."

"Yes, indeed," I agreed, giving his hand a squeeze. We worked our way through the crowd, finally returning to my father.

I was never sure which way introductions were supposed to be made, so I took my best shot. "Dad, I would like you to meet Jason," I stated. The two men shook hands. I indicated Zelda. "And this is dad's girlfriend, Zelda," I continued. Another set of hands shaking.

My father looked Jason over. "So I hear you work for the forest service," he said, intrigued. "Does that make you sort of a warden, watching for people shooting out of season?"

Jason nodded. "Certainly that's part of it, but mostly it's about helping injured hikers or people who have wandered off the trail. We also do regular trail maintenance – chopping away trees which have fallen across the path, trimming back bushes, and that sort of thing. Sometimes we run educational programs."

My dad smiled. "When I was younger I used to take Morgan on long hikes along the Nipmuc trail in Connecticut. We would look for old homesteads and foundations. Sometimes we'd find a graveyard deep in the woods and make rubbings from the stones."

"It's amazing what you can find in the woods," Jason agreed. "This land has been used by our ancestors for almost four hundred years, and of course by its native inhabitants for much longer than that. We come across old graves, remnants of ancient foundations, arrowheads, buckles, and much more."

My dad's eyes brightened. "So, what is your heritage?"

Jason rubbed a hand on his chin. "Well, on my mother's side …"

I sat back to listen. I had helped my father enough with genealogy over the years to know this conversation could go on for hours. Jason's family, like many in these parts, had an intermingling of just about everything. Some English, some German, some Native American, a smidgen of Irish, a dash of French, and of course there were always the mystery lines you could never quite pin down.

It was just after two before our name was finally called and we were ushered into the back card room. I was happy for the quiet. The Publick House was true to its heritage, retaining the plank floors, wood ceilings, and bare walls from its 1771 construction. That meant that the main dining room was often quite loud and hard to hear in. This back room held only four tables and was much quieter than even the reception room. We settled into our chairs. Dad and Jason went merrily back to their genealogy track, with Dad explaining how we connected back to the Oxendine family in North Carolina, part of the Lumbee tribe. On another line we traced to a poet in England.

I glanced around occasionally, but while our waitress came in and out to service the other tables, it took another half hour until we even had our water glasses filled, the apple cider poured, and our order taken. Certainly I understood they were busy, but Thanksgiving here sells out a month in advance. The administration knew exactly how many people were coming and surely they should have been prepared with ample staff and properly spaced out seatings. It seemed that not only had they tried to cram seatings in too close to each other but they hadn't brought in adequate staff to handle the flow.

Our salads came with the traditional maple dressing along with the cloth-covered basket of bread baked in their very own bakery. Finally, something to eat! I declined eating any bread, but the others selected from the cornbread, sticky-buns, and fresh rolls.

The interruption had finally shaken the two men loose from their genealogy conversation, and Zelda took advantage of the break to lean forward. "I want to hear more about this research you've been doing on the man you found in the woods. His name was John?"

I nodded. "We had thought he was accidentally shot by a hunter, but it seems more and more likely it's murder."

Her brows creased. "Are you sure you should be poking around in a murder?"

I nudged Jason with my elbow. "I have Jason by my side," I pointed out. "I doubt someone who could only handle an elderly man by sneaking him into a barely-used corner of the woods would want to take the two of us on in broad daylight. I imagine when we get close that he'll simply run for it and we can turn the whole matter over to the police."

She pursed her lips. "Why not just let the police handle it now?"

I gave a soft shrug. "They are doing all they can, of course," I agreed. "But they still seem to think the death was accidental."

Her eyes sharpened. "And you think it's not?"

"There was this drowning back in 1968, in Lake Singletary," I explained. "I just have this sense it's related to that somehow. I can't explain why. According to Jason's contacts the police don't agree, so I'll do my best on my own."

The waitress came by and replaced our salad plates with our appetizers. My plate sported three pink shrimp with a small pool of cocktail sauce. My father had gotten the same thing. Jason took a spoon and carefully tapped on the crust that had formed on his corn chowder. Zelda took a careful sip of her harvest bisque, then sighed. "Barely lukewarm," she reported.

"Well, at least we're eating now," I pointed out with a chuckle.

She took another sip. "Tell me everything from start to finish. Maybe I can help with a pair of fresh eyes."

I turned to Jason. "Zelda has her doctorate in psychology," I explained. "She spent decades providing mentoring and advising services at UConn. She might be able to see something from a different angle."

Jason smiled. "Sounds good to me," he agreed. "The more minds we get on this, the better."

The appetizers were eaten, and I was up to our lunch with Charles when the waitress arrived with our main course. Here was Thanksgiving dinner in classic New England style. There was a mound of stuffing, another of mashed potatoes, and yet another of orange squash, layered with thick slabs of turkey and gravy. A silver boat of chunky cranberry sauce was placed at the center of the table.

I smiled widely. "Ah, here we go," I sighed with pleasure.

This was the one time of year I splurged on less-than-healthy food. There was no doubt that I'd be quite sleepy in under an hour. People used to think it was the tryptophan in turkey which brought on the post-Thanksgiving nap, but studies had since showed that there is not enough tryptophan in turkey to have that kind of effect. Instead, it's simply the high-carb starches consumed in quantity that put us to sleep.

Luckily I had a designated driver, so I enjoyed every last bite. Still, I couldn't finish it all and left perhaps a third of it to be wrapped up for a snack later on. I dove back into the story, relating the rest of what we'd been up to during the month of November.

The waitress had come back with boxes for our leftovers by the time I finished. Zelda had templed her fingers and was pondering what I'd told her.

"Certainly it does seem like there were many powerful emotions swirling around Eileen's death," she agreed. "Each boy had different perceptions about their role in her life. That makes perfect sense, in terms of how men and women look at relationships."

I leant forward. "What do you mean?"

"Well, in an evolutionary sense, women look at dating as a long-term project. When they hook up with a guy they need him to stay around for a while. If they get pregnant, that's a solid two to three years they are in need of assistance before the baby can easily walk on its own. Women tend to be fairly deliberate in making their decision about who to be with and like to keep their options open."

I smiled at that. "And men?"

She glanced at my father with a twinkle in her eye. "Men, again strictly evolutionarily speaking, can have their fun and then take off. In an ideal world they would get as many women pregnant to guarantee as many offspring as possible. The odds are that at least some portion of those mothers can either raise the kids on their own or find another man to do it with."

Jason chuckled. "Some of us do like to stick around," he pointed out.

"Oh yes," Zelda agreed. "We can all overcome these urges. Men even willingly become celibate, which goes against every drive in their nature."

My mouth tweaked at that. "Sometimes it doesn't work very well."

She nodded in agreement. "I imagine it also has to do with a variety of other factors. Testosterone levels vary from man to man. One man might find it perfectly contenting and serene to be celibate. Another man might find it nearly impossible to last a week under that restriction."

Zelda looked between us. "Testosterone is also linked to other aggressive traits," she expanded. "Studies of men in prison find that they tend to have higher levels of testosterone than men outside of prison. So it might be fair to say that a young man's chance of ending up in prison is in part based on something completely out of his control – his body's genetic make-up. Certainly he can take anger management classes, meditation classes, and do other things to help him fight the rising tide. But there will always be that fight within him, that drive to be more aggressive than our society permits. It will be a challenge he has to handle daily."

"Like an extra burden," I mused.

"Exactly," she agreed. "If two men start their day out, Male One with low testosterone can focus all his energy and brainpower on doing his daily tasks. He can talk with his boss, attend a meeting, and do his assignments with a focused, attentive mind. He can make progress toward his goals."

She took a sip of her cider. "In comparison, Male Two with high testosterone is going to be spending much of his energy simply keeping his emotions in check. When he meets with his boss, he has to restrain himself from speaking out of turn. At a meeting, he has to struggle to refrain from scolding the co-workers with whom he disagrees. When he's working on a spreadsheet he'll have a drive to move, to be active, and by the end of the day he'll be worn down. There's only so much a person can do in a day to fight against their nature."

Desserts finally arrived. Dad had asked for his pecan pie to be pre-packed, and Jason had gotten the apple pie. Zelda and I both went for the chocolate cake. Dad and Zelda had coffee, while Jason and I had tea.

Jason poked at his apple pie in curiosity. "I think this is more like apple pudding," he teased, then took a bite. "Yup. The slices pretty much dissolve in my mouth."

"Well, I'm quite pleased with my chocolate cake," I countered with a smile. "This is absolutely perfect."

He grinned widely. "Well, with the amount of turkey you ate, I'm guessing that you won't be able to finish that cake. So I'm sure I'll have a chance to find out."

"O-ho, is that a challenge?" I asked with a chuckle.

He was right, of course, and I finally gave in about two-thirds of the way through. I handed over the plate, then turned back to Zelda.

"How do you feel the testosterone issue might apply to our situation?"

"It's the shooting," she pointed out. "There are so many ways to kill a person. You said that John left his home open for people to come and go. Someone could quite easily have slipped new pills into his pill bottle or a commonly available poison into something in his kitchen. It would have been challenging for the murderer to be identified, if the poisoning was ever detected. In addition, the murderer could be far away when the actual death occurred."

I pondered this. "Maybe the murderer hoped the shooting would be seen as a hunting accident. That is, after all, what they're calling it."

She shook her head. "The only reason the police are considering that is they have no other choice," she mused. "A planned murder would have presented itself with a neatly wrapped solution, so there was no question."

She took another bite of cake. "No, I think this was a crime of anger and passion. Someone wanted to pull that trigger, to feel the explosion of the bullet, to see the look on John's face when he was shot."

"And that points to higher testosterone?"

"Not absolutely, of course, but I would take it into consideration." She held my gaze. "For example, Charles the banker. You said he avoided you for over a week because he didn't want to face the past?"

"Yes, that was him."

"Well, then, he doesn't seem the type to want to confront John and shoot him face to face," mused Zelda. "He would be much more likely to go the poison route. He'd want to be as far away as possible when it happened. He'd probably enjoy the planning part and the idea that everything was neatly taken care of."

"All right, I see that makes sense," I agreed. "So how about Sam or Richard?"

She finished off her last bite of cake. "Sam seemed to have a temper when he stormed off from the restaurant. That shows a person who is willing to take strong action when necessary. So it might be him. But what would his motive be?"

I pondered this. "Well, the others went off to build experience and strength elsewhere. All Sam had was the reputation of his farm and his standing in the local community. What if John was going to publish something that might risk it all – something he did that would turn the community against him?"

Zelda thought about this. "Like ...?"

Jason finished off the last of my cake. "Well, what if Sam had gotten Eileen pregnant and forced her to get an abortion because he wasn't ready to start a family yet? What if he still held out one last hope for escape from the farmer's life?"

Zelda nodded. "That might do it," she agreed. "All his friends and family would be shocked. The thought that Sam had done that to such a beloved member of the community could resonate strongly, even now.

I looked between them. "All right, so Sam seems to have the temperament and we can imagine a scenario that would cause him to do it. How about Richard?"

Zelda put a finger to her lips. "The lawyer? It sounds like he's done a good job over the years of putting a refined veneer over his passions. However, I've met few lawyers who were both successful and timid. I would have to guess that he has great fires within him and he has trained himself to focus them with precision."

I nodded. "I got that sense too. I wouldn't want to cross him."

Jason leant in. "And the same type of scenario would be just as threatening for him," he pointed out. "His reputation is founded on his solid ethics. If he was found to be doing unethical things it might not look good to the crowd at the country club."

I sat back. "And the missing money?"

Jason glanced around. "Wasn't Eileen's sister supposed to be working here today? Maybe she has some insight into that."

I rubbed my forehead with my hand. "I had completely forgotten about her," I admitted. "However, the restaurant is a madhouse. We are barely getting our own service and I'm sure the other waitresses are just as frazzled. We might do better to try to meet with her off-hours on another day."

Dad nodded in agreement. "It might not hurt to ask at the desk to see what her hours are," he pointed out. "Are we ready?"

I stood. "Yes, indeed – I am both over-full and exhausted."

The main lobby was only half-stuffed with waiting people; it was now past five. I only had a short wait in line before I was able to speak with the maître d'.

"Is Cheryl working tonight?" I asked.

"Yes, certainly. You can see her in the back corner."

I turned and stepped into the entryway to the dining room. It was a large, open room with a pleasant fire crackling in a stone fireplace to the right. About twenty dark-wood tables of various shapes and sizes filled the room, with wood plank floors and curtain patterns that seemed right out of the Revolutionary War.

I spotted Cheryl where she said, pushing a tendril of brown, shoulder-length hair back from a harried face as she leant over a table of six elderly patrons. They were scolding her about one of their orders, and she was nodding in patient agreement.

Jason was at my side. "Maybe calling her tomorrow might be a better idea," he offered with a wry smile.

"I would tend to agree." We turned and walked with my father and Zelda back through the maze of twisty passages until we reached the entry area again.

My father held his hand out to Jason. "Great to meet you, Jason," he offered. "I look forward to seeing you again soon."

"I hope so," agreed Jason, and soon we had exchanged our farewells and moved out into the courtyard.

Jason smiled at me, taking my arm as the other two headed off to their car. "That seemed to go well," he offered.

"It did, indeed," I smiled back at him. We strolled toward the back of the parking lot.

I pointed in mild surprise. "Oh, look, a helicopter. I've been coming here for fifteen years and have never seen one of those in this back field."

"Must be a wealthy visitor," chuckled Jason.

He looked out beyond the field and shook his head. I followed his gaze to where a dense forest had once stretched. A year ago Massachusetts had experienced a freak tornado. We barely got one every fifty years and apparently we had been due for a monster. It had come straight across the forest, shearing off the tops of the trees at about twenty feet up as neatly as if a giant had set his lawnmower for that height and groomed with a steady push. Their limbs had been ripped off. So now there stood a field of dead poles, stark against the night sky, a reminder of that stunning day.

I shook my head. "It's a bit grisly."

He gave me a hug. "Eventually they will fall, their decomposing bodies will nourish the ground, and we'll get a fresh forest to grow," he reminded me.

"Still, it looks pretty somber right now."

"Ah, but it's your mind that makes it somber," he pointed out. "Everything in life is neutral until our minds interpret it."

I stared for a few minutes at the woods, thinking of this as being the first stage in a cleansing process. Soon the poles would collapse, melt into the earth, and fresh, green sprouts would stretch willingly to the sky. I could imagine it all; a smile slowly spread on my lips.

"I believe you're right," I agreed, and his arm drew me in close.

Chapter 21

Black Friday's morning was the opposite of its namesake – bright, clear, and redolent with a flurry of chickadees enjoying the buffet at the feeder out the side window. Jason was working on concocting his spinach shake. I had my traditional chocolate protein shake with my wealth of orange chewy vitamins.

I smiled at him. "So, off to do your shopping?"

He nodded. "Sure you don't want to come with me?"

I laughed out loud at that. "If there is one thing you're going to learn about me, it's that I absolutely abhor shopping crowds. It would be sheer torture for you to drag me through those mobs of price-hungry zealots. You really don't want to see me in that situation."

He smiled. "In that case, you remain safely home. I will be the hunter. You can enjoy the quiet."

My phone chirruped and I picked it up to glance at it. "Or maybe it won't be quiet," I mused. "Cheryl has agreed to come over for a little while and talk about her sister."

His eyebrows arched. "Oh? How did you manage to track down her email address?"

I waved the phone at him. "Why, Facebook of course. A quick query, a few clicks, and I had a message off to her."

He smiled. "You may convince me to set up an account yet," he teased.

I flashed him a smile. "How else am I supposed to connect to you, if I ever decide to change my status from 'single'?"

His gaze stilled for a moment, becoming more serious. "Oh? And do you think you're ready for that?" he asked, a note of cautious hope entering his tone.

My grin widened. "Well you know how this works. You men want to lay your claims, take us women off the market, at least while you have us. But us women, we want to make sure our options are open until we're quite sure we have what we want."

His brown eyes held mine. "And what do you want?"

My cheeks warmed and I looked out to the feeder. A male cardinal had alighted there, his rosy feathers nearly glowing in the morning sunshine. As I watched, his mate fluttered down to join him on the opposite side. Her garb was more subdued, in quiet browns and greys, but I sensed a strength there.

"I have to say I am fairly content," I stated at last, looking over at him. "Boyfriend and girlfriend, then?"

His hand reached over to take mine. "That sounds just right."

* * *

I'm not sure what I expected in Cheryl, but the woman who stood on my doorstep wasn't quite it. Squat, heavy, dressed in a too-tight hip-hugging pair of black jeans and a paisley top which squeezed her breasts into a high, unnatural shape. Her face was weathered and rough, as if an apple had been left in a corner for far too long.

I drew back, welcoming her in. "It is great to meet you, Cheryl," I greeted. "Thank you so much; I imagine you had many things to do today."

"It was on my way," she stated, a sharpness edging her voice. "And besides, you said we could have a glass or two of wine while we talked."

I glanced at the clock on the cable box – the green, segmented lines indicated it was a few minutes after noon. "Of course," I agreed with a smile. "Come on in."

She looked around as we moved through the living room, her eyes lingering a little too long on the large-screen TV hanging over the fireplace. A shiver moved through me; I dismissed it with a deliberate push. Surely she was not simply here to case my house for a robbery.

She plunked herself down on the chair facing the back suet feeder and looked over at the waist-height maple wine rack which stood against the center island of the kitchen. "I prefer red," she called out.

"Red it is," I agreed without censure, drawing out a bottle of Velvet Devil merlot. It was a screw-cap, so it was only a moment before I had the glass in front of her. She drank half of it down in one draw.

I moved to the fridge and pulled out a Tupperware of cheddar I'd sliced into squares, and laid them out on a plate with some Triscuits. I placed the snack at the center of the green tablecloth, settling myself to her right where my mug of Chanakara tea waited, steaming.

She ignored the food offering. "So, what'd'ya wanna know?"

"Tell me about your sister."

She made a swirling motion in the air with her hand. "Eileen the perfect. Tall. Elegant. Blonde. Blue-eyed. Every guy within fifty miles wanted to have sex with her." She gave a chortle. "In all the movies she'd be the other woman, the reason the guy drowned his ugly wife. It figures she somehow took the martyrdom glory and the starring role for herself."

"The glory?" I asked, baffled.

She leant forward. "Oh, sure," she insisted. "The papers were talking about it for months! How did she drown? Was it one of those four guys? What could the motive be? What kind of a brilliant actress had the world lost?" She rolled her eyes, and it was as if a petulant thirteen-year-old had been trapped inside the sagging body of a middle-aged woman. "She would have absolutely loved it."

"What did you think the motive was?"

She downed the rest of her wine and her eyes went meaningfully to the empty glass. I stood, brought back the bottle, and put it on the table beside the plate of cheese. She filled her glass to the very brim; I was impressed how the surface tension kept the liquid from rolling over the lip onto the table.

Another mouthful and she was talking again. "Oh, I'm sure it was simply her stupidity. My sister thought she was perfect.

She never had even the slightest inkling that she could fail."
Cheryl scowled. "And of course, she wouldn't. If she did
something wrong in Algebra class, she would just smile and
wink at Mr. McGuthers. He would give her extra tutoring after
class and pass her. If she got caught speeding down 146, a wink
and a flash of her cleavage would get her off with a warning."
Her look soured. "I got caught in that exact same spot and the
ticket was tossed at me without a second glance."

I took a sip of my tea, sliding my fingers along the smooth
burgundy ceramic handle. "But surely one of the boys could
have done it?"

She took another gulp of the wine, pondering the thought for
a moment. "Maybe Richard or Sam," she stated at last, "But
certainly not Charles. I've never seen a bigger coward." She
gave a snorting laugh. "I saw him at the Publick House a few
days after he was fired from OmniBank for his inappropriate
loans to the senator. You should have seen him. He would have
jumped if someone had tapped him on his shoulder." She
scoffed. "And he calls himself a man."

"How about John?" I asked.

She looked at me as if I'd spoken in tongues. "John? John
was her lap-dog. I'm surprised he didn't dress in matching
outfits with her. He was beyond obsessed with her." She took
another long drink of wine. "Calling every day on the phone,
throwing pebbles at her window every night, it was beyond
belief."

"How did your sister take it?"

She laughed out loud. "As my sister took everything in life.
As her due. She was the queen, and John was her groveling
subject. If she was ever surprised, it was because not every man
collapsed like a puddle of quivering Jell-O when entering her
presence."

I thought about that, looking out the side window. The
cardinals from the morning had long since gone. Now a blue jay
sat stationed at the feeder, picked a sunflower seed out of the
feeder hole, tilted his head back, and swallowed it whole.
Another seed, another tilt. I saw a chickadee flutter tenuously

down toward the opposite side, then veer off, nervous. The blue jay was not giving up his perch; for now the smaller birds would have to wait.

Cheryl looked sullenly down into her wine. "Eileen always got everything," she sulked. "My parents sided with her on every argument. At Christmas she got exactly what she wanted, while I had to settle for 'nearly good enough' presents. And at school –" She snorted. "Every teacher would look around in delight when they read my name on the first day, and then I could see it in their eyes when their gaze finally settled on me. Disappointment. Throughout the year I would be exhorted to do as well as my sister, reminded when I failed that my sister would have succeeded."

"That must have been rough," I commented.

"You bet it was rough," she snarled. "I was always in her shadow. A black, grimy shadow I could not escape. That was what life was like with her around. Inky dark, and not even a glimmer of light could penetrate it."

I kept my voice low. "So you were … happy when she died?"

"You betya," she agreed with a nod, "and I'm not ashamed to admit it. It was her own stupid fault she got drunk on that beach. It's her own idiotic choice to insist they go out on the water. She probably stirred those boys up into a jealous frenzy and got them fighting about her. It was her favorite pastime. And what kind of an idiot spends time on a lake and barely knows how to swim?" Her voice took on a sing-song effect. " '*I wouldn't want my skin to wrinkle,*' she would say. *'I might look all gross and old.*'" She laughed. "Well, looks like she doesn't have to worry about that now."

"But there was money missing when she died, wasn't there?" I asked.

Her eyes darted to the window, staring at the blue jay, and her fingers wrapped tightly around the stem of her empty wine glass. I reached forward to pour it full again. I pitched my voice to be reassuring. "I don't care about the money," I reassured her. "I just want to eliminate it as a motive for foul play."

She snorted at that, bringing the wine to her lips, her shoulders easing as she drew the liquid down her throat. "There would be plenty of motives for drowning her, with the enemies that girl made, but the two thousand dollars wasn't one of them."

So she knew the amount. I kept my voice calm. "Oh?"

Her voice began to rise. "After all I went through? After all those years of neglect and failed promises? Every single item of clothing I owned was a hand-me-down from her. I never got a new coat. Never a new pair of shoes. Everything was worn and scuffed and stained and torn. Every. Single. Thing." The years of pain echoed in her voice. "I deserved that two thousand dollars. I earned it. I bled for it!"

"So nobody knew?"

She shook her head. "She thought she could lock me out of her room but I figured out how to pick that door years ago. I knew exactly what shoebox she kept her treasures in." She snorted. "She couldn't help but boast to me the moment she came home with the cash, how glorious her life would be and how nasty mine would end up. She was going to live in an elegant mansion in Hollywood, with an in-ground swimming pool, a sauna, and a personal masseuse. I would be lucky to have a roof that didn't leak."

She took another drink. "The moment my parents told me she had drowned, I ran upstairs. They thought I was upset, but I was only making sure that I could get into her room as quickly as possible. I took that two thousand and hid it underneath my dresser. The moment I turned eighteen I moved out and got my own apartment. I was going to take charge of my own destiny and be out from under her shadow forever."

I looked her over. Her top was frayed around the neckline and the necklace she wore had imitation turquoise in it. My voice became soft. "Did you find happiness?"

The corners of her mouth turned down. "It was too late," she snapped. "She had spoiled everything. Every family gathering focused on the loss of Eileen and how tragic it was. There weren't even any more hand-me-downs for me. Everyone around here treated me like an outcast for not wearing black and moping for the loss of the *world's greatest treasure*."

"So why didn't you leave?"

She blinked in surprise. "And go where?" she asked. "I wasn't a star. I couldn't go to Hollywood."

I looked at her for a moment. "But surely there are many other places in the world that would interest you?"

Her blank gaze seemed to indicate that she'd never thought of that.

Her eyelids began to droop. A nervous spear of energy lanced through me at the thought of inflicting her on the busy roads in this state. "I just got in Brave on Netflix," I offered. "It's a DVD about a girl who chooses her own destiny. It sounds like it's right up your alley. Would you like to watch it?"

"Sure," she agreed listlessly, and together we moved to the futon in the living room. I set her up on the left side, with the pillows against the arm and a draped comforter over her. I pulled the ivory tapestry curtains over the windows to dampen the light a bit.

The movie had only finished its opening sequence before I heard a low snore.

* * *

Jason's truck pulled into the driveway in the dusky glow and I moved to the door. I pulled it open as he came up the stairs, putting a finger to my lips.

His brows creased in confusion, then his eyes moved to the futon and lit up in surprise. He moved with me quietly into the kitchen.

I kept my voice to a whisper. "She might have had a bit too much to drink," I murmured.

His eyes were steady on me, with a glint of amusement in them. "Did you help?"

The hint of a grin tweaked the corner of my mouth. "I might have had a tiny bit to do with that but it hardly needed any encouragement," I pointed out. "She would have drunk the entire bottle if I had not distracted her."

There was a yawning from the other room and we moved to the living room. Cheryl stretched, shrugging off the blanket, seemingly quite comfortable with the idea of having slept in a stranger's living room for the afternoon.

"Well then, I have some shopping to do," she stated, drawing herself to her feet.

I glanced back toward the kitchen. "Would you like some coffee, or water, or something else before you go?"

She shook her head. "Nah, I'm meeting some friends at TGI Friday's for drinks at five." She glanced at the clock. "That gives me a half hour – just about perfect." She gathered up her purse and coat. "Thanks for the wine. Hope I was helpful."

"You were indeed," I agreed, moving to open the door for her. "Thank you for your time."

"Yeah, sure," she waved, and then she was moving down the steps toward her car.

Jason came up behind me, watching her go. She backed her car up smoothly; apparently the nap had prepared her well enough for the short drive into Millbury for her next round of drinking.

His voice was rich and warm at my ear. "So, did you really learn anything?"

I turned against him and his arms automatically came up around me. "Welcome home," I murmured, drawing him in to a kiss. It was many long minutes before we pulled apart again.

I smiled up at him. "That always comes first," I pointed out.

"Of course," he agreed with a smile.

I took his hand and we moved back into the dining area. I made us some tea and took the cheese out of the fridge, putting it out on the table with the Triscuits. Jason took a pair and layered them, popping them into his mouth.

I took a sip of my tea. "Yes, I did fill in a few holes," I agreed. "For example, it was Cheryl who took the money."

"Oh?" he asked, his eyebrows raising. "She stole from her own sister?"

My mouth tweaked. "She didn't quite see it like that. Her sister was dead already, and Cheryl felt it was owed her after the injustices she had suffered."

Jason ate another pair of squares. "So what did she feel about the drowning?"

"She felt it was an accident and wholly her sister's fault. She seemed to have a fairly poor view of her sister."

He chuckled. "Not uncommon between siblings," he pointed out. "There can be issues there that even decades don't resolve."

"When pressed, she singled out Sam and Richard as the two who might have the strength to have done something to Eileen," I continued. "Although I don't think she took it seriously. She figured her sister just drowned through her own stupidity. Apparently Eileen couldn't swim very well."

"Well, it seems that she and Zelda concur on the suspects," mused Jason. "It seems worth looking into, at least."

"I agree. What do you think our next move should be?"

His eyes held mine, and a smile drew across his face. "I'm sure we could discuss that in the morning," he murmured.

Chapter 22

We were in our own little world - tucked into a quiet booth at MargaritaGrill in Auburn. I loved the booths. There were three of them along the right side of the main dining area. Each featured high-backed wooden benches, the right side abutted the wood wall, and the left side had figured woodwork edges creating a private space. A hanging tin light provided a constellation of patterns and a red-glass candle on the table added to the ambiance.

I took the last bite of my beef burrito, dousing it fully in sour cream. It was as delicious as the first. "Someday I need to try one of their other dishes," I admitted. "I just love this one so much – it's hard to think of anything else when I come to order."

He chuckled, offering me a toast with his Dos Equis beer. "If you find something you adore there's no harm in sticking with it," he reminded me. "So many people out there have to make do with things they're not fond of. Treasure your satisfaction."

I smiled. "So true."

The opening notes of *Can't You Hear Me Knocking* echoed softly from my purse and I reached down into its depths. "Nobody ever calls me," I apologized to Jason. "I wonder who it could be?"

The contact name said Matthew and I brightened. "Hi, Matthew," I spoke into the phone. "How are you doing?"

His voice was rich with delighted excitement. "I sent you an email, but you didn't answer. The scanning program found the password!" He gave a merry laugh. "It was *My1Love*."

I smiled. "It figures," I answered. "Although if we had tried every combination of love and desire and adore it might have taken us years. It's a good thing we found that program."

"So what did you want to do now?" asked Matthew. "I think you wanted Jeff present when we opened it up?"

"Definitely." I glanced at my watch. It was just about eight. "Is it all right if we come over now?"

"Absolutely," he agreed with heart-felt warmth. "I want to know what's in this file as much as you guys. How about I call Jeff and you two plan to get here at half-past? Does that give you enough time?"

"We're just finishing up dinner now in Auburn," I let him know. "That will be perfect; it gives us time to pay the bill and head over. Probably back roads will be the fastest. You're sort of in the middle of nowhere out there."

"Eight-thirty it is," he confirmed, and then he clicked off.

Jason took my hand from across the table. "I heard most of that. So the password has been revealed?"

I nodded, waving to the waitress. She cleared off the plates and Jason handed her his credit card. She headed off into the back room with the lot.

I leant forward. "He hasn't actually opened the file yet," I explained. "He's going to wait for us to get there with Jeff. That way we can all see it together."

He tilted his head to one side. "You still think there might be a chance it's Jeff?"

"I think it's *not* Jeff but I figure there's no harm in being sure," I stated. "It's hard to think that anybody could have shot an old man simply for writing his memoirs. But then again, I was born in 1969. To me that is long ago and not worth worrying about." I took a sip of my sangria. "But what if it was something out of my high school years, something I was quite ashamed of? For example, what if I had been raped? Even though it was over twenty years ago I might still be quite upset at the idea of it being broadcast to everyone I knew. If I got wound up enough, I might get pushed to my limits."

His eyes were steady on me. "You would never murder someone, though."

I smiled, squeezing his hand. "Certainly, I know that I would not murder anyone. It's not in my nature. But I'm also wise enough to know that we all have different natures, and we all have different triggers. It could very well be that, to another person, life holds less value."

The waitress brought back the receipt to sign, placing it down before Jason with a warm "thank you". Then she was off again.

Jason opened the folder to add the tip and his signature. "Maybe someone who chops the heads off of chickens every day, and who raises young cows in tiny sheds barely large enough for them to turn around, might consider culling an elderly man to be an act of mercy."

"You're thinking of Sam." I took his offered hand and slid out of the bench. "The thought has come to me too."

"Then again, Richard and his lawyer business have undoubtedly destroyed many a man as completely as death could," mused Jason as we walked through the bar area to head out of the restaurant. Sound blared from several TVs tucked over the bar. To the left was a counter which often held free food during sports nights.

"I suppose that's true," I agreed. "Richard has spent his life building a wall between him and his victims. He prizes the victory and probably doesn't worry about the debris he leaves behind."

In a moment we were climbing into the F-150 and turning left onto Route 20. I watched the headlights shine in the dark. "So, out of the two of them, which do you think it would be?"

He pursed his lips. "Maybe I'm a softie, but I just don't think it could be Sam," he admitted at last. "Sure, he has rough edges, but his life hasn't been an easy one. He's been there for his family and made the best he could of it. And yes, they kill animals, but most of us eat meat. Maybe he's the more honest one in that he cares for and raises the meat he then eats. The rest of us only look at it sealed, trimmed, and without any thought as to the life that was taken away."

I smiled at that. "So you think we should all raise our own cows and chickens?"

His eyes twinkled but his mouth remained serious. "It might not be such a bad thing," he murmured. "People would have more thought as to what they were eating and how it was cared for. We probably wouldn't have chicken factories with animals jammed into tiny cages where they can't even move. Each chicken gets barely a foot of space. Their entire existence – from chick to death – is that one metal cage. They go blind from the ammonia levels of the excrement they stand in. The poor animals are even 'de-beaked' so they can't hurt each other out of frustration."

"It is awful," I agreed. "We should all be far more aware of the things we buy. We support industries with our money. We should choose wisely."

A leaf tumbled across the road and I gave a small jump. He smiled at me. "Worried about the leaf's health?"

"I thought it was a frog," I insisted. "It looked like it was leaping with its little legs."

"In late November?" he pointed out. "All the frogs are safely tucked into their mud beds, dreaming their dreamy dreams until spring. I doubt any frogs are out roaming the night."

"I know that logically," I countered. "And yet, when I saw that motion, I was convinced it was a frog."

"Our mind can delude us sometimes, trying to make sense of what it sees. Right now it's a frog and next time –"

A car came racing up behind us, its high beams on, and he sighed. "This time of year comes with its challenges," he muttered. "Everyone seems in such a hurry. They miss the entire concept of the season." He slowed and pulled further right to allow the car to pass.

I glanced off to the right. Ramshorn Pond glittered under the dark sky, soft ripples glistening with the light of the moon. We were on the northern, Millbury side of the pond; Matthew's house would be down on the opposite end. I wondered, if I stared hard enough, if I could make out the distant shape far across the water.

The car pulled to the left, passing us. And then, with a sudden squeal, the car sliced sharply right, its large form cutting hard across our path. Jason spun the wheel hard right, driving his foot on the brakes. Our truck spun, the forequarter slammed into the car in front of us, and we lunged toward the inky blackness of the pond. A blaring squeal of tires pierced my ears. The car vaulted off into the distance while the world spun in dizzying chaos.

To my surprise, there was no splash, no rotating of my world upside-down. We hung at a forty-five degree angle pointing down toward the pond but thankfully the truck had maintained its purchase on solid earth. Still, the water seemed dangerously close and my heart was pounding so loud I could hear nothing else.

"Are you all right?" came Jason's voice in my ear. I realized he must have said it a time or two before it made it through to me. I nodded shakily, unable to draw my eyes from the surface of the water.

"Are we going in?" was all I could think to ask.

He shook his head. "Not if I can help it." He hit the buttons on his arm console and both windows rolled down. "Just in case," he added. "Have your hand on your seatbelt buckle."

I did as he suggested and forced myself to breathe. It seemed as if holding my breath was a natural reaction.

He carefully shifted into reverse, turned the wheel a slight amount, then pressed with light pressure onto the gas. The truck rocked slightly, then the tires began to slip. He released immediately. He took in a breath, then carefully lowered his foot down. There was a soft whir, the tires began to move, the truck gave a shudder ... and the traction held. We inched carefully back up along the rocky bank, regaining our spot on the pavement.

I disconnected my seatbelt and flung myself across his body. His arms came around me immediately, holding me close, soothing me. His voice was a soft murmur in my ear. "It's all right. We're all right," he repeated. "We are fine."

After a few minutes he put on the hazards and got out to walk around the truck. He gazed carefully along the front parts of the chassis, then examined the rest before regaining his seat.

"It's beat up, but it's still drivable," he reported. "Did you want to go home?"

I glanced across the quiet lake; suddenly deep concern hit me. "Get us to Matthew's house," I insisted.

Understanding lit his eyes and in a moment we were racing down the road, taking the remaining curves in quick order. We pulled into Matthew's driveway. Only his car was there – Jeff's was nowhere in sight.

Jason turned to me, his gaze serious. "Stay in the truck. Lock the doors," he ordered. I didn't question it; the moment he got out I hit the lock button. I fumbled for my phone, drawing it into my hands as he moved down the path on the right side of Matthew's house. The lake spread blackly out before him, stretching into the distance.

My phone rang in my hands, startling me. I hit the answer button and brought it to my ear, my eyes steadily on Jason's form as he approached the door. "Yes?"

Jeff's voice echoed in my ear. "There you are! Come on out already. We're here waiting."

I blinked. "What? Wait, who is waiting? Where are you?"

"Matthew and me," he stated, and there was a hint of exasperation in his voice. "You emailed us and said we should get to your house quickly – that you had something to show us before we looked at that file. We're here in your driveway but you're not answering your door."

Jason stepped to the left, through Matthew's doorway, and vanished. My heart pounded in my chest. What was happening?

"Jeff, we're at Matthew's house. Someone tried to run us off the road. Jason's in there and –"

Jeff's voice came sharply. "What? Are you all right?"

Jason came sprinting up the dark path toward the truck and I hit the unlock button. He pulled open the door. "The door was kicked in and the computer's gone. The whole thing."

An oath sounded in my ear; apparently Jeff could hear what Jason had said. "Someone broke into Matthew's house?"

I could hear Matthew's outraged cry from the background.

I called into the phone, "Get back here immediately. We're fine. We'll wait here for you."

"Be there in fifteen," agreed Jeff, and he clicked off.

I looked up at Jason. "Was the house in bad shape?"

He shook his head, looking in at me. "There was no sign of anything else out of place, at least from my cursory glance. The living room, dining area, kitchen – it all looked neat and untouched. Only the computer was missing from the table's center. Even the monitor and keyboard were sitting there, their cables loose."

He settled himself back into the driver's seat; I turned up the heat to fight off the sharp winter's chill.

I looked at him. "The door looked forced?"

He nodded in agreement. "The lock area was shattered. Someone kicked through it. That was the only thing I could see that showed any sign that someone had been there."

It seemed no time at all before Jeff's car pulled in beside ours and all four of us were walking down the narrow path toward Matthew's front door. Matthew paused for a moment by the door, looking at the damage, then we walked inside. He strode around the room, looking at everything, then vanished into the back of the house for a few minutes. At last he returned, relief shining in his gaze.

"Nothing else was touched, thank God," he informed us. "It was just the computer they wanted."

Jeff looked at Matthew. "You didn't look at the file to see what was in it?"

Matthew glanced at me for a moment before shaking his head. "We thought it best that we were all here to see what it said," he stated. "I have no idea what was in there."

I sighed. "Now we may never know."

Jason put an arm around me. "Nobody was hurt," he pointed out, "and now we know that someone cared immensely about us finding out the contents of that file." He looked over at Matthew. "Maybe time to make a call to the police?"

Matthew lifted the phone off its cradle. "Absolutely."

Chapter 23

My tree pose was wobbly. I focused on the burly oak at the far end of the yard, the one with the neatly carved hole which occasionally housed the family of squirrels. I thought of its two up-stretched limbs as my own reaching toward the sky. And yet my center was gone. I swayed, as capricious as a willow in a springtime gust, and finally I had to put my left foot down.

Jason sat at the table, sipping his tea, his eyes on the feeder out the side window and the titmouse who sat there. The soft grey tuft on the bird's head made him seem a wild-eyed teenager, eager to shock his parents. The titmouse snatched at a sunflower seed, settled it in his beak, and then swooped off to an aspen to diligently peck into it.

Jason's voice was soft and reassuring. "Anyone would be shaken up by last night," he murmured.

I stretched my right leg back, angling that foot perpendicular to the mat. My left foot went point-forward in parallel. I stretched out my two arms, one back, one forward, becoming a human starfish. But unlike that noble beast, if one of my limbs had been cut off, it would not regenerate. It would be gone forever, an eternal reminder of how close I had come to that final crossover.

I reined in my mind. *Pose: Warrior II.*

I looked forward, settling my left knee down, stretching my arms out fore and aft as if I was surfing on my yoga mat. I strived for that balance – half the weight on my front foot, half on back. Balance on my back foot's right edge, the furthest point there. Press my forward, left foot firmly into the mat.

Breathe.

My thoughts were floating, drifting clouds. Yes, certainly, they were sometimes storm-clouds, sizzling with an energy that

I could feel through every atom of my body. And yet they were simply thoughts. Simply bursts of electrical energy that, if I released them of attention, would eventually drift away. The more I practiced, the more I could disengage from being controlled by them. Surely I would never be perfect – but that was not the point. Even the most adept monks were still troubled by circling thoughts. The aim was solely to become slightly better at separating oneself from the control of those thoughts. To have the ability to stand apart, to watch them, and to view them objectively.

A smile came to my lips. And when I did that, was it simply another corner of my mind which watched that first set of operations? And if I drew back again, was it a third corner of my mind watching the first two? Just how many vantage points did my mind hold? At what point could I look down at all of the lightning-storm operations of my brain, the reptilian core, the esoteric beauty center, and believe I beheld it all?

I moved through the various stages of my routine, the rolling cat, the bridge pose, the bliss of savasana where I lay flat on my back and simply breathed in the luxury of being alive, of having a roof over my head and food in my pantry. So many on earth dreamt of such luxuries. I would not take them for granted.

At last I sat cross-legged, looking through the slider at the back yard. A downy woodpecker hung on the suet feeder, nibbling contentedly at his morning meal, and I pressed my hands together at my chest.

"Namaste," I offered him and the world.

"Namaste," echoed Jason, smiling down at me.

I stood, and he went to the fridge, filling a glass with ice and adding in my protein shake. He brought it to me as I sat with him at the table.

His eyes held mine as I began drinking my breakfast. "The police seem to be taking our theories more seriously now," he commented.

"Well, we were nearly run off the road, and someone did break into Matthew's house," I agreed. "Whoever it is seems willing to take some drastic action to keep his secret safe."

"I checked in this morning. Neither Sam nor Richard has a good alibi for last night."

I looked down into my shake. "I suppose that doesn't mean much," I mused. "Until recently, if someone had asked me what I'd done on a given night, I would have said I was home alone. There would have been no one to vouch for where I was or what I was doing."

His hand came over mine. "And now there is," he murmured.

A smile came to my lips and I looked up, nodding. "And now there is."

After a moment I took another sip. "I wish they had been able to trace that email message Jeff got down to something more specific, though."

Jason's eyes twinkled. "Our modern technology may be good, but it's not *that* good," he pointed out. "They know it came from somewhere in Sutton. Did you want a street address?"

"That would be nice," I agreed, a grin growing despite my discouraged mood. "And then we could look it up in Google Maps, and there'd be a big arrow pointing at someone's house. With a note on the side saying *solution right here*."

His smile widened. "I suppose you were looking forward to a Hercule Poirot style gathering, then."

I laughed out loud at that. "Oh, could you imagine?" I asked. "Me, the shy one, gathering every single suspect into one room? Questioning and grilling and challenging them, and then spinning to stare the guilty man straight in the eye?"

"But we don't have a butler," pointed out Jason with a chuckle. "Isn't it always the butler?"

"It always seems to be the person least suspected," I countered. "Maybe that means that somehow Charles is the guilty guy. Maybe all of his doddering and avoidance is some sort of an elaborate act that he's kept up for decades."

Jason shook his head, doubt creasing his brow. "I always preferred the tenets of Occam's razor," he countered. "Those convoluted, twisted plots that movies adore rarely make sense in the real world. In that 1935 Singletary Lake drowning it was straightforward. Man has wife. Man falls for seventeen-year-old girl. Man decides he'd rather have the fun than the duties of a wife-plus-two-kids, so man drowns wife. Man is shocked when his brilliant plan doesn't work."

I took another sip of my shake, looking out at the feeder. A pair of chickadees attempted to land on the same perch simultaneously then erupted in a flurry of feathers and squawks. As they flew off, a dove whirred in and complacently took the spot.

"OK, then, what is the simplest solution here?"

He thought about that for a while, sipping his tea. The circular clock gently ticked away the seconds, its face offering an herbal marker at each hour. I thought, as each tick sounded, how that was one less moment of my life. Each breath was gone forever into the past, never to be retrieved. That was my life passing and I needed to be attentive to each precious drop.

"I think John's death might have been an accident," he said at last. "I cannot think of anyone we've met who would slay another person either for the joy of it or as a deliberate desire to end their life."

I ran a hand through my hair, drawing out the pony-tail holder I'd worn during my yoga session. "So why would the assailant have had a gun?"

"Maybe to scare him into complying with something? There had to be a conflict of some sort."

"The book," I posited. "Whatever was going to come up in the book?"

"That sounds reasonable," he agreed. "So this book was being worked on. Something was going to be made public that the assailant didn't want to be known. It was a fairly serious topic for him."

"Something that he felt would destroy his life."

Jason nodded. "So he wanted the book to stop. That's all. He didn't want to hurt anybody or do anything rash. He simply wanted this book, which after all didn't even exist yet, to go away. If the book went away then everything would stay the way it was. They wanted to keep the status quo."

I leant forward. "So this person, nervous about the potential book's contents, went to talk with the author."

Jason held my gaze. "Just to talk. But maybe he worried that John would be too wrapped up in his author's pride to listen clearly. Perhaps he was concerned that John had already been talking up the book to his friends and wouldn't want to just put aside such an attention-gathering project."

"Right," I agreed. "So the person brought along a bit of insurance. Something to help guarantee that John took this request as seriously as it warranted."

"John could be too focused at times after all. He might not see how critically important this was to the other party. He might need a bit of jarring to understand another's viewpoint on the issue."

It was starting to seem plausible. "During their talk, John scoffs. He says that he already has loyal fans encouraging him. He has a publisher friend designing covers. How could he let them down? How could he explain just abandoning his project?"

"And then the assailant brings out his gun to make his point. But maybe he doesn't quite know how to hold it properly."

"Maybe John gets panicked and lunges for it to knock it away. Or maybe John becomes furious and dives to grab it himself."

"Heck, maybe the guy with the gun trips over something."

I nodded. "Then there is John lying on the ground, a bullet hole blasted through his chest, and there's no turning back now. There's only the specter of years of legal battle ahead. So he runs."

Jason sat forward. "Once the lies begin, it's that much harder to turn around and tell the truth. It's so much easier to just keep marching forward and hope it all dies away after a time."

I took a sip of my shake. "Just like Eileen's death," I mused. "It was a flurry of excitement for a while. Then they ruled it an accident and it faded into the background. Life went on."

I looked at Jason. "So who is it then?"

He thought for a long moment, then shook his head. "It could be any of them," he sighed. "Once that hard drive vanished we lost our ability to trace it from that end. Whoever hacked into your account, to know when we found the password, simply used it to lure Matthew and Jeff away from the vicinity. Really, the only dangerous part of it all was side-swiping us. But all we saw was a dark SUV. There are probably thousands of those in this vicinity."

"All three of them have access to one, apparently," I sighed morosely.

"As does half of the town," he pointed out. "It seems to be the vehicle of choice in these parts."

"You remember that snowstorm of 2011? We had snow piles literally taller than cars! I'm thankful I sold that Mustang of mine years ago. It was little more than a sled when the white stuff came down."

He chuckled. "I'm sure it was fun in the summertime, though."

I grinned at the memories. "Yes, it was."

I tilted up my glass, finishing off my shake. "Well, where does that leave us?"

"We know the hard drive had something meaningful on it. So it does seem related to John's story he was writing. I think we can safely say Jeff isn't involved."

"Unless he hired someone," I commented morosely. "It could still be pretty much anybody."

"I think I'm leaning toward his innocence," he stated. "Occam again. The idea of him overseeing a complex conspiracy just doesn't make much sense. If he wanted to stop his father, he could just have sabotaged his father's computer. He was the one who gave his father the system in the first place. A few computer issues, a few other distractions, and he could have dragged the process out until his father finally succumbed to his illnesses." He shook his head. "No, I get the sense that Jeff honestly was trying to help his father finish those memoirs as best he could. He knew it might bring up childhood dreams and loves, and Jeff seemed all right with that."

I smiled. "I am glad to hear that you feel that way too," I commented. "I like Jeff. He seems a good soul."

He raised an eyebrow. "So what do we do, then? Gather up the three boys down at Lake Singletary, put them into canoes, and see who flinches first? In traditional Agatha Christie fashion?"

Mirth bubbled up in me at that scenario but I shook my head. "We had enough trouble wrangling interviews with them separately," I pointed out. "The chance of getting all three of them to agree to meet us, and then to head out onto the frigid surface of Lake Singletary when the air temperature is barely over freezing, is slim to none. No, we have to think of something else."

"And what might that be?"

I shook my head. "I'm not sure." I brightened in a smile. "But I do have a stack of three Midsomers Murders DVDs waiting in the living room. We could have a marathon and see if inspiration hits us."

He made a sweeping motion with his arm. "A perfect way to spend a wintry Sunday afternoon," he agreed. "Settle yourself in and I'll make the popcorn."

"A perfect gentleman," I sighed, and he drew me in against him, his warmth enveloping me.

Chapter 24

Matthew spotted me the moment I stepped through the doorway of the Sutton Senior Center; he came over to draw me into a warm hug. "How are you doing?"

I was comforted by his embrace and looked into his blue eyes when I stepped back. "I am fine, but how about you? It was your home that was broken into."

He shrugged, guiding me back toward the main room. "Nothing was taken, besides the computer of course. The door has already been replaced, we are as good as new."

Jeff and Adam were waiting for us at a table. Jeff's eyes held concern. "Thank goodness there was nobody home at the time," he mused as we sat. "If that man has already killed once, who knows what lengths he might go to in order to further protect his secrets."

Adam nodded. "That's true," he agreed. "We can only hope that the danger for y'all is past now. After all, the computer is gone. Whatever data was on it has presumably already been destroyed. There shouldn't be any reason at all for this person to come back and harass you any further."

Jeff nodded. "I adored my father," he stated. "He meant the world to me. But I know he would not want other innocent people slain because of whatever is going on here."

Matthew looked to him. "What have the police said?"

Jeff shrugged, his oval face becoming shadowed. "Certainly they see that this is all related somehow. However, as you know, they found too many fingerprints. The computer itself is gone. As Adam says, the thief has probably destroyed it beyond repair. Really, that is all we had to go on, in terms of figuring out what this was all about." He looked to me with only faint hope in his eyes.

I nodded in resignation. "We have vague feelings, of course, about one of the three men being involved. But we don't even have a guess as to what it might have been about. Eileen's sister had no idea. Even a motive we thought we had – the missing money – ended up being a dead end."

I laced my fingers into each other. "Sure, we could make guesses until the cows came home about what Sam might have felt or what Richard might have dreamt about and so on. But it was over forty years ago. The men won't say. Nobody else knows what was in their hearts. Nobody even watched the whole situation unfold, besides the four men who were there."

Adam nodded his head. "Well, and that decrepit woman out at Marion's Camp," he pointed out.

I glanced up at that. "There was a witness?"

He spread his hands before him. "I'm not sure she could be called a witness, exactly," he cautioned. "She heard a scream and a yelp. The night was layered in mists and she had no idea what was going on. She figured it was just some teenagers at horseplay on the lake. It was only the next day, when the police began interrogating everyone on shore, that she realized just what she had heard."

My pulse quickened. "Is she still around town?"

He laughed out loud at that, his eyes brightening. "Dodgy Mrs. Moggle?" he asked in delight. "Heck, she was older than Methuselah even when I was young. Always waddling along the shore in the bruise-purple dress of hers, with the grimiest hiking boots you could hope to see. Looking for reeds or pond scum or something." He shook his head. "Nah, she probably died back in the seventies."

My shoulders slumped again. Another dead end. I looked between the men. "Maybe there is something we missed here? Some tiny detail that seemed unimportant?"

Matthew shrugged. "Maybe the reports of the time would have more details. Did you try looking them up?"

"I did some Google searches," I began hesitantly.

He laughed out loud. "You know, we do in fact have a library in town," he pointed out. "Maybe you should take a visit down there."

"All right," I agreed with a smile. "I'll swing by there tomorrow and see what I can find."

Chapter 25

I pulled into the small parking lot at the back side of the Sutton town hall, my tires making gentle creases in the light layer of newly fallen snow. Winter was finally starting to arrive. Soon there would be a semi-permanent layer of white on the ground through February. Sometimes the snow would reach two feet deep or more and at other times there might be patches of grass showing through. But if we had a traditional winter there would always be some white around to add a glistening sparkle to the day.

The town hall's rear was on the lower end of a slope, so while the front of the building, on the opposite side, featured an elegant series of marble steps, I was down on the basement level. To the right were some garages for town trucks, and the General Rufus Putnam Hall, a.k.a. Sutton historical museum, was also alongside the parking area. It was closed up tight now, only open on certain days, but I knew well what was within that 1800s two-story building. It held a wealth of civil war items, historic farm tools, apple presses, and much more.

I moved forward toward the small door of the library. Glass panes on either side let me see into the narrow lobby which opened up into a small room. To the left were four shelves of children's books, while the right held perhaps six of adult material. The traditional check-out counter was straight ahead.

There was not a customer in sight.

I held a special, fond place in my heart for libraries. My father had worked in a library. My stepmother and one of my best friends had been librarians. Perhaps it was telling that they had all retired. It seemed that news stories kept talking about how libraries were shutting down, how web research was taking over library visits, and how people were turning to ebooks instead of physical books. It was over a year ago, in May 2011, when Amazon announced that their ebook sales had surpassed their physical book sales. And that trend seemed to only be continuing.

I myself was a part of the change. Certainly I had an appreciation for physical books. I had eight full bookcases of books in my home, everything from classic literature to science fiction to modern novels. But in terms of buying new material, I had reached my physical limit. I was buying on my Kindle. Not only was it instant, it wasn't adding to the clutter.

The elderly woman behind the counter had tight, mist-grey curls and wore a fawn-brown dress over her slim figure. Her eyes brightened with delight as I approached her. Her voice creaked with age, but held genuine warmth.

"Welcome, how can I help you?"

I snugged my notepad against my side. "I am looking into a drowning that happened back in 1968 at Lake Singletary," I explained. "Do you have the old newspapers on microfiche?"

She put a slim hand in front of her mouth to hide the laugh that began to erupt. "I'm afraid that machine was hauled away years ago," she explained. "We used to maintain a database subscription with the Worcester Telegram & Gazette, to look through their archives but then they began to price that far out of our range. I suppose they had to find some way to stay afloat."

Discouragement settled over me. "Do you have any sort of archives then?"

She waved a hand. "Over there ..."

I turned and saw the section. "Thank you very much," I said. "I can figure it out, I'm sure."

I moved to the shelf, took down a pile of likely material, and brought it over to the low table. It certainly was a different experience than Googling material and having it flash by in neat order. I read through a wealth of unrelated items, flipping through page after page to look for a glimpse of what I sought.

Finally, I came across something that caught my eye. It was a special interest piece on the history of Marion's Camp. The land was first purchased by Mrs. Harry Goddard in 1928, just ten years before the 1938 drowning. Mrs. Goddard had set up the area as a camp for the Camp Fire Council, naming her project after her daughter, Marion.

The camp was enjoyed by thousands of children over the years, but at last the Goddard family decided to sell it. The Town of Sutton stepped forward in 1989, buying it for public use and turning the camp into the town beach.

I thought about the people living and working at the camp, knowing that the lake they treated as a playground had also hosted a number of tragic events.

There – a mention of the name Adam had brought up. Mrs. Beatrice Moggle. Apparently her mother had worked at the camp when it first opened, and Beatrice had grown up there, taking over from her mother in turn. She had been a fixture at the camp, handling cleaning and light maintenance tasks. Several of the articles on the camp seemed to use her for filler quotes about the camp's history and traditions.

I flipped through some more pages. Yes, there was a note of her passing, in the early seventies, and how many locals had fond memories of her quirky behavior. I sighed. It hadn't been much of a lead, in any case. The newspaper reporters hadn't even thought to mention her vague thoughts in the write-ups they had made of the drowning.

I replaced the material on the shelves, gave a wave to the librarian, then headed back out into the snowy day. It seemed I was drifting further from a solution with every step I took.

Chapter 26

A metal bar stretched across the driveway to the Sutton Town Beach, blocking the entrance. The parking lot beyond had been turned into a field of white by the snow. I pulled the Forester along the right hand side of the road, then walked around the edge of the gate. My footsteps made a soft crunching noise in the snow as I crossed the parking lot and walked down the long, sloping, curved pathway toward the edge of Lake Singletary.

One of the original buildings from Marion's Camp still remained to the left, a sagging wooden building with boarded up windows. In the summertime it had a decrepit air, but now beneath its layer of snow, it looked almost romantic.

The lake glistened in the afternoon light, gentle ripples moving toward me with the wind. There was nobody here, of course - just me, the crunch of the sand, and the crisp wind stinging my cheeks.

I stood for a long while gazing out at the lake. Forty years ago an elderly woman had walked these shores, had heard a cry or noise out in the water, and perhaps had peered uncertainly into the fog, wondering what had caused it.

My cell phone rang, shaking me out of my distant musings. I picked it up absently. "Yes?"

Sam's gruff voice sounded from the other end. "It's me, Sam," he stated. "We were wondering …" His voice trailed off uncertainly.

"Were wondering?" I gently encouraged.

"Well, with your talking and such, it made me think. It's the holidays and all; a time for forgiveness. So I called Charles and Richard. Tomorrow was her birthday, you know. So we were going to go down to Marion's Camp. You know, the Sutton Town Beach. And ... maybe say a few words for her."

I glanced around me. "That sounds lovely," I offered.

"We would like you to be there," he added. "You were the one who brought us back together, after all."

A chill wind whistled against me and I held in a shiver. "Would it be all right if Jason came too?" The thought of being alone on this desolate beach with the three men had sent a shaft of unease through me.

"Yes, of course," he agreed promptly. "Jason has been just as much a part of this as you have."

I wasn't sure that gave me a sense of ease, but knowing that Jason would be by my side did. "What time would you like to meet?" I asked.

"How does four sound? That should be right around sunset."

"We'll be here," I agreed.

Sam had barely clicked off before I was pressing the button to call Jason.

"Tell me you're not busy tomorrow at four," I began without preamble.

"What's up?"

"The trio is planning some sort of ceremony here at Marion's Camp and they want me to join them."

"In that case, absolutely I will be there with you," he agreed. "I'll make sure some friends know where we are, too, just in case."

"You're having those thoughts too?" I asked, relieved.

"I was a lifeguard for my teen years, out on the Cape, as well as an Eagle Scout," he pointed out. "Be prepared."

I glanced up at the camp building. "Well, this was a Camp Fire campground before it became the town beach," I mused. "They were for girls only until 1975, but they had the same type of self-reliant mottos. I guess back when they were getting started in 1910 that there were only scouting organizations for boys, and not one which would accept girls."

"It's good to train all children – male and female – to be able to look out for themselves," he agreed. "It sounds like a good thing that the Camp Fire Girls were founded."

I pulled my scarf closer around my neck, then turned and headed back up the long slope. "Well, you and I will be prepared for tomorrow's meeting, that's for sure," I said. "See you soon?"

"Absolutely," he murmured, and warmth spread through me like spring sunshine.

Chapter 27

I leant against the metal bar by the entrance of Marion's Camp, my arms hugging my chest, watching anxiously for Jason's truck. It was still only quarter-to-four, but I had wanted to get there early and Jason was coming from his job. At last I saw the approach of his white vehicle down the long, straight road toward me and I sighed in relief.

The snow from yesterday's light flurry had nearly all melted away. Scattered patches of white speckled the edges of the road. Jason pulled in behind my car and parked, coming over to offer me a warm embrace.

"We're the first?"

I nodded, taking his hand in mine. "Let's go and wait by the water," I suggested. We covered the same ground I had yesterday, across the parking lot, down the serpentine path which ended at the small beach area.

He wrapped his arm around my waist as we stared out to the lake. The wind was gentler today, only the slightest ruffling added texture to the smooth surface.

There were footsteps behind us and Sam came down to join us, a heavy red-checked flannel jacket holding off the cold. He nodded to us without speaking, then stared out at the lake, a shadowed look on his face. His hands dug deep into his pockets.

In another few minutes Charles joined us. His jacket was blue and red with an embroidered Patriots logo on its back. Like Sam he didn't speak a word, just moved to a spot on the beach slightly apart from us and hunched his shoulders.

Richard was the last to arrive, elegant in a dark blue wool jacket. He walked up to each of us in turn, offering a hand to shake, muttering a greeting in a low, somber voice.

At last Sam turned from his musings and looked between us. He reached into his jacket and drew out a screw-cap bottle of blush wine.

"It was her favorite kind," he muttered, then twisted off the top and tucked it into his pocket. He stared at the bottle for a long moment, then turned and held it up toward the silent lake.

"To Eileen and all her dreams," he toasted. "She had a heart of pure sweetness." He took a long swallow, then brushed at his eyes with his free hand. He offered the bottle to Charles.

Charles took the bottle, his brow creasing for a long moment. Then at last he sighed; it was as if all the air eased out of him. He held up the bottle. "To Eileen. A woman who knew her path in life and who could have achieved anything she'd set her mind to." He took a long swallow.

Richard was next. He gave a wry smile, raising the rosé. "To Eileen, an amazing individual. She could have changed the world. She could have advanced our culture. She never got her chance." He took a long drink, his cheeks burnishing in the wind.

He then turned to me with the bottle. I hesitated. I wasn't sure I felt right sharing in their personal sorrow. Richard offered it again and I could see the support in the other men's eyes. So as not to hurt their feelings, I took the bottle, staring at it for a moment.

"To Eileen," I offered, holding it aloft. "A woman of many facets. She was kind and gentle. She was intelligent and driven. She had great hopes for changing the world. Most of all, she treasured the friendship of those closest to her, those who supported her in her dreams." I met each man's eyes with my own, then took a long drink. I could see the appreciation in each pair of eyes as we turned to look out over the dark waters.

I leant against Jason, and moved the bottle toward him, but he gave the slightest shake of his head. I could feel the controlled tension along his arm where he had wrapped it around my waist.

Several long minutes passed in silence. At last Sam took the bottle back from me, re-sealing the cap. He looked as if he wanted to say something, but after a long minute he stared back out to the lake.

Richard rubbed his hands together, and spoke to the group. "My family is having a small get-together at my house on the eighth, for the holidays," he stated in a low voice. "Nothing special, just some drinks and appetizers. Seven p.m. I would love to have you all come."

Sam and Charles looked up to meet his eyes, and then both nodded, cautious smiles warming their faces. Sam spoke up first. "I should be free."

"As will I," agreed Charles. "Should we bring anything?"

Richard shook his head; there was an easing to his shoulders. "Just yourselves," he offered. "It has been too long."

As one, the three men turned and headed back up the path. Jason took my hand in his and we followed them back up the slope. Something had changed in the way the men walked. They were no longer held aloof from one another; there was a familiarity in the way they moved together.

We reached the cars as the sky glimmered into sunset. Each man came forward to give me a gentle hug before returning to his vehicle and driving off. At last it was just me and Jason standing at the quiet entrance.

His eyes stared down the long road, considering. "I suppose I honestly believe it was an accidental drowning. They seem to be, at long last, healing and moving on," he murmured.

"I would have to agree." I sighed. "But where does that leave us with John's murder?"

He gave his head a shake. "Maybe it's really not related. Maybe this has been a wild goose chase the entire time. Maybe it has to do with his current investments, or a love triangle at the senior center, and whoever was involved only deleted the story to throw suspicion in another direction."

I gave a wry smile. "It certainly worked."

His cell chirruped, and he looked down at it. "It's work, they need some final details sorted out for that event we're hosting tomorrow at the Asa Waters Mansion in Millbury," he explained. "See you at home later?"

"Of course," I agreed. "I just want a few more minutes here alone."

His eyes shadowed, but he nodded. "Keep your phone on you, and call me when you head out," he murmured. He drew me into a warm hug before climbing into his truck. It rolled down the path toward Boston Road. A turn to the right, and then it was gone.

I walked back down the path toward the lake. Something had been tickling at the back of my mind; it had been hard to get a handle on with the others present. I hoped with just me and the wind that I could draw it into focus.

As I came down toward the beach I stopped in surprise. A man was standing there, his tan coat held tightly against the wind, his lean face staring out toward the slate-blue depths.

"Adam?" I asked in surprise.

He started, turning, then relaxed when he saw who it was. "Howdy, Morgan."

"Why didn't you join us?"

He gave a soft shrug. "It looked like Sam and the others wanted a private ceremony," he explained. "I had come out of duty to John. I knew this day was special to him. But I am only a stand-in for him, of course. I wanted to allow those three men their own private time, to spend as they wished. They were, after all, the ones who were there with her."

"They were indeed," I agreed, my voice low.

I stared out at the waves for a few minutes. At last I broke the silence again. "It seems so peaceful," I stated. "As if nothing could have happened on its surface. It just doesn't seem real."

His voice was hesitant. "I was going to ... no, never mind."

I glanced over in curiosity. "Going to what?"

He looked down. "Tomorrow is supposed to be warm and gentle. I was fixin' to take my rowboat out and lay flowers out on the water, at the center of the pond. To commemorate her passing." He glanced back up toward the parking lot. "I was going to do it today, but Jeff told me that the other three were planning on coming out for their own ceremony. I thought it might disturb them to see a rowboat in the water while they were reliving their memories."

"That was very thoughtful of you," I murmured.

"Maybe you would get a sense of closure if you could see the actual spot?"

I nodded. "I think I would like that a lot," I agreed. "Something is nagging at me about this. Maybe it's because I keep seeing everything from the shore. Maybe seeing it from the water is exactly what I need."

"All right, then – how about four? Just like today?"

"That sounds great."

We walked up the path together, skirting the edge of the gate. I looked around. "Where is your car?"

"I parked it around the corner," he explained. "That way it wouldn't upset the others. I didn't want them to think I was intruding." He offered a thin hand. "So, tomorrow at four? Over at the boat ramp on the Millbury side?"

"I will see you then."

Chapter 28

The Millbury boat ramp parking lot was deserted. I wasn't surprised - in less than twelve hours December would arrive with its frosty gales and nose-biting chill. The water stretched sullenly in flat, dull grey. I walked over to the asphalt boat ramp, looking down into the shallows. In the summer there would be a school of tiny, silvery minnows gathered here, eager for bits of bread or crackers to nibble on. Now only gravel and silt lay there, motionless, still.

I squatted down by the water's edge to stir a small whirlpool with my finger. The water was chill, maybe 40°F. I stood and pulled my parka close around my neck. At least there was no wind, but the air was crisp. My breath had a delicate tracery of white puff lining its edges.

At last Adam pulled into the lot in his marlin blue Santa Fe, trailering a small wooden rowboat behind. The boat was clean and looked well cared for, with a white body and natural wood trim on the edges. Adam deftly backed his vehicle up to the ramp and eased the rowboat into the water. When he was in position he jumped out to hand me the tow line before finishing the release. In a moment he had parked the car and was holding the boat so I could climb in.

Once I had settled myself onto the back seat he joined me, one arm cradling a large bouquet of wildflowers. He placed them reverentially in the center of the small wooden craft. The aroma drifted up around me, of daisy and goldenrod and something crisp.

He gave a push with his oar and we were gliding through the water, moving through the narrow inlet and toward the lake proper.

I slid my hand into my pocket, feeling the reassuring presence of my cell phone there. Jason had been less than thrilled with my plans and had made me promise to keep my cell on me at all times. He was deep in the middle of his training event and would not be free for another hour. By then an ebony darkness would have immersed us.

Adam smiled at me as he worked the oars, turning us right to head out into the main lake. As they said in Ireland, the day was soft. A gentle mist added an ethereal glow to the water's surface. The setting sun was drifting toward the horizon, its shimmering golden wash reflecting off the tiny water droplets in the air.

Adam's voice creaked out of the mists. "I only know what John told me, of course," he murmured. "Still, I think I have a sense of where to go. In any case I am sure Eileen will appreciate our efforts, as clumsy as they might be."

"I'm sure she will," I assured him.

He rowed in silence, drawing us out toward the center of the lake. It was immensely serene. A small flock of mallards flew across our heads toward the south, but otherwise nothing stirred on the lake. There was no sign of life from the shore. I was beginning to understand how Eileen had slipped from life all those years ago. It was like being in another world.

Adam pulled in the oars, settling them into their metal rests. We were about centered now equidistant from the various shores. The mist ebbed and swirled around us, sometimes hiding the twinkling lights of docks, at other times washing them into a muted glow. Marion's Camp, to the far south, was a distant blur on the shore.

Adam leant forward carefully, his thin frame balanced in the boat. He took up the flowers and looked at them for a long moment.

"For Eileen, a precious jewel amongst women. With hair of spun sunshine, with a laugh of a thousand dancing butterflies. A soul which warmed the world and a heart which knew no boundaries. We will always love her and miss her."

He made a gentle sweeping motion with his hand, strewing the flowers in a shimmering cascade across the waters. They floated, delicately, speckling the surface, turning the area near the boat into a radiant meadow.

I nodded to him in appreciation. "That was lovely."

"Thank you," he murmured hoarsely, staring down at the flowers.

I looked out toward Marion's Camp again. The fog had swirled and I could make out one of the buildings now. "Oh, you can actually see it," I commented absently.

"What?" he asked distractedly, his gaze still elsewhere.

"The camp," I clarified. "You can see it even from here."

"Oh, yes, of course," he agreed. "When I was a kid you could see the girls' campfires long after dark if you took a rowboat out here. They were like fireflies in the mist."

Thoughts swirled and ebbed in my mind as I stared at the distant structure. "You grew up in Texas."

He gave a soft shrug. "My grandparents had their house here. I would visit."

I nodded, breathing in deeply. The wildflowers were all around us now, filling the dense air with their delicate fragrances. Goldenrod, daisy, and ...

I slid a hand into my pocket, pressing the call button for Jason. I knew it was the featured icon on my screen, knew that he would pick it up no matter what else was going on at his event. I tilted the phone so the microphone pointed toward the opening of my pocket and hit the volume-down button a few times to mute his voice.

"Is that juniper I smell?" I asked Adam in a quiet tone.

He glanced over sharply. His gaze slowly evolved from surprise to resistance to acceptance in the way a sand dune shifts under a steady wind.

At long last he nodded, a look of almost relief coming to his features.

"It is juniper," he stated calmly. "A widow donated a case of the after-shave to the senior center. Few others seemed to like the scent so I took it home with me."

"I never smelled it on you before," I mused, keeping my voice even. I drew in long, slow, steady breaths, imagining myself balanced in a safe place. I was the willow in the wind.

He gave a wry smile. "Some of the women at the senior center are quite sensitive to fragrances," he pointed out. "Now that John is gone, I might have a chance with a few of them. I wanted to make sure I gave it my best shot."

"John was your rival," I murmured softly.

Adam's face turned hard. "John was an idiot," he snapped, his eyes going cold. "He held the most precious jewel in his hand and he tossed her away as if she were a worthless piece of coal. He let Eileen slip through his fingers!"

The pieces were shimmering into alignment, each one connecting with the other in logical succession. "Your grandparents had a cottage here," I echoed, his previous statement finally coming into focus. "You moved into it when you retired."

He nodded, leaning forward. "As a child I used to come up every summer. Texas would get as hot as the hinges of Hell; I was thrilled to escape. My parents would bring me to Sutton and leave me here in my vacation paradise." His voice caught for a moment. "When I was seven I met Eileen."

His face gentled and his focus became hazy. "I still remember it as if it were yesterday. She was wearin' a pale blue dress with white daisies embroidered around the neckline. She looked like a flower fairy come to life. Her voice was a love song in three part harmony. When I said 'howdy' with my Texas accent, she burst into a delighted laugh." His breath held. "It was the most beautiful sound I had ever heard."

He looked down to the white petals floating alongside the boat. "Every year I counted the days until I would come up and be with her again."

I pursed my lips. "Why didn't the other men know you, then?"

He gave a quick shake of his head. "What, them, associate with mere help? My grandmother was the cook for the camp, while my grandfather handled maintenance and heavier tasks.

Even the local farmers felt they were above such meager connections." His eyes shadowed. "Also, my grandparents had only recently arrived from Hungary. I spent much of my time translating for them or helping them with chores. It didn't leave me time to socialize."

I leant forward, drawn in despite myself. "So what *did* happen that night on the lake?"

He looked at the grey water, his brows heavy with sorrow. "She was an impetuous fool, as always," he sighed. "She loved wrapping them around her little finger to show them just how much power she had over them. I have no doubt she drank too much and flirted too much." He gave a short laugh. "For all I know she half wanted to fall overboard to see which one of her brave suitors would rescue her." His hand shook as it ran through his hair. "She should have stayed on shore. She should have stayed with me."

My voice was soft. "You loved her."

His eyes glittered with tears when he looked up at me. "I adored her. I worshipped the air she breathed. She was more than an angel to me. She was life itself."

I held his gaze. "And you blamed John for her death?"

He gave his head a quick shake, snorting in disbelief. "John? That buffoon. He wouldn't have hurt a fly." He swept his gaze across the flowers drifting in a spreading collage around us. "No, I blame all of them – and I blame none of them. They were caught in her silvery web as much as everyone else was. They were foolish kids. They thought they were immortal."

I knit my brows together in thought. "But if there wasn't anything incriminating about Eileen's drowning in the book John was writing, why did it have to be stopped?"

He stared at me in shock. "Because it was about *her*!" he cried out in abject misery. His voice echoed with a staggering amount of pain, more than I would have thought his thin frame could bear.

My face must have reflected the utter bewilderment I felt. "Of course the book mentioned her," I finally responded.

"Wasn't that the point, for John to write about his life and the people in it?"

Adam gave a quick shake to his head, his face darkening. "John said he was writing a *memoir*," he clarified, as if to a young toddler. "I thought the content would be focused on his explorations in Asia, the romantic way he met his wife, his grand adventures around the world. I even encouraged him in the project. It would have been a meaningful legacy to leave to his son. Jeff has never been to his mother's homelands."

Adam's lips pursed into a tight line. "But then, the more John worked on the early years, the more he began to babble about his relationship with Eileen." A growl came to his voice. "*My Eileen.*"

A kernel of understanding began to coalesce in my thoughts. "He was going to write about how much he loved her."

Adam's voice was tight. "That I could have taken. Heck, every man in Sutton loved her, as well they should have. She was a beautiful angel who graced our world. Every person she came into contact with was stunned by her. To have yet another man praise her would only have added to her legend."

I shook my head in confusion. "But then what was it?"

He leant forward, his eyes flaring with heat. "He said that she loved *him*!" he cried in outrage, his body shaking with fury. "That he had an engagement ring in his pocket and that she was going to accept his proposal that night! That is why he took her out in the rowboat. He was trying to get away from the other boys. He wanted her all to himself!"

I shook my head in confusion. "But Charles said that she was going to leave shortly for Hollywood," I pointed out.

He scoffed. "As if Charles knew anything," he countered. "That incompetent dullard could barely get two sentences out together." His shoulders firmed. "She was going to wait for me to save up that nest egg she knew I was working on. We would live in Sutton for a year or two and get married at the camp, with daffodils and daisies. When we were ready we would buy a beat-up Ford and drive across the United States."

His eyes looked toward Marion's Camp, and past it. "I had the whole route mapped out for us. We would stop by St. Louis and listen to music at the blues clubs in Soulard. We would visit Mesa Verde and the cliff dwellings in Colorado. Every day would be a marvelous adventure."

I kept my voice gentle. "But she didn't need to wait for a nest egg," I pointed out. "Her sister said –"

"That sister of hers was a joke!" he scoffed. "Always teasing me, telling me I wasn't good enough for their family. She would say anything to cause trouble. I'm surprised she's sober long enough to say anything at all these days."

I took in a deep breath. Clearly logic was not going to work here. Perhaps the safest route would be to humor him. "So you felt she was going to end up with you?"

His eyes shone with fervor, reflecting the rich glow of the setting sun. "I *knew* it with absolute truth," he corrected. "Just that afternoon she had told me to meet her on the shore the next morning. She said she had something to tell me, something wonderful. She knew I would be thrilled." A child-like smile spread on his face. "I know with crystal-clear certainty what it would be. She would tell me that she would be mine and that once she graduated we would be married."

I leant forward. "So you adored her and she adored you. Why would you be concerned about what John might write as his mistaken version? You said yourself that every man in Sutton adored Eileen. This memoir would just be one more part of her myth."

He shook his head fiercely. "John had political connections, he had access to loans, and he had a network of friends which staggers the mind. He was fixin' to have the memoir turned into a screenplay. He was even discussing casting ideas! The whole world would come to believe Eileen was *his*." His face twisted in a grimace. "My Eileen, my precious, beautiful, personal treasure, would be known all around the world as *John's girl*." His eyes became blazing coals. "There was no way in Hell I was going to let that happen."

I nodded. "So you went to talk with him."

His arms crossed defensively in front of his chest. "I just wanted to make my point clear," he insisted. "I didn't want to hurt the man. He didn't have long to live, in any case. I told him he had to change the project. Write about Vietnam. Write about Asia. Write about anything else he wanted."

I could see the scene as clearly as if I had been there. "But John didn't want to change it."

His brows furrowed in anger. "The bastard claimed she was clearly the focus of his story. When I tried to explain that she loved *me* and not him, he laughed in my face! He laughed! He laughed about Eileen's love for me." His brows became rigid lines in the mist. "I had to defend her honor."

"Of course you did," I agreed soothingly.

Relief eased his tightness. "I'm so glad you understand," he murmured, reaching under his jacket. His hand came out with a black matte pistol with an oddly long barrel. It took me a moment to realize he had a suppressor attached to it.

Adam's voice was calm and reasonable. "You'll see why you need to get into the water now."

My world coalesced into the end of the barrel, its nonjudgmental length pointed straight at the center of my chest. A long moment passed before I remembered to breathe again. "In the water?" I echoed, my mind not quite connecting thoughts properly.

"It seems a fitting tribute to Eileen," he commented, his eyes not leaving mine. "It's a shame, of course, but it has to be done. John has inspired me, after all. I will tell my story. It will be *my* name linked with Eileen's for the world to appreciate." His lips eased into a smile. "Her eternal summer shall never fade." He made a small motion with the gun. "But first you have to go."

I strove to keep my voice steady. "You can't shoot me – I might cry out. Every homeowner around the lake would hear my scream."

He gave a dismissive glance at the thick fog which swirled around the boat in the last fingers of sunset. "Half of the homes are now empty for the winter season. For the other half?" he shrugged. "Your body will be found in a few days with a hole through it," he agreed. "By then I'll have crafted a story that explains exactly what happened, involving a mysterious assailant."

His eyes grew steely. "So, your choice. Quick death or slow. Either is fine with me. Which would you prefer?"

I could almost see the muscles in his finger tightening on the trigger; I made my choice. There was no way I could spring at him quickly enough to disarm him before he shot me. Even if I tried to tip the boat, I would undoubtedly end up both with a hole in me and in the near-freezing water. At least if I went in uninjured I had a chance.

I moved toward the side of the boat, easing myself over its edge. The barrel of the gun stayed squarely on me every second. My body slipped into the water and I gasped as the cold hit me. It was like an iron vice squeezing at my chest. My lungs began to spasm with hyperventilation, and it took all my years of yoga training to rein them in, to hold myself to shaky, long draws.

The water soaked into my clothes almost instantly; the leaden weight of them pulled down with an insistent drag.

I kicked off my shoes and yanked my arms free of the heavy jacket, letting both fall into the murky depths. The weight gone, my struggle to stay afloat became less frantic, but the cold pierced me with a pain that nearly overwhelmed all other thought.

My voice shook with the cold and my efforts. "P-p-p-lease – don't –"

His tone was almost gentle as he kept the pistol pointed at my body. "Don't fight it, dear. Give in to the silence. I hear it's like falling asleep. Think of your most wonderful vision. Let it take you away."

I closed my eyes and brought up an image of Jason before me – his strength, his dedication, his resolute loyalty. For a moment my shivering almost stopped.

Something tugged at my hand.

If I could have, I would have screamed. As it was, the chill had soaked so deep into my bones that I felt myself an ice sculpture barely managing a tremor of life. I reverberated with a deep coughing noise.

The touch came again. Strong fingers closed on mine.

He had come for me.

I took a last look at Adam, at the gun aiming down, and I tried to fill my voice with resignation. It probably didn't matter. My teeth were chattering so hard that the words could barely get past my frozen lips.

"Good bye."

I stopped kicking, took in a deep breath, and immediately my body sank down beneath the surface.

Jason spun beneath me, wrapping my arm across his shoulder, and then he was swimming hard, pulling me with him, as sleek as a seal through the dark depths.

It was a dream. It had to be. Maybe my mind had already begun to shut down. Maybe when I closed my eyes I had slipped into unconsciousness and the sensations around me were merely my body turning off its various functions one by one. The pain had vanished, after all. I was left with numbness, sluggishness, a sense of release.

I could not seem to connect thoughts to each other. Just the slow trickle of air from my mouth, the steady motion of limbs beneath me, and the firmness of Jason's back pressed into my chest.

My air reached its end and I pondered what my next breath in would feel like. What was it like to breathe water? It seemed so unimportant now. I was already crossed over into the final frontier. My frozen body knew it. It was only my mind which was resisting the inevitable. The opening of my mouth was a mere formality, a final punctuation mark on the long, winding essay which had been my life. My lips began to part -

Jason breached the surface and I gasped in unison with him, drawing in as much air as I could hold. The world swam with spots, as if a mischievous child had scattered chocolate jimmies in profusion across a greying landscape.

He rolled me over onto my back, wrapping an arm around me in a lifeguard's rescue and setting out at a hard pace. I stared up at the swirling clouds, glimpses of Orion peeking through. My eyelids were heavy, but I forced them to stay open, to stay concentrated on those bright lights. Time lost all measure.

Jason staggered, caught his feet, then swept me up in his arms. There was a murmur of voices around us, the thick weight of a blanket swaddled over me, and we were hurried toward a house. I barely saw the rec room; we were ushered into a large bathroom where a shower was already going at full blast. My hands were curled into claws and my body shivered with violent tremors. Jason stripped off my pants, then shirt, then half carried me into the shower, propping me up with his own body.

I knew logically that the water was not very hot – there was no sign of steam coming from it – but it felt as if they had set the shower on sauté. Jason immediately reached behind me to turn the temperature down even further and at last the liquid tumult became tolerable.

I stood there, full in the stream, focusing on my breath, on Jason's arms around me.

At long last the shivering began to ease, he carefully inched the water temperature up, and my hands released their tight curl. I moved them around his body, drawing him in against me, and he let out a low moan as he cocooned me in.

His voice in my ear was half anguish, half joy. "Oh, Morgan …"

"It's all right," I sighed, and I wasn't sure if I was reassuring him or me. "Everything is going to be all right."

Chapter 29

The Union League Café in New Haven, Connecticut was decked out in full holiday splendor, from the ivy draping the elegant staircase to the half-sized reindeer by the fireplace. The décor was forest green with natural wood highlights, perfectly complementing the season.

Jason sat to my right, his hand resting warmly on mine, his eyes oblivious to the beauty around us. He looked at me as if he still could not believe I was here with him, that two days ago we had crawled from the murk of Lake Singletary like primeval creatures gasping their first breath of air.

A black-suited waiter moved behind us, and Jason released my hand with visible hesitation. A pair of elegant gold-chased plates was set down before us.

I looked down and smiled. "Entrecóte de Bison," I murmured.

Another waiter came behind us, pouring the wine. Jason's eyes lit up. "Château Angelus 1989," he commented, picking up his glass and giving it a swirl. "Now here is a fitting tribute to what you have been through."

I lifted my own glass, raising it to his. For a moment the rest of the room misted away and it was just the two of us together, as it had been when we made our way up the sandy shore of Lake Singletary.

It was a long moment before he breathed again, taking a sip. His eyes closed. "A treasure," he murmured. His eyes opened again. His voice became hoarse. "It still only comes close."

I smiled, putting my own glass down. "So the police were able to apprehend Adam without any issue?"

He nodded, taking a long moment before looking down at his bison and starting to cut. "One of the officers at the event lived on Singletary; I think we made it to his house in four minutes flat. We had to be cautious to ease the boat out near you without spooking Adam." His eyes were somber. "Once I pulled you under, the officer gave Adam a few minutes before carefully approaching. Adam seemed quite agitated; the officer didn't want Adam to start shooting at the water in a panic."

He pressed his lips into a line. "Adam took a while to settle down, to agree to hand over his weapon. It seems he felt he was justified in what he had done, and in taking any further steps necessary to protect Eileen's reputation."

He put his knife down and reached for my hand, taking it again. "If you had not made that phone call –"

I smiled gently at him. "But I did, because of your continual warnings," I soothed him. "It had never occurred to me that he would somehow be involved in this. I thought he was so distant from the issues that were swirling around. It was your alertness that had my phone ready." My voice dropped low. "It was your prompt arrival that saved me."

His face shadowed and his gaze held mine steadily. "I should never have let you go out alone with him," he repeated for perhaps the fiftieth time in the past two days. "I should have canceled my training."

I reached up to lay my hand against his cheek. "You couldn't have shadowed me forever," I pointed out. "We had no idea that this threat existed. You had me prepared. When there was trouble, you were there to rescue me."

His hand came up to cover mine. "I remember the moment as if it was etched in crystal. The officer's boat stopped just on the edge of the mists." His fingers tightened. "You do not know how hard it was to see you in that boat with Adam, to know that any stray sound or motion might cause him to tighten that finger. One momentary swirl of fog and it would all be over."

My eyes brightened. "I do know how hard it must have been for you to slide into the icy water."

He almost chuckled at that and our hands lowered again to the table. "When I realized he was going to give you the 'option' of drowning, everything became perfectly clear. It was six hundred feet to shore – and we already had a house waiting for us there. I've done many water rescues over the years; I know the numbers by heart. I traded those frigid nine minutes against getting you as far away from Adam's gun as possible."

His gaze held mine. "You entered the water, and Adam's gun was on you. I had no doubt after that moment."

I reached out with my left hand to take up the glass of Bordeaux. I looked at the label on the bottle resting at the table's center. "There were thirty years between the 1935 drowning and Eileen's drowning in 1968. And another thirty years between that tragedy and when this superb bottle of wine was laid down. Maybe the gods of Lake Singletary were thirsty."

The corners of his mouth tweaked up and he raised his own glass in a toast without relinquishing my hand. "Then let us hope another thirty years go by before anyone else is put in this situation."

I held my glass up. "To another thirty years of joy, then."

His eyes held mine and I was lost in their depths, in the smoky brown which wrapped me in adoration. His voice shimmered with emotion. "To a *lifetime* of joy."

The bowls of the glass rang. The crystal chime resonated throughout my body, echoing with a certainty I knew to the depths of my very soul.

Dedication

To Paul and Anne Holzwarth, long time Sutton residents whose patience, advice, and support were invaluable.

To Chief Dennis J. Towle of the Sutton police department who provided details to assist in my research.

To Joan May, who inspires me with her writings and who offers wonderful feedback on my stories.

To my Mensa Writing Group, especially Ruth, Tom, Lynn, and Ken, who provide valuable commentary on my projects. Jody Zolli provides vast reams of notes and suggestions.

To my uncle Blake, who provides enthusiastic cheerleading. My Dad is great at finding typos everyone else has missed.

To my Geek Girls who support me with nurturing encouragement in all my projects.

To my BellaOnline editors, including Lisa B and Denise C, who inspire me to be the best I can.

Neptune's Car is an amazing local band featuring the talented musicianship of Holly Hanson and Steve Hayes. Be sure to visit NeptunesCar.com to hear their music and support their efforts.

Most of all, to Bob See, my beloved partner of seventeen years and counting. When I mentioned my mystery series project to him, he never hesitated. He went with me on scouting visits to the Sutton Forest and Lake Singletary, he hunted through brush for likely sites of murders, and he photographed hundreds of turkey-tail mushroom, nuthatches, aspen trees, and other local delights. Without him none of this could have been possible.

All references to the 1968 drowning of Eileen are fictitious and were invented for the purpose of this fictional story.

Glossary

1906 Drowning – On July 11, 1906, Chester Gillette took his pregnant 20-year-old girlfriend Grace Brown out on a boat and capsized it, so he could pursue a wealthy woman instead. The murder fascinated the US and was reported coast to coast.

A Place in the Sun – This film from 1951 featured Elizabeth Taylor and Montgomery Cliff. It was based on the 1925 novel An American Tragedy by Theodore Dreiser.

An American Tragedy – Published in 1925, this novel by Theodore Dreiser quickly became a best seller. It was closely based on the 1906 murder. It features Clyde Griffiths and Roberta Alden as the unfortunate couple. Dreiser deliberately gave his protagonist the initials CG to match Chester Gillette.

Newell Sherman – On July 20, 1935, Newell Sherman took his young wife Alice out onto Lake Singletary in Sutton MA and deliberately drowned her. He did so because he had fallen in love with seventeen year old Esther Magill, who worked with him at a machine shop in Whitinsville. The trial became a nationwide sensation, and was called "An American Tragedy" in many news reports, relating it to the book and the 1906 drowning-murder of Grace Brown by Chester Gillette.

Lake Singletary – Lake Singletary is partly in Sutton, partly in Millbury. About 330 acres in size, Lake Singletary has a maximum depth of 37 feet. The one boat ramp is on the northern side in Millbury, while the Sutton Town Beach, former site of Marion's Camp, is on the southern side.

Purgatory Chasm – a chasm caused perhaps 14,000 years ago by the sudden releasing of a glacial ice dam. The granite cliffs on either side rise up to eighty feet high.

Ramshorn Pond – Ramshorn Pond (pronounced *rams-horn*) is a private pond in Sutton and is about 110 acres in size.

Sutton MA – Founded in 1704, Sutton is located in lower central Massachusetts, close to the Rhode Island border. The town has two large lakes, the beauty of Purgatory Chasm, and is primarily farmland and forest.

About the Author

Lisa Shea was born in Maryland during the Vietnam War to a father in the Air Force and a mother who worked as a journalist. She grew up in various towns along the eastern seaboard, raised in an environment where writing and researching the past were as natural as spending weekends tromping through old-growth woods looking for stone wall foundations. Her concept of art focused on cemetery stone rubbings and photos of old homesteads.

When Lisa moved to Sutton, Massachusetts in 1995, she finally found her true home. Sutton's rustic charm, dense forests, and bucolic farmland all resonated with her creative spirit. The stories she had been writing since she was young now had a fertile ground in which to flourish.

Lisa's first book set in Sutton, *Aspen Allegations*, was written in November 2012 in a chapter-a-day style. Each day she explored Sutton and its surrounding areas and then wrote those experiences into the chapter. The mystery-romance earned a gold medal from the 2013 IPPY awards. Her second book, *Birch Blackguards*, was written in the same chapter-a-day style in August 2013. The third book in the series will be written starting on May 1, 2014.

All proceeds from the Sutton Mass Mysteries series benefit local battered women's shelters.

Lisa Shea has written 21 fiction books and 67 non-fiction books.

About Aspen Allegations

Aspen Allegations is the first in a series of mystery novels set in Sutton Massachusetts. Information on this series can be found here –

http://SuttonMass.org/SuttonMassMysteries/

Aspen Allegations was written in "real time." Each day's chapter was first written on the actual day the events took place. Locations were visited and described as they appeared on that day.

For example, here is the hickory nut found on November 1st, 2012, in Sutton Forest.

More photos of the sunsets, rainbows, and foliage described can be found at SuttonMass.org.

All proceeds from this series benefit a local domestic violence shelter.

Lisa Shea's library of medieval romance novels:

Each novel is a stand-alone story set in medieval England. These novels can be read in any order and have entirely separate casts of characters.

All proceeds from sales of these novels benefit battered women's shelters.

As a special treat, as a warm thank-you for buying this book and supporting the cause of battered women, here's a sneak peak at the first chapter of *Birch Blackguards* – the second book in the Sutton Mass. Mystery series.

Chapter 1

When you are in doubt, be still, and wait;
When doubt no longer exists for you,
*   then go forward with courage.*
So long as mists envelop you, be still;
be still until the sunlight pours through
and dispels the mists
*   as it surely will.*
Then act with courage.
~ Chief White Eagle of the Ponca Tribe (ca. 1840-1914)

Sometimes life is too much like a pathless wood, but for me, today, on this grassy patch of sun-smeared Earth, at this specific moment in time, it was the right place for love. I twined my fingers in Jason's as we stepped along the overgrown pavement, moving beneath the crumbling granite arch of the drive-in entryway. I half-suspected the dangling wires and aged stonework would collapse on our heads as we passed beneath. Against all odds the structure stayed upright, remained monumental and silent as we approached the long-abandoned triangular ticket booth and the massive screen beyond.

Jason smiled at me, his short, chestnut hair shining in the August afternoon sunlight. "So, did you ever go to drive-ins when you were a kid?"

I nodded, looking ahead to the distinctive undulating pattern of the pavement. The hills and valleys would give each car an ideal angle to the screen. The posts with speakers were long gone, though. Only the aging projection house remained, the collapsing main screen stretching before it. An assortment of spindly trees poked up through the blacktop like unruly grey hairs on a Nigerian grandfather's balding head.

I smiled as I looked across the fading scenery. "My mom would take me to the drive-in during the summers when I was young, back in the seventies. Our family had a dark green AMC Hornet. I would bring my sleeping bag and pillow and think it a grand adventure."

I shook my head, turning to the massive screen, my eyes drawn to the shadowed areas where the whiteness was interrupted by decay and collapse. Philip K. Dick would have said it was a clear sign of *kibble* – the inevitable progression of all of life into a messy chaos which smothers us.

I shrugged. "Even when I was a teenager, in the eighties, drive-ins were becoming a thing of the past. They were something seen in vintage settings, like *Grease*. My friends and I went to the multi-plexes, waiting in line for *Ghostbusters* and *Footloose*, eager for chemically-dusted popcorn and filtered air conditioning."

Jason looked over the landscape around us. "This drive-in opened back in 1947," he mused. "It survived McCarthyism, the Cold War, and Kent State. It was only the traffic patterns on 146 which finally did it in. I hear a key reason it was shut down in 1996 was that the cars backed up too much on the highway."

I let out a sigh, brushing my long, auburn hair from my face. "A shame. So much is becoming lost. Lost and decaying, while people are mesmerized by their smart phones and block out their surroundings with tiny white ear buds." My eyes drew up to the large screen, the pale squares slowly, inexorably, curling away from each other. "I wonder what they were watching back in 1947."

Jason's voice came without hesitation. "*A Gentleman's Agreement.*"

I glanced over in surprise. "Oh?"

He grinned. "My mother was an avid fan of Gregory Peck. The movie won three Academy Awards and I believe was nominated for eight."

I smiled. "Maybe we can Netflix it tonight," I offered. I looked around the wasteland. "However, right now we have a task to complete."

He nodded. "And a challenging one it is, too. Though why Jeff can't come out and track down his own gear ..."

I nudged him in the side. "We had the day free," I reminded him. "And with Citadel Airsoft being asked to stop using the grounds for their games, we need to figure out where he tucked that rifle before the new owner takes over. For all we know, they'll be bulldozing this paradise to turn it into a parking lot."

He ran a hand through his hair. "Well, so far it's gone from classic drive-in to pseudo-military combat field." His eyebrow raised. "Complete with a boat."

I followed his gaze and chuckled. Parked to the left of the projector building was a fifteen-foot motorboat. As we approached it, we could see a scattering of white pellets in its bow along with several small trees poking up through its floorboards. Apparently the opposing factions in the Battle for Sutton Drive-In had found the beached boat made for good cover.

Jason shook his head, looking around. "All right. Enough sight-seeing. Where did Jeff say he forgot this rifle of his?"

My mouth quirked up in a smile. "He didn't *forget* it," I teased him. "He *secreted* it, so he could grab it at an opportune time and sneak up on his enemy unawares." I grinned. "Then, unfortunately, he lost track of where he had put it."

I walked toward the western side of the clearing, heading away from the highway. The growl of slow cars was faintly audible in the background. It was nearly six p.m. but traffic was still backed up to the Millbury line. The legislators had talked often about removing the light at Tony's pizza, to remove this evening log-jam, but somehow nothing ever was done.

I looked at the stretch of trees before us. "Jeff said something about a stand of white birch," I commented. "There isn't anything but forest for over a half mile in this direction. Lots of options."

Jason chuckled. "Probably why the drive-in was so popular," he joked. "You know how teenagers are."

I smiled at him, and then we both dug into our pockets and pulled out leather gloves. Jason's years in the forest ranger service had made him well aware of the issues with poison ivy, poison sumac, and disease-bearing ticks. I had been dating him for just about nine months now, and I had learned quickly. No need to risk Lyme disease just to track down a plastic replica of an AR-15.

I glanced up at the sky. Earlier in the day the world had been softened by gentle showers, but now only drifting grey clouds remained, filtering the sun and adding a romantic cast to this first day of August. I took a breath and delved into the phthalo-green shadows of the forest. The landscape was different from the nearby paths in Sutton Forest and Purgatory Chasm that Jason and I enjoyed hiking. This was an overgrown tangle, once a tame edging to a family fun spot, now left to its own insidious devices. Dense patches of Virginia creeper were interlaced with gnarled stretches of goldenrod and wild strawberry.

I smiled, enjoying my explorations, keeping a sharp eye out for a straight shape amongst all the curves. Whatever the excuse, I was immensely content to be exploring the summer wilderness with Jason. His presence was a balm to me, and I had still not quite gotten used to having him in my life. Perhaps I would always hold a tinge of surprise and appreciation that he fit so easily into my world.

I certainly hoped so.

I tripped over an upturned root and went down hard on my knees into the club moss and aster. I shook my head. I wasn't elderly, but at forty-four I was hardly a toddler either. My yoga routine kept me flexible, but I respected my body's limitations. I put both hands down to press myself up off the fragrant forest floor.

My left hand settled over something smooth and cylindrical, and I smiled. Perhaps the tripping had been fate, after all. I brushed away the layer of dirt and sediment, my voice gathering to call out to Jason that I'd found the elusive weapon.

The victory cry died in my throat.

The object beneath my gloved fingers was stained with time, discolored with grime, but was clearly not a metal or plastic gun barrel. Rather, it was that delicate ivory which so clearly connected with my soul.

I stared at the bone, and time stood still.

Jason must have been calling my name, for by the time he strode over to me his face was set in half exasperation, half worry. He drew up at my side – and stopped. His gaze snapped into that serious focus that I knew so well. His hand was at his hip, he dialed the three digits, and then he dropped to one knee by my side. His arm wrapped around me, drawing me in, while he spoke into his phone.

"Jason Rowland here. I'm at the Sutton drive-in. We've found a dead body. No flesh on the bones that I can see – at least three weeks is my guess. Maybe much longer." He listened for a moment. "We'll be here."

He drew me to my feet, easing me back. I could see now the outline of the rest of the corpse. It seemed the person had been as tall as me – about five foot six – and curled onto one side. I had disturbed the femur, but the remainder remained hidden under a layer of dirt and moss. It almost seemed that a natural, earth-brown blanket comforted the dead person, nestling them in against the birch.

It was only minutes before the sirens began, before there were police officers and yellow crime-scene tape and endless questions. But I had no answers to give. The chaos came from all sides and a thought flickered in my mind. Perhaps the skeleton had been content to lie there. Perhaps we had disturbed its serene resting place with our brash, noisy intrusion.

At last the final interview was complete. I climbed in beside Jason in his white F-150 to head back home. He glanced over at me as he turned through the deepening dusk onto 146, now free flowing with light traffic. "How are you holding up?"

I rolled my shoulders. "It still doesn't seem real," I admitted. "How long had the body been there?" I looked down at my hands, pondering the sinews, the scattering of light brown freckles which made my unique constellations. "How quickly does a person go from flesh and blood to a skeleton?"

His brow furrowed, and he thought about it for a minute. "It's August first. These past few weeks have see-sawed between record heat and steady rain. Between that and summertime insect activity, in that shallow grave, full decomposition could easily have happened within the month." He looked ahead as we turned onto our street. "But it could be longer, of course. Years. Maybe decades. During the time of the drive-in's use that land would only have been visited on weekends. I imagine few of the customers ever left the pavement area." He gave a soft shrug. "For all we know, the body could even date back to before the drive-in was operational."

We drew to a stop in our driveway. He came around and took my hand, walking me up to the door. "I'm sure we'll find out more tomorrow," he assured me. "Once they start looking more closely at the bones."

Juliet, my stripy cat, was waiting for us when we opened the door, and I knelt down to pet her. I felt unsettled, lost, and I wasn't quite sure what I wanted to do.

He nodded his head to me. "Go on upstairs and settle into bed. I'll bring up some Triscuit nachos. We can watch *A Gentleman's Agreement* on Netflix. It'll keep your mind off of things and help you sleep."

I nodded and made my way upstairs. In only a few minutes he was up with the plate, as well as a glass of red sangria with frozen peaches in it. I smiled and propped up the pillows.

The movie drew me in. I had always adored *To Kill a Mockingbird*, but this showcased a different type of discrimination. It was stunning to think, so soon after the real-life horrors of Auschwitz and Dachau, that people in the US could still feel it quite reasonable to have "restricted" hotels and establishments which kept out Jews.

The movie finally spun to an end and I rolled over to look at Jason. "Even though the movie made it clear from the beginning that Phil was going to end up with Kathy, I'm not sure I like it,"

I murmured. "Throughout the courtship Kathy made disparaging remarks about Jews, even equating them to being old and sick. In comparison, Anne is honest, intelligent, and compassionate. She bares her soul to Phil and he seems to respond. Then, *poof*, Kathy makes one minor concession and he goes running right back to her."

He grinned. "Anne did win the Academy award," he pointed out, "while the rest only got nominated. So it seems others agreed with you there."

I lay against his chest. "Still, the plot is a good portrayal of how prejudice can be an insidious force. This wasn't as in-your-face as *In the Heat of the Night*, for example. Characters in this movie would not state right out that they had an issue with Jews. They would just turn away or make quiet comments."

He nodded, running a hand along my cheek. "And then we have, just today, Rhode Island accepting gay marriage with nary a rumble of an issue. Back in 2004, when Massachusetts was the first state to allow gay marriage, there was a huge outcry. Now, nearly ten years later, all of New England allows gay marriage, and life goes on, serene and content."

I held his gaze. "The world is making strides. Still, there are so many ways in which people are marginalized. Obese people are thought of as lazy. People in wheelchairs are thought of as mentally slow. When will we stop jumping to conclusions? When will we start allowing each person to shine with their natural abilities and hopes?"

He smiled at that. "They may say you're a dreamer," he murmured, "but you're not the only one."

I chuckled. "Of course not. I have you, don't I?" My throat tightened. "Every day I give thanks that you found me."

His eyes grew smoky, he drew me down to him, and the world faded away.

To read the rest of *Birch Blackguards*, you can find details about the paperback and ebook versions here:

http://SuttonMass.org/SuttonMassMysteries/

Made in the USA
Charleston, SC
10 May 2014